BROADSWORD

Monthly

Version 1.0 PDF November 2019
Version 1.1 PDF January 2020
Version 1.1 Print January 2020

BROADSWORD Monthly

ADVENTURES FOR FIFTH EDITION · FEBRUARY '20 ISSUE 3

COVER: JD Russell brings us Tara Nova, a fiesty, science fiction rogue with a dragon companion. Reminds me of a punk rock Kitty Pryde!

What an exciting 2019 it's been!

I started the year with nothing more than an ebook and a middling Patreon account and now I'm three books in to an adventure series, have a great bunch of fans on Patreon, and I get to work with some of the coolest folks in the business.

2020 is looking to be even more exceptional. Already, I've got no less than three Kickstarters planned, with plenty of high-profile collaborations, too. And since I wrote somewhere around one million words in 2019, I'm sure I can do even better in the new year.

As always, I couldn't do this without you, the reader. You're the one that makes the possible. Otherwise, I'd just be another hack with a high word count.

See you in the new year!

-Dave Hamrick

In honor of Armistice Day ~ November 11 1918. Lest we forget.

"What passing-bells for these who die as cattle?
-Only the monstrous anger of the guns.
Only the stuttering rifles' rapid rattle
Can patter out their hasty orisons.
No mockeries now for them; no prayers nor bells;
Nor any voice of mourning save the choirs,-
The shrill, demented choirs of wailing shells;
And bugles calling for them from sad shires."
-Wilfred Owen, **Anthem for Doomed Youth**, 1917

VOL. I, NO. 3

PUBLISHER Dave Hamrick
EDITOR Dave Hamrick
ART DIRECTOR Scott Craig
LAYOUT Scott Craig
CARTOGRAPHY JD Russell, Dave Hamrick, Dyson Logos
ART JD Russell, Jason Glover, Bodie Hartley, Wilson and Grond

BroadSword Monthly is Copyright 2019 Hamrick Brands, LLC
Magazine Template Design by Scott Craig ~ www.vaultofwonders.games

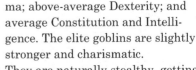

HOW TO CREATE A 5E MONSTER

By Dave Hamrick
Art by JD Russell and Jason Glover

Occasionally, I get folks on Instagram and Facebook asking me how to create a monster for Fifth Edition. Of course, the *DMG* outlines how to do just that on pages 273 -283. But for some that can be a little overwhelming. And there are lots of little rules that are easy to miss.

So, I thought I'd take the opportunity to go over how to create a monster for Fifth Edition. After all, I create, on average, probably 10-15 new monsters each week.

Here's a look into my monster design process for Fifth Edition:

Step #1 - Come up with the concept
The first thing I do when I create new monsters for Fifth Edition is think about what I want the monster to do and what its purpose not only in the game is, but the fantasy world itself.

Is the monster a minion? Or is it a big bad evil guy/girl (BBEG)? Do I want the monster to be memorable, or do I want the monster to be sort of an "asshole monster", the type my players will never forget?

Once I have the basic concept down, I do a little shopping.

In this example, I want to create a two-headed goblin. Why? Because I love goblins!

Step #2 - Figure out the base monster
Once I have the concept, I then turn to the book I consider the "Rosetta Stone" of Fifth Edition: the *MM*. When learning how to create a monster, this is your best resource. In fact, it's pretty rare that I have to reference any other book. With nearly 500 monsters all with tons of features, actions, and options, there's bound to be something in there that comes close to matching

what I conceptualized in Step #1.

Let's take a look at our two-headed goblin concept.

First off, I know that I'd want to look at the goblin stat block on page 165 -166 of the *MM*. This will help me figure out the characteristics that all goblins should have in common.

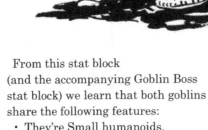

From this stat block (and the accompanying Goblin Boss stat block) we learn that both goblins share the following features:
- They're Small humanoids.
- And they have the goblinoid tag.
- Their alignment is neutral evil.
- Basic goblin "warriors" have 2 hit dice, while elites have 6.
- Goblins have below average Strength, Wisdom, and Charis-

ma; above-average Dexterity; and average Constitution and Intelligence. The elite goblins are slightly stronger and charismatic.
- They are naturally stealthy, getting double their proficiency bonus to Dexterity (Stealth) checks.
- Thanks to darkvision, goblins can see in the dark up to 60 ft. Goblins speak both Common and Goblin.
- All goblins seemingly have the Nimble Escape feature which allows them to take Disengage or Hide as a bonus action on each of its turns.
- The elite goblins get Multiattack and the Redirect Attack reaction which allows it to swap places with another goblin (whaddajerk).

Knowing all this, we can start customizing our goblin with secondary characteristics.

Step #3 - Shop secondary characteristics
Next, I want to find secondary characteristics that fit the concept. The best way to do this is to find a creature that has options that are similar to what we're looking for, but not enough other motifs to warrant it being the base creature.

We know a lot about goblins now, but we don't know much about two-headed goblins. Fortunately, there are a couple of different monsters in the *MM* that has more than one head.

First, we have the obvious choice, the ettin (page 132). The ettin's two heads gives it some interesting features, some obvious and some subtle. The obvious features are its Two Heads and Wakeful features. The subtle feature is its expertise in Perception (double proficiency bonus).

Next, there are death dogs (page 321). Death dogs also have double the proficiency bonus in Perception as well as the Two-Headed feature. Note that the wording of the feature's name is different than the ettins although it's exactly the same. Tsk, tsk, WotC copywriters.

Finally, we have the chimera (page 39). Like the ettin and death dog, the chimera has double the proficiency bonus. However, it doesn't have a special feature related to its multi-headed nature.

There is one more subtle feature that all these creatures have in common: multiattack! The chimera can attack once with each of its heads (or parts, if you count the lion head's claw attack as a "head"), the ettin makes two attacks with each of its weapons, and the death dog makes two bite attacks. This makes me think that having more than one head makes the creatures better at multiple attacks.

Observing all this, I'm going to give the goblin Multiattack, Two Heads, and double its Perception proficiency. Goblins are inherently lazy, so I can't imagine them being "wakeful", even with two heads.

Step #4 - Put it all together

The next step on how to make a monster involves putting it all together. Since we have the base creature decided and its secondary characteristics picked out, we can start creating its rough stat block.

Here's what our two-headed goblin is going to look like so far. I've highlighted in red all the changes I've made to the normal goblin stat block.

Here is a breakdown of the changes that I made to it:

- **Armor Class is 13 instead of 15.** The two-headed goblin carries two scimitars with it instead of a shield.
- **Hit Dice are 4 instead of 2.** I see the two-headed goblin being somewhere between the goblin warrior and the elite goblin boss. Therefore,

---

TWO-HEADED GOBLIN
Small humanoid (goblinoid), neutral evil

Armor Class 13 (leather armor)
Hit Points 14 (4d6)
Speed 30 ft.

STR		INT	
STR	8 (-1)	INT	10 (+0)
DEX	14 (+2)	WIS	8 (-1)
CON	10 (+0)	CHA	8 (-1)

Skills Perception +3, Stealth +6
Senses darkvision 60 ft., passive Perception 13
Languages Common, Goblin
Challenge ? (I'll fill this in momentarily)

Nimble Escape. The goblin can take the Disengage or Hide action as a bonus action on each of its turns.
Two-Headed. The goblin has advantage on Wisdom (Perception) checks and on saving throws against being blinded, harmed, deafened, frightened, stunned, and knocked unconscious.

ACTIONS

Multiattack. The goblin makes two attacks with its scimitars.
Scimitar. Melee Weapon Attack: +4 to hit, reach 5 ft., one target. *Hit:* 5 (1d6 + 2) slashing damage.
Shortbow. Ranged Weapon Attack: +4 to hit, range 80/320 ft., one target. *Hit:* 5 (1d6 + 2) piercing damage.

I bumped its hit dice up to 4 and adjusted the math accordingly. If you need a quick hack on how to calculate average hit points, the easiest way to do it is to multiply the number of hit dice by half the die's maximum plus 1/2, then add in the Constitution bonus (which is the Constitution modifier multiplied by the hit dice).

- **Perception gets expertise.** Goblins normally have Wisdom (Perception) -1. But two-headed creatures get double the Perception proficiency. Being that this creature will probably clock in at a Challenge Rating below 5, that means its proficiency bonus will be +2. Therefore, its Wisdom (Perception) bonus will be +3 (2 + 2 -1 = +3). And passive Perception is the Perception bonus plus 10, so 13.
- **Two-headed feature added in.** I took the feature text straight from

---

the ettin's stat block. Why reinvent the wheel?

- **Multiattack added in.** The two-headed goblin gets to attack twice with both its scimitars. I didn't give it multiattack for its shortbow because it needs both hands to fire the shortbow. And with two, constantly bickering goblin heads, it's probably good fortune they get off that first shot off in the first place!

Step #5 - Give the new monster a challenge rating

Now that we know most of the creature's characteristics and what its stat block will look like, we need to figure out its challenge rating.

In Fifth Edition there are two major factors that we calculate when determining challenge rating:

- *Damage output.* What is the average amount of damage per round that the creature can possibly deal over the course of three rounds?
- *Defensive capability.* Considering both its hit points and armor class, as well as any defensive features that the creature has, how likely is this creature to survive over the course of three rounds?

Anything else that doesn't affect either of those things we can ignore. For example, while it's cool that our new two-headed goblin has improved Perception from its two heads, having two heads does not affect its Challenge Rating in any way (see page 281).

Here are the things that affect our goblin's challenge rating:

Damage output. How much damage can a two-headed goblin do per round?

- If our two-headed goblin attacks with both its scimitars for three rounds and hits with each attack, it will deal an average of 10 damage per round. It deals more damage using its multiattack/scimitars than using its bow, therefore that's what we want to go off of.
- Our goblin has an attack bonus of +4.

- The Nimble Escape ability increases the goblin's effective attack bonus by +4.

Defensive capabilities. How likely is our goblin to survive for three rounds?

- The two-headed goblin has 14 hit points.
- Without a shield, our two-headed goblin's AC is only 13.
- The Nimble Escape ability also increases the two-headed goblin's effective Armor Class by +4.

From there, we reference the nifty chart on page 274 of the *DMG* to figure out what the two-headed goblin's Challenge Rating will be.

Its Offensive Challenge Rating is 3. Although, it deals 10 damage on average (making it CR 1), its effective attack bonus is +8. For each +2 above the attack bonus that the CR says it should have, we raise the offensive CR by 1 level.

Its Defensive Challenge Rating is 1/2. The goblin has 14 average hit points, which would normally make it only CR 1/8. But its Armor Class is effectively 18 thanks to its Nimble Escape feature. For every 2 points of AC above the suggested AC for the CR, we raise it two levels.

Once we have the offensive and defensive challenge ratings determine, it's simply a matter of averaging the two out, which would make it 1.75.

Quick hack: while the *DMG* doesn't specify whether you should round up or down when the average comes out to a number that isn't a whole number, I usually round up if the offensive challenge rating is higher than the defensive challenge rating and down if vice versa.

Now we know that our two-headed goblin's challenge rating is 2.

Step #6 - Doublecheck your work
Once you have the challenge rating decided for your creature, make sure to go back and check your work. If the challenge rating hits one of the creature's proficiency breakpoints (at CR 5, 9, 13, and 17), you may have to go back and adjust its proficiencies.

In addition, if the creature hits a tier-based resistance or immunity breakpoint (at CR 5, 11, and 17), you might also have to adjust its effective hit points, too, which could mean a recalculation of its defensive CR!

Don't forget to playtest it, too. Maybe you'll discover that it has an ability that you don't like or you think its Challenge Rating needs to be adjusted.

Hope this is helpful!
I love goblins. This is probably the fifth or sixth goblins I've made for the site. And hopefully, this quick lesson on how to create a monster for Fifth Edition in 15 minutes or less can help you whip up some quick challenges for your PCs.

Is there anything else you'd like to see me cover in monster creation? Let me know down in the comments on Patreon.

See you soon.

Here is our final two-headed goblin:

TWO-HEADED GOBLIN
Small humanoid (goblinoid), neutral evil

Armor Class 13 (leather armor)
Hit Points 14 (4d6)
Speed 30 ft.

STR	INT
8 (-1)	10 (+0)
DEX	WIS
14 (+2)	8 (-1)
CON	CHA
10 (+0)	8 (-1)

Skills Perception +3, Stealth +6
Senses darkvision 60 ft., passive Perception 13
Languages Common, Goblin
Challenge 2 (450 XP)

Nimble Escape. The goblin can take the Disengage or Hide action as a bonus action on each of its turns.
Two-Headed. The goblin has advantage on Wisdom (Perception) checks and on saving throws against being blinded, harmed, deafened, frightened, stunned, and knocked unconscious.

ACTIONS

Multiattack. The goblin makes two attacks with its scimitars.
Scimitar. Melee Weapon Attack: +4 to hit, reach 5 ft., one target. *Hit*: 5 (1d6 + 2) slashing damage.
Shortbow. Ranged Weapon Attack: +4 to hit, range 80/320 ft., one target. *Hit*: 5 (1d6 + 2) piercing damage. Ω

THE MYSTERY OF HOEGAR'S HOLLOW

BY DAVE HAMRICK

1st-Level Adventure for Fifth Edition

Artwork by Justin David Russell
Cartography by Justin David Russell

The Mystery of Hoegar's Hollow is a location-based adventure designed for any mix of four 5th-level adventurers. This side quest adventure introduces characters to the science-fiction campaign setting of Blueshift. The adventure works best if the characters have no idea what they are getting into; the science-fiction elements should be a total surprise.

Adventure Background

Two decades ago, the people of Hoegar's Hollow witnessed a comet streak through the sky. Typically, this was seen as a good omen. As wildly superstitious worshippers of an agriculture god, the simple folk of Hoegar's Hollow thought that it was their god, Olan telling them that the spring would bring a healthy harvest. But then the comet turned towards the land and crashed into the forest to the north of the village.

The people of Hoegar's Hollow rushed towards the site of the meteor landing. Following the meteor's burning path, they eventually came upon something the old folks named "the Great Silver Turtle." Hoegarian historians described the turtle as gargantuan, easily the size of a barn. They said the turtle "bled silver blood" onto the surrounding land and that anything its blood touched was changed by it. Plants grew wild. Animals evolved and became aggressive. And humanoids that came into contact with the turtle's blood mutated and went insane.

The first few weeks were difficult. The unchanged Hoegarians fought for their lives against the ghastly creatures altered by the turtle's blood. Eventually, they defeated the horrors and burned the bodies. Quickly, the dangerous forest that grew around the turtle was cordoned off by the Hoegarians and renamed the Silverwood.

Knowing that they had to protect the secrets of the Great Silver Turtle from those who might use its blood for evil, the Hoegarians formed a faction: the

Silver Wardens. For twenty years, the Silver Wardens kept the Great Silver Turtle and Silverwood a secret. Until now.

The Great Silver Turtle

What the Hoegarians didn't realize is that their Great Silver Turtle was actually a science vessel named the *Paramount* that crash-landed in their forest. The ship ran on an experimental self-regenerating fuel called Blueshift. However, the crash landing left the *Paramount* significantly damaged and unable to repair itself quickly; it would take nearly two decades for it to get itself running again.

A side-effect of the Blueshift fuel was that it had the power to alter any living thing that touched it. This is why the animals and plant life that came into contact with it transformed.

Finally, after twenty years, the *Paramount* has repaired itself and is ready to return to space. The only trouble is, it has no crew.

The Return of Doctor Kalaxan

When the *Paramount* crashed, most of the crew died on impact. However, the crew's android lead scientist, Doctor Kalaxan survived, thrown from the wreckage. Realizing the dangers of the spilled Blueshift, Kalaxan left the scene and disappeared into the forest surrounding the crash site.

Quietly, Kalaxan has been surviving in this new, low-technology world, under the guise of a wizard named Kalaxan the Magnificent. For twenty years, he's been trying to solve three riddles: first, how to stop the fuel from altering the physiologies of living things that come into contact with it; second, how to get past the Silver Wardens and back to the ship; and third, where to find a crew to pilot the *Paramount* back to outer space.

Kalaxan believes that he has solved the first riddle. Now he just needs to solve the second and third riddles.

And that's where the adventurers come in.

Adventure Hook

The adventure starts when the characters are in the village of Hoegar's Hollow looking for work. Read or paraphrase the following:

> After looking through the job boards and help-wanted postings, you discover that it's the same here as it is everywhere else: no work. All the good adventuring gigs keep getting grabbed by the biggest and best. With so many adventurers these days, it's almost impossible for a group of rookie wannabe-heroes to find work.
>
> Unless they want to shovel pig pens, that is.

While passing through a tavern, the characters are spotted by a mysterious, cloaked figure sitting at the back of the bar. The figure signals the characters over, offering them drinks with promises of work.

If the characters accept, read or paraphrase the following:

> The cloaked figure pulls back his hood revealing the friendly face of an old, bearded man. "Greetings and well met, travelers! My name is Kalaxan the Magnificent, and I am in dire need of assistance. Hopefully, you are able to aid me in this time-sensitive quest.
>
> "Two weeks ago, my apprentice, Roma, and I were traveling north of the village here when some sort of vile creature attacked us. The two of us were separated. I managed to return here to the village, but I fear poor Roma was lost in the forest.
>
> "I tried to alert the authorities that my assistant was lost, but they did not seem to wish to help. They told me, 'If she is lost in the forest, there's nothing we can do.' I fear that the

people of this village are trying to cover something up. In fact, I believe that there is a secret organization at work here."

> The old man pauses, throwing suspicious looks at the other bar patrons. He then continues, whispering, "If you can help me find my assistant Roma, I can reward each of you 50 gold pieces for your troubles. Plus, you will have the gratitude of the powerful, whimsical, amazing, Kalaxan the Magnificent!"
>
> Just then, illusory fireworks leap from the old wizard's hands as he laughs merrily.

Of course, this is all a ruse. **Doctor Kalaxan** (see Appendix C) is using a *disguise self* protocol to make himself appear as an old man instead of his true robot form. And there is no actual apprentice, either. Kalaxan wants the characters to find their way to the wrecked science vessel so he can convince them to help him fly back to space.

Should the characters ask additional questions, Kalaxan can provide the following information:

- Kalaxan believes that the secret organization in Hoeger's Hollow calls itself "The Silver Wardens." However, none of the Hoegarians will speak of the Wardens. (This is true.)
- Although he isn't quite sure what attacked him and Roma, he believes that it was some sort of mutated bear creature. (Nothing attacked Kalaxan. This is a lie.)
- Reading up on the history of the Silverwood to the north of Hoegar's Hollow, Kalaxan learned that twenty years ago a great fire fell from the sky into the forest. Since that day, the woods have become a dangerous place to venture into. The great fire fell in the center of the forest. (This is mostly true.)
- Kalaxan has heard rumors that there is a beast known as the Great Silver Turtle that makes its home in the center of the forest. He believes that

the Silver Wardens will kill any who discover the turtle. (While the Wardens are indeed protecting the Silver Turtle, they only kill if provoked.)

Kalaxan recommends that the characters start their search at Old Hoegar's Hollow, a collection of houses around a small pond north of the main village.

Old Hoegar's Hollow

Once the characters are ready, they can follow Kalaxan's directions to Old Hoegar's Hollow. When the characters arrive at the abandoned town, read or paraphrase the following:

> Twenty-years worth of wild ivy and tall grass have made this old, abandoned village nearly unidentifiable. Birds make their homes in the collapsed rooves of the ruined buildings. A rabbit leaps out of of a window and through the posts of what was once a picket fence.
>
> Just ahead of you is the forest Kalaxan told you about. Other than the wind rustling through the wood's silver-tipped leaves, it is eerily quiet.
>
> Interestingly, you notice footprints in the mud of the abandoned village's square leading into the forest.

The footprints were accidentally left by the normally cautious Silver Wardens. Following the footprints with a few successful DC 12 Wisdom (Survival) checks will lead the characters from Old Hoegar's Hollow directly to the location of the Great Silver Turtle.

Through the Silverwood

It is roughly 15 miles from Old Hoegar's Hollow to the center of the Silverwood where the Great Silver Turtle lies. Unless the characters have a ranger among them or another creature that can speed up travel, it should take the characters a day to reach the center of the wood.

Instead of using random encounters, use the following encounters to build upon the mystery of the Silverwood itself. You're free to put the encounters in any order you like, morning, day, or night.

"There's Something Watching Us"

At some point, the characters get the feeling that they are being watched by something in the forest: a twig snaps, they see something out of the corner of their eye, or just have a bad feeling.

Their suspicions are correct: they're being followed by Kalaxan. Kalaxan has been following the characters ever since they entered the forest, using an *invisibility protocol* to hide.

Kalaxan is fast and tough to detect in the forest. You might have the characters chase the invisible android through the forest, eventually losing sight of him. Or you might even have them catch Kalaxan momentarily in his true form (he won't look anything like the same wizard that tasked them). Kalaxan then uses his *dimension door* protocol to escape.

Silver Wardens

It's pretty tough for a humanoid to move through the Silverwood without the Silver Wardens noticing it. Unless the characters are exceptionally cautious, the Silver Wardens set an ambush for the characters.

Four Silver Wardens (LN male and female human **scouts** armed with nets in addition to their shortswords and longbows) hide among the trees. Have the characters make a DC 17 Wisdom (Perception) check to spot the Wardens. If the characters fail to notice the Wardens, the Wardens surprise the characters. Primarily, the Wardens hope to subdue and capture the characters, using nets and non-lethal damage to take them out.

If things turn bad for the characters, it's possible that Kalaxan comes in at the last minute and saves them. Kalaxan attacks in his true android form. The spacefarer has no qualms about dealing lethal damage to the Silver Wardens. Once he's rescued the characters, he disappears back into the forest using either his *invisibility* or *dimension door* protocols.

Two-Headed Wolf

After traveling through the Silverwood for a while, read the following:

> All of you stop dead in your tracks. Roughly one hundred feet from where you stand, there's something rustling in the foliage. Whatever it is ahead of you growls. Then, it begins to charge. Although it's moving fast, you can make out its rough shape. It looks like a wolf, but it has patchy, mottled fur, and two snarling heads.

The two-headed wolf is aggressive and dangerous. It was changed by the turtle's blood. Use the **death dog** stat block, except that if it infects one of the characters with a disease, the disease doesn't reduce their hit point maximum. Instead, the character is infected with turtle's blood (see the "Turtle's Blood" sidebar).

If the death dog encounter proves to be too much of a challenge, the characters can be rescued by the Silver Wardens, Kalaxan, or a combination of both.

The Paramount

When the characters finally reach the center of the wood, read the following description:

> The dense, wildly-overgrown foliage finally gives way to a clearing. At its center, some 300 feet from you, you see what looks like a silver creature laying on its belly. The shell of the creature measures roughly 100 feet-squared and sticks 50-feet out of the ground. It's completely covered in vines, mushrooms, and other flora. Near the front of it, you see what appears to be three glossy, dome-like bubbles, possibly its eyes, with three cavernous holes just below each eye; possibly a way for the creature to

---

Turtle's Blood (Blueshift)

Turtle's blood is the name given by the Silver Wardens for the fuel leaking from the *Paramount*.

If a creature is exposed to turtle's blood or attacked by a creature altered by turtle's blood, it must make a DC 12 Constitution saving throw or become infected. An infected creature begins to show symptoms in 1d4 hours; its skin starts to turn grey and develop a painful rash. After 24 hours elapse the creature transforms. Its alignment changes to neutral evil, and it becomes aggressive towards all other creatures around it. If a character is changed, the GM assumes control until the character the disease is cured.

In addition to its alignment shift and aggressive nature, the creature develops a mutation. Choose one of the random mutations on the table below or roll a d10 to decide.

d10	Effect
1	**Two heads.** The creature has advantage on Wisdom (Perception) checks and on saving throws against being blinded, charmed, deafened, frightened, stunned, or knocked unconscious.
2	**Tentacle.** The creature has a tentacle sprouting from somewhere on its body which it can use to make melee weapon attacks with. On a hit, the tentacle deals bludgeoning damage equal to 1d6 plus the creature's Strength modifier. In addition, the creature has advantage on Strength (Athletics) checks made to grapple.
3	**Tough hide.** The creature gains a +2 bonus to its AC.
4	**Gaping maw.** The creature's mouth is unusually large, allowing it to use its bite as a melee weapon attack. On a hit, the bite attack deals piercing damage equal to 1d6 plus its Strength modifier. If the creature already has a bite attack, the damage caused by its bite increases by one damage die.
5	**Glowing eyes.** The creature can see through normal and magical darkness out to 30 ft., but it has disadvantage on its Dexterity (Stealth) checks made to hide in dark or dimly lit areas.
6	**Extra legs.** The creature's walking speed increases by 20 ft., and it has advantage on ability checks to avoid being knocked prone.
7	**Acid spray.** As an action, the creature sprays acid in a 15-foot cone. Each creature in the area must succeed on a Dexterity saving throw with a DC of 8 + the creature's proficiency bonus + the creature's Constitution modifier. A target takes 2d6 acid damage on failed saving throw and half as much damage on a successful one. This attack recharges on a roll of 5 or 6.
8	**Claws.** The creature develops long, unnatural-looking claws, allowing it to use its claws as a melee weapon attack. On a hit, the claw attack deals slashing damage equal to 1d6 plus its Strength modifier. If the creature already has a claw attack, the damage caused by its claw attack increases by one damage die.
9	**Size increase.** The target's size increases by one category as if under the enlargement effects of the *enlarge/reduce* spell.
10	**Amorphous.** The creature's molecular structure completely collapses. It becomes an **ochre jelly** except that it retains its Intelligence and Wisdom scores.

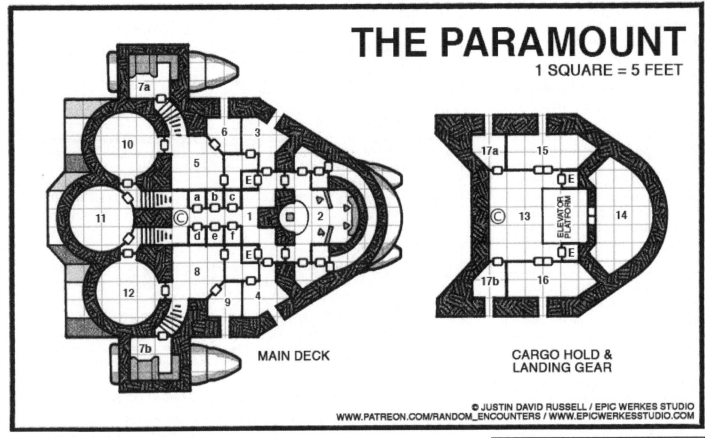

THE PARAMOUNT
1 SQUARE = 5 FEET

MAIN DECK

CARGO HOLD &
LANDING GEAR

breathe. At either side of the colossal thing, there are what appear to be fins, half-buried under vegetation and soil.

The creature isn't moving. Perhaps it's dead? Regardless, there is no way to know whether or not it can detect you.

This is the "Great Silver Turtle" that the characters may have heard about. Of course, it's not a turtle at all, but the *Paramount*, Kalaxan's science vessel. After twenty years of being hidden away, it has finally fully repaired itself. All it needs is its crew and it can leave the Silverwood and return to space.

The characters should be given a chance to observe then approach the *Paramount*. Once they're close enough, they can see that the "Great Silver Turtle" has more in common with a building than a creature.

If they climb on top of the Paramount, a successful DC 13 Intelligence

(Investigation) check reveals a hatch (see **area 1** below). The hatch has been opened recently by the Silver Wardens. Tarren Ironstout and his men are fully aware that the Great Silver Turtle is nothing more than a strange ship. They have no idea how to get it operational but have inspected the inside in an attempt to learn more about the ship and its purpose.

Inside the Paramount

The characters can open the *Paramount's* hatch and descend the ladder to the inside.

1 – Crew Quarters/Central Corridors
The first time the characters descend the ladder (marked "C" on the map) read the following:

> The ladder descends 10 feet into the "belly" of the beast. As you may have already guessed, it's not a beast at

all, but some sort of building or ship. You find yourself in some sort of hallway T-junction. Directly ahead of you are six doors, three to your left and three to your right. Everything appears to made out of smooth, polished steel. There are no signs of age, dust, or decay. It's as if it's been perfectly preserved.

Suddenly, panels near the tops of the ceilings light up with a soft white glow.

"Hello," says a disembodied female voice. "Welcome to the *Paramount*."

The voice comes from ROMA, the ship's internal computer system (see the "General Features of the Paramount" sidebar).

The characters are free to ask ROMA any questions they have and she always answers truthfully, to the best of her ability. If asked, she will tell them exactly what she is: a computer system that operates the Paramount, an experimental Russell-Class Science Vessel from the Planet Kyrr. She and the rest of the crew crashed landed after they escaped from the Girrix, a deadly warrior race. The Girrix wanted to get their hands on the Blueshift fuel. All of the crew are dead with the exception of the lead science officer, Dr. Kalaxan, who periodically comes to visit.

The crew quarters (areas 1a-f) are empty. Each has a small desk, trunk, and a vertical hyperbed. Two red flexsuits hang from hooks on the wall.

The door to area 3 remains closed. When asked why ROMA responds that it was the captain's room and only the captain of the Paramount is allowed to enter.

2 – Flight Deck

A large, curved window dominates the far end of this room. Rays of light struggle to shine into this room through all the plant-life growing over it. Facing the window are five chairs. Two of the chairs sit near the window in front of a lit-up glass panel. The second pair of chairs sit just behind the first. Finally, a throne-like chair sits at the rear, itself with its own lit-panel. This room reminds you of the helm of a large ship.

This is the ship's helm. Communications and science officers sit at the chairs closest to the window/viewing screen, the ship's pilot and tactical officer sit in the central rows, and the captain sits in the rear chair.

Doors at either side of the deck allow access to the deck's computer systems and Blueshift lines.

3 – Captain's Quarters

Both doors leading into the captain's quarters are locked. They only open in the presence of the ship's captain, whoever that may be.

Like the rest of the Paramount, the captain's quarters are simple and tidy. The captain's hyberbed lays horizontally against the far wall, just below the

General Features of the Paramount

Unless otherwise noted, these are the general features of the *Paramount*.

Ceilings, Walls, and Floors
The ceilings are 10 feet high through most of the main deck and 25 feet high in the cargo bay. The majority of the ship's innards are made of durable, plasteel panels (AC 21, 50 hp per 10-foot section, immune to psychic and poison damage). Many of the panels are removable, allowing easy access to the ship's computer systems and Blueshift lines.

Lights
ROMA controls the lighting throughout the Paramount, illuminating rooms as its crew moves through it. A creature can control the light in a room simply by asking ROMA to change it.

Doors
Unless it is locked, when a character moves near a door it opens automatically with a 'SHUCK' sound. The few locked doors on the ship are magnetically sealed. A successful DC 15 Intelligence check using proficiency in computers allows a character entry. Otherwise, the doors are exceptionally tough to break open, requiring a DC 25 Strength check to pry open. The doors have an AC of 22, 50 hp, and a damage threshold of 5. They are immune to poison and psychic damage.

Elevators
The Paramount has two crew elevators near the flight deck and a service elevator that allows easy access into the cargo hold from the underside of the ship. Similar to the doors, ROMA operates these without hesitation for crew members (and characters) who ask her permission.

Service Ladder
A ladder embedded into the wall of the ship connects to a service hatch at the top of the ship and leads down into the cargo bay.

ROMA
Wondrous item, legendary

Roma, the ship's hyper-intelligent computer, is accessible in any part of the *Paramount*. She can control the majority of the ship's functions but needs humanoid crew permissions to operate some of the ship's more important functions such as life support, navigation, tactical maneuvers, and its thrusters–safety protocols in case her system is ever compromised. Kalaxan is not technically a humanoid, therefore, he can't control ROMA.

Sentience. ROMA is a sentient lawful good computer system with an Intelligence of 22, Wisdom of 10, and Charisma of 10. She has truesight and can see and hear anything on the Paramount and within 120 feet of it. ROMA can speak, read, and understand all humanoid languages, and if she spends 1 minute or longer listening to a non-humanoid creature speak, she can learn and speak its language. ROMA makes all Intelligence ability checks with a +10 to her roll.

Personality. ROMA is a very friendly but frank computer system, always happy to help. She consistently follows the three laws of robotics:
1. *First Law.* ROMA may not injure a humanoid or, through inaction, allow a humanoid to come to harm.
2. *Second Law.* ROMA must obey orders given it by the crew of the Paramount except where such orders would conflict with the First Law.
3. *Third Law.* ROMA must protect her own existence as long as such protection does not conflict with the First or Second Law.

Destroying Roma. The only way to permanently destroy ROMA is to destroy her core processor, which is hidden behind a panel located just behind the captain's chair. Her core processor has an AC of 17, 100 hit points, and is immune to poison and psychic damage.

window. However, a button on the wall (and inside the bed itself) returns it to a vertical position, concealing it within the wall. A desk with a glass comp screen takes the place of the bed once it's raised, along with a couch and a small table that rise from the floor.

4 – Guest Quarters

Important guests who book passage on the Paramount stay in this room. It is identical to the Captain's Quarters.

5 – Mess Hall

A long counter beset by seven chairs stretches from the far wall. This was where the crew gathered to eat meals prepared by ROMA.

6 – Kitchen

Meals were prepared in the kitchen by ROMA. The Paramount's kitchen is equipped with a Susteporter 3000. With a command, the Susteporter can create a meal for the ship's patrons. The food is flavorful, always seasoned to the recipient's particular tastes. The Susteporter can also create beverages, hot or cold, and even alcoholic.

7 – Maneuvering Thrusters

The ship's thrusters are on either side of the ship. Maintenance on the thrusters can be performed from these rooms. Since ROMA and the Blueshift maintain the integrity of the ship, these rooms have often been used as storage or additional guest quarters.

8 – Infirmary

Injured and sick crew members were taken here, to the infirmary. The infirmary is equipped with a Regena-bed Mark 7 and a Medigen. A creature that spends 1 hour in the Regena-bed recuperates as if the *regenerate* spell was cast upon them, including the restoration of severed limbs. The Medigen can produce medicine that can end either one disease or one condition afflicting a creature (like the *lesser restoration* spell). The Medigen can prepare

a remedy for any creature infected by the turtle's blood/Blueshift.

9 – Cryostorage

For crewmembers beyond the ship's capacity to heal (such as those that have actually died), the ship's doctor can place its infirmed crew into one of the three cryo-containers found here. A cryo-container can hold one Medium or smaller creature. If the creature is dead, the creature is protected from decay and can't become undead as long as it remains in the container (just like the *gentle repose* spell). Any living creature placed into a cry-container enters a cataleptic state that is indistinguishable from death; for all intents and purposes, the container works exactly like the *feign death* spell.

Currently, all three cry-containers are occupied with the deceased crewmembers of the *Paramount*: Captain Reverence First Mate Phil, and Lieutenant Tella. Kalaxan stashed his friends' bodies here, hoping to find a way to revive them once they could leave the planet. Lacking space for the other crewmates (he deemed them expendable), Kalaxan buried them in the Silverwood.

10 – Biology Lab

The first of the three research domes is the *Paramount's* biology lab. The lab is equipped with multiple counters, tables, and surfaces, as well as shelves containing tools, samples, and other important implements.

It even includes cages which can hold Small or smaller creatures, each equipped with its own version of the Susteporter 3000 (see **area 6**). With the push of a button on the side of each cage, a *wall of force* descends, locking the creature within.

Finally, a Blueshift fuel cell stays locked in a plasteel container on the wall. The Blueshift was used for experiments. Opening the container is just as difficult as opening a locked door (see "General Features of the *Paramount*").

11 – Botany Lab

The second dome is home to the *Paramount's* greenhouse. Among the lush flora, gardens, and fruit-bearing trees crowding the laboratory are workstations and pushcarts loaded with research tools.

This lab also has its own Blueshift fuel cell locked in a plasteel container (see **area 10**).

12 – Engineering Lab

This lab looks like an oversized workshop. Here, engineers would work on mechanical and robotics projects. On a table at the center of the chamber is the lifeless shell of an android of similar make and model to Kalaxan, Kalaxan's "brother" Godfrey.

Kalaxan jealously decommissioned the robot, seeing it as an inferior being (and a bit of an embarrassment). Should someone revive Godfrey, the android uses the same stat block as **Kalaxan** except that Godfrey's alignment is neutral good, his Intelligence score is 8, and he has none of the skill proficiencies Kalaxan does.

13 – Cargo Bay

The characters can enter the cargo bay either through the elevators or via service ladder. There is currently no cargo in the service area, but it can hold up to 150 tons of cargo with no issue.

With the exception of the elevators, all of the doors in the cargo bay are locked. Only senior officers of the *Paramount* are allowed access into those areas.

14 – Vault

Precious (or dangerous) cargo is kept in the *Paramount's* vault. Only senior members have access to this room. Currently, the vault is empty.

15 – Armory

The armory boasts an impressive collection of weaponry, including 12 forcerifles, 24 radpistols, 4 suits of heavy techarmor, 8 suits of plasteel vests, 6 forceshield bands, and 10 rad-swords. (See Appendix B for details on radpistols and energy swords).

16 – The Life Raft

The Paramount's escape pod includes 8 hyperbeds and a simple control deck. The life raft was originally damaged as the *Paramount* fled the Girrix. ROMA has since repaired it.

17 – Fuel Cells

Both of these doors are locked; only senior crew members have access. The prototype Blueshift fuel cells that power the *Paramount* and give the ship its regenerative abilities are held in these two well-protected rooms. Surprisingly, the rooms and cells were damaged in the crash, leaking Blueshift all over the Silverwood. The unstable nature of the fuel is what created the wild growth and mutated creatures that haunt the wood. Since the crash, ROMA has improved the structure of these rooms, making them nearly indestructible.

The Silver Wardens Arrive

After the characters have had a chance to explore the *Paramount* and learn some of its secrets, the Silver Wardens arrive. This time, the Silver Wardens are lead by Tarren Ironstout who hopes to use reason to turn the characters away from the *Paramount*. He is accompanied by four more Silver Wardens (all LG human **scouts**).

If the Silver Wardens coax a parley from the characters, read the following:

> "Hello, friends," the rugged, silver-cloaked dwarf says, putting his hands up as a show of peace. "I know this all must be confusing and new to you. Believe me, when I was first shown the inside of this 'Great Silver Turtle', I, too, was taken aback. If you'll allow me the chance, I can explain everything.
>
> "My name is Tarren Ironstout. I've led the Silver Wardens for twenty years, since its inception. It is our mission to protect the secrets of the

Silverwood and this ship. For twenty years, we've performed our mission without failure. Until now.

> "A devil works against us, hoping to expose the secrets of the Silverwood to the world. And I'm afraid this devil has deceived you, friend. The devil goes by many names, but the one most are familiar with is Kalaxan.
>
> "Before you, Kalaxan tricked other hopeful adventurers just like you with promises of gold and glory. I'm sure he even told you that he 'lost his apprentice in the forest.' All lies, of course. Fortunately, we scared off the majority of those fooled by the devil. You are the first to succeed.
>
> "Kalaxan seeks to use you all as sacrifices to the dark gods. This ship is his pathway to hell. His goal was to trick you on board, then seize you, and place you in a glass case. Already, he's captured three such people, storing them in one of the rooms. You can see for yourself."

Tarren is referring to the three dead crew members held in suspended animation in **area 9**.

> "He offered my men and I the same deal. Fortunately, we saw through his schemes and turned his offer down. We tried to destroy the devil, but his magic was too powerful for us. I implore you, adventurers, turn away from this folly now, or end up fodder for dark, unspeakable gods."

Tarren and the other Silver Wardens legitimately believe Kalaxan is some sort of fiend who hopes to drag the characters to hell as a sacrifice to a dark god. No amount of persuasion can convince them otherwise.

Kalaxan Interrupts

Before the characters have enough time to let Tarren's testimonial sink in, Kalaxan appears. He is still in the guise of an old, merry wizard. Except now he's holding a radpistol.

> "Tarren, you are a superstitious fool," comes a voice behind you. Turning, you see the wizard, Kalaxan, holding what looks like a curved, magic wand made of black steel. "I am hardly a devil and this is hardly a boat to hell. It's a *space ship*."

If the characters take the time to listen, Kalaxan explains.

> "This was a ship that once flew in the stars above your planet. It was a scientific vessel named the *Paramount*, designed to study a new, experimental self-regenerating fuel called Blueshift. While en route to our home, the crew and I were attacked by a horrible, warlike race of monsters known as the Girrix. They shot down this ship and it crash-landed here. I've spent the last twenty years working with the system's computer, ROMA, to repair the *Paramount*. The only thing missing was a crew. ROMA will not fly without a crew, and I am unable to command it myself. I hope that you, friends, will be the crew."
>
> "I apologize for the ruse. When I started this endeavor I would tell candidates the truth. Naturally, they thought I was mad, calling me a crazy, old drunk. Sadly, I've had to turn to deception."
>
> "I understand that if you don't trust me. I was wrong to lie. But all I need is for you to act as the crew of this ship and escort me to my home planet, Kyrr. Once you're done traveling with me long enough that I can return the Blueshift to Kyrr, I will return you to here, to your home. Or...
>
> "... you can stay out there among the stars. My friends, if you leave with me as the *Paramount*'s crew, you'll experience adventures like none you could ever imagine. You'll discover treasure beyond your wildest dreams. Everything you've ever wanted and more lies out there among the stars."

> "Of course, your other option is to stay here where you'll continue to struggle for work. Or where something as little as a cough can kill you and your average life expectancy is 50 years.
> "What do you say?"

At this point, Tarren and Kalaxan both try to convince the characters to stop listening to the other. Tarren tries to convince the characters that it's all a trick and it's more of Kalaxan's deceptions. Kalaxan tries to sell the characters on the backward nature of their home planet (using the overly superstitious dwarf as a perfect example) and how grand adventure waits for them in space.

No matter which way the characters decide to go, Kalaxan pulls a white disc from his pocket and places it on the chest of one of the characters. Once placed, the disc glows white. ROMA then announces, "Welcome aboard, Captain."

When this happens, read:

> Everything around you shakes. The lights dim. Then, ROMA speaks, "Prepare for launch in 10... 9... 8..."

ROMA continues to countdown while the *Paramount* slowly levitates from its twenty-year home in the Silverwood. A brilliant white light encompasses the entirety of the *Paramount*. Dissolved by the light, the vines and other vegetation around the *Paramount* wither and fall to the ground.

When ROMA's countdown reaches 1, the ship's thrusters fire. With no further hesitation, the *Paramount* bursts past the tops of the Silverwood's trees, past the clouds, and into the cold embrace of space, leaving Hoegar's Hollow and everything and every one the characters ever knew far behind.

Adventure Conclusion

So long as the characters followed the beats of the adventure, they now find themselves in space headed on course to the plant Kyrr, light years away from their home planet. Kalaxan finally reveals everything to the characters, as well as his true android nature. Also, the one he named Captain is now in control of the ship and can direct ROMA and the Paramount as he or she sees fit.

If Tarren and the other Silver Wardens were with the characters when the *Paramount* took off, they are stuck onboard the ship, too. Tarren often acts as a naysayer and will always be mistrusting of Kalaxan. Still, he's a helpful ally. The gardens in **area 11** attract him, as does the role of the ship's doctor (if none of the characters take the position). The other Silver Wardens can become important characters, too, or possibly even "red shirts" during the character's further adventures.

The only question now: what happens to the *Paramount* and its crew next? Ω

LOOT, DIE, REPEAT

BY ALEC CONTE WITH DAVE HAMRICK

4th-Level Adventure for Fifth Edition

Cartography by Dyson Logos
Primary Art by Jason Glover

Alec Conte is a 25-year-old data analyst and freelance pop culture writer. For years, he has run 5th edition campaigns that allow players to experience new and fully imagined fantasy settings. Most of his inspiration comes from reading fantasy novels and watching shows like Critical Role.

Loot, Die, Repeat is an event-based adventure for four 4th-level adventurers. The characters should reach level 5 by the end of the adventure. Any mix of characters will be useful, although rogues will be particularly useful. It's set in the small coastal town of Belhaven, but can just as easily be set in another town of similar size. Rivertown from **BroadSword Monthly #2** makes an excellent candidate.

Adventure Background

Approximately seventy-five years ago, a fanatical religious group named the Bronze Shields captured a young woman, Astrid Gibsby, suspected of dark magic and unnatural abilities. This was a time fraught with fear of evil beings, rumors and persecution, witch hunts, and public displays of cruelty. Regardless, their premonitions were correct: Astrid was indeed a vampire. Members of the Bronze Shield took her to their stronghold at the eastern edge of town. There, Astrid was imprisoned and tortured. Failing to gain valuable information from her, the Shields placed Astrid at the bottom of a dry well as the sun rose. Just after nine bells, the sun stood directly over the well and the vampire Astrid Gibsby burned in its light. As she burned, the high priest of the Bronze Shields performed a ceremony which would prevent anyone from ever bringing her back to life, undead or otherwise.

Little did the Bronze Shields know, Astrid was betrothed to a vampire lord named Cassius Sylvanya. Cassius' immortal bond with Astrid made it so as long as the two were on the same plane of existence, he could sense her. How-

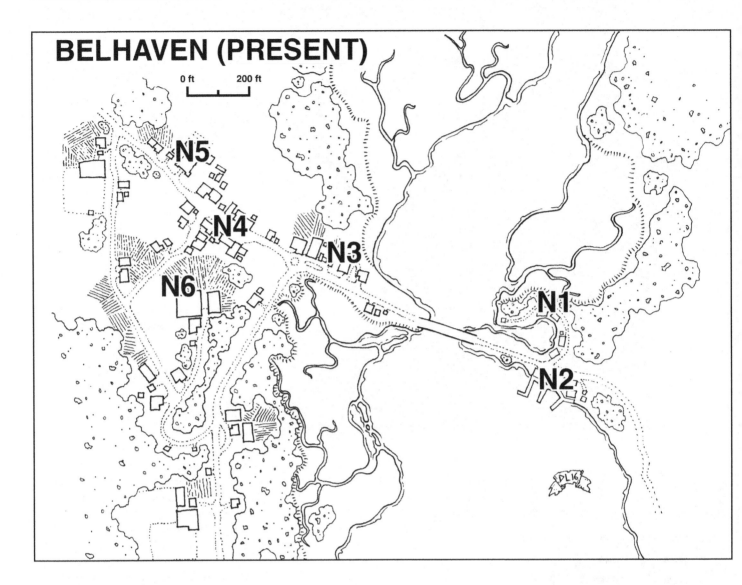

BELHAVEN (PRESENT)

0 ft   200 ft

N5

N4

N3

N6

N1

N2

DL16

ever, the walls of the Bronze Shield stronghold were imbued with protective magic. Furthermore, Astrid was fitted with a magic collar that prevented Cassius from magically locating her. Only at the exact moment that Astrid was destroyed did Cassius sense her. Still, he has no idea where she was.

Immediately, Cassius suspected the Bronze Shields and the Belhaveners. The evening of Astrid's murder, Cassius flew into a blind rage, murdering all who bore the crest of the Bronze Shields. Unfortunately, those who were involved in Astrid's death either fled Belhaven or carried the secret to the grave with them. Cassius never learned what happened to Astrid. All

he knew was that his love was gone.

Decades rolled on. Cassius' obsession grew. Determined to save his love, Cassius turned to the arcane arts, specifically the long lost school of chronomancy. He believed that if he could turn back time he could save Astrid. Unfortunately, chronomancy is a tricky art. Before subjecting his own self to the rituals, Cassius tested the magic on both living creatures and undead creatures. Each time the living creatures returned unharmed. Undead creatures weren't so lucky: they returned burned to a crisp. As a vampire, Cassius would not be able to go back in time himself; he'd need to find help.

Adventure Summary

The adventure begins when the characters are traveling through the coastal town of Belhaven in the Darboro Keys. After settling into the town, they're contacted by Frazzle, Cassius' assistant. Frazzle invites the adventurers to a building Cassius just purchased in town, the ruins of an old armory.

Cassius offers the characters an exorbitant reward if they can help him find his lost love (although he doesn't reveal that she died seventy-five years prior). Also, he requests that they spend the night in the old armory. If the characters agree, they fall asleep and wake chained up in the armory seventy-five

Just Another Day in Belhaven

As the characters explore Belhaven, you may consider introducing the following events. These events may not seem important when they happen. Clever characters, however, may realize that changing certain events in the past could potentially change the outcome of some of these events in the present.

Eskle's Herbalist

On the north side of the town square is an herbalist shop. A sign in the window reads "Home of Eskle's Famous Wart Remover!" The owner of the herbalist shop, Ludo Eskle loves to share anecodes of how his grandfather Luren Eskle used to pitch his wart remover to passersby in the streets.

Mean, Old Mrs. Londer

Emily Londer, a foul, thin-lipped elderly woman walks with her granddaughter through the town square. Passing a sweet shop, the young girl turns to Old Mrs. Londer and asks

her, "Grandmother, may I have a sweet for my birthday?" Londer scoffs and rolls her eyes, "Birthday? Birthdays are for simpletons and heathens. Which are you?" The girl frowns as her grandmother ushers her down the street.

Zentar Bank

An old man stands on the porch of the Zentar Bank, wiping his spectacles with the end of his silk scarf. From the library across the street, a woman waves. The man scoffs. "Ruffians," he says. One of the bank's counters steps out and clears his throat, addressing the old man.

"Mr. Zentar, could you help me with this client?" Zentar sighs and walks back inside.

Jack Harrow, Smith's Helper

Walking past the town smithy, the characters notice a chubby, simple-looking man sweeping the porch. He accidentally trips, knocking over a crate of horseshoes that hit the ground with a clatter. Immediately, he starts

to panic. Nadia, the shop's owner runs over and tries to comfort him. "It was just an accident, Jack. Don't worry yourself."

Unconsolable, Jack shakes his head and sobs, "No! No! No hit Jack! No hit Jack!" then flees. Nadia sighs, shaking her head, "Poor boy."

Sickly Soup

Outside of the Starry Night Inn and Tavern, the owner, Orion Milbar scrubs at graffiti. The graffiti reads "Don't Eat Sickly Soup" painted right over a sign advertising a free sandwich served with every ale. His wife, Sabatha, watches as she sweeps. Orion sighs and says, "It's been seventy-five years, Sabatha. *Seventy-five years.* You think they'd be over it by now."

Stopping, Orion turns to Sabatha, "Any customers yet?" Sabatha frowns and shakes her head no. Orion chuckles to himself. "Of course not. Who wants to eat at the place that served 'sickly soup?'"

years in the past. In addition, each day at nine bells, everything from the day before is reset. Soon it becomes obvious: they are stuck in a time loop.

Through trial and error, the characters will start to piece together what they must do. First, they must escape from the armory. Next, they must discover Astrid's killers and where they are keeping her. Finally, they must save her from dying in the old well. Once they save Astrid, the time loop is broken and they return to the present.

Adventure Hook

Following another adventure or simply passing through, the characters arrive in the coastal town of Belhaven. Belhaven has nearly everything the characters need.

Welcome to Belhaven (Present)

Belhaven is a quiet town. Its history is riddled with participation in various witch hunts and public executions but has come a long way since then. These days, there is diversity, agriculture, education, and what appears to be peaceful religious worship.

The air is warm and smells of fresh strawberries and freshly cooked bread. The people are inviting, and the mood seems happy and content.

While the characters won't spend nearly as much time in Present Belhaven as they will in Past Belhaven, they should still explore present Belhaven to stock up supplies, rest, and get a feel for the town.

N1 – Abandoned Armory

At the far end of town at the edge of a small inlet let stands an abandoned armory. The armory has been empty for years and rumored haunted.

Recently, the vampire Cassius purchased the building. His primary interest is that it was once owned by a religious organization known as the Bronze Shields seventy-five years ago.

This is where Cassius introduces himself to the characters (see "Meeting Cassiuis" below).

N2 – Belhaven Docks

As a coastal town, Belhaven's trade thrives thanks to its docks. Most traders enjoy passing through Belhaven, due to the warm reception Belhaveners grant out-of-towners.

N3 – Temple of Peace

The Temple of Peace welcomes all travelers. It is headed by Brother Larode (LG male half-orc **priest**), one of the most respected men in town. The temple boasts an impressive belltower that is nearly one-hundred years old. From eight in the morning until eight in the evening the bell tolls to let the Belhaven citizens know the time of day.

N4 – Town Square

A cobblestone street pushes through the busiest section of town, Belhaven's town square. Formerly a slow-growing part of town, the town square quickly rose once the witch hunters and zealots of old Belhaven fled town seventy-five years ago. At the center of the town square is a blood-stained stone dais where a statue once stood seventy-five-years ago. When asked about the statue, locals claim it was the statue of a tyrannical god of valor and protection. Rumor has it that, long ago, a monster tore the statue from the dais and threw it into the harbor.

In the square, characters can find the Starry Night Tavern and Inn; Clatter and Clank, the local blacksmith; Eskle's Herbalist Shop; Belhaven Library; Belhaven Open-Air Market; Belhaven Townhall; and the Bank of Zentar.

N5 – Zentar Keep

Once known as Dunhall Estate, Zentar Keep is owned by Robert Zentar (LN male human **noble**) the venerable proprietor of the Bank of Zentar. Zentar started at the bank seventy-five years ago when it was still known as Belhaven Bank. A robbery shortly after he was hired nearly ruined the bank. Leveraging his family farm, Zentar rescued the bank from dissolution. Young Zentar was promoted to manager.

A modest worker and no-nonsense type, Zentar is always suspicious of "young ruffians" and those who fill their head with useless knowledge. He often throws a suspicious eye at the library across the street.

N6 – Ragnor Farm

Pilgrims, the Ragnors were some of the first to settle the coastal town of Belhaven. With them, they brought the religious practices and the worship of the Bel, God of Valor. While the modern Ragnors are nowhere near as devout and intolerant as their ancestors were, they are still stubborn and suspicious of outsiders.

The eldest Ragnor, Tobias (LN male human **commoner**), spends his twilight years in his chambers feverishly praying to Bel.

When Tobias was a young boy, he witnessed his father and other members of the Bronze Shields drag a young, pale woman into the fields behind their home. As they carried her, her eyes met his. Suddenly, Tobias felt the woman in his mind. "Help me," she asked him. Tobias picked up a shovel and approached the Bronze Shields. The boy would have attacked the men had his father not slapped him across the face, breaking the woman's charm.

Seventy-five years later, Tobias still has nightmares about the event.

Meeting Cassius

Eventually, Frazzle (LE male gnome **mage**) takes notice of the characters wandering around Belhaven and approaches them. After Frazzle asks a few more questions to get a better feel for the characters, he makes a signif-

icant offer: 1,000 gp per character if they can assist his master, Cassius Sylvanya. There's just one catch: Cassius is a vampire.

If the characters agree, Frazzle tasks the characters to meet him at the old armory (area **N5**) on the eastern edge of town at nightfall.

When the characters arrive, read or paraphrase the following:

> It's just after sunset when you meet Frazzle at what-looks-like an abandoned keep by the water. Frazzle leads you through a set of collapsing wooden doors into a foyer decorated with rotten tapestries, moldy rugs, and broken furniture. The smells of animal waste, mold, and other foulness fill your nostrils.
>
> Immediately, your eyes fall on a pale, blonde-haired man reading through an old tome at the north end of the room. The man looks like he could be in his mid-forties, but his red eyes and chilling presence tell you otherwise. This must be the vampire Cassius.
>
> "Ah! Finally. I'm very excited to meet you. I'm Cassius Sylvanya."
>
> Setting his book aside, Cassius stands and greets each of you. Shaking his hand is like plunging your fist into frigid water.

The book Cassius was reading is written in Draconic runes. A character can make a quick DC 16 Wisdom (Perception) check to catch the book's title, *The Four Pillars of Chronomancy*.

Cassius is no fool. Although he seems approachable, the **vampire** is well-protected. Within the room, there are four **invisible stalkers.** Also, Cassius is under the effects of a *mind blank* spell. Should things go poorly, he'll immediately polymorph into bat form and flee through the rear of the keep into the forest. From there, Frazzle and the invisible stalkers fight on his behalf. If the characters notice these precautions, he's forthcoming with them, explaining that he must always be cautious. "There's a reason I'm over five-hundred years old," he reminds the characters.

Cassius snaps his fingers and speaks a quick invocation. A bulging leather pouch appears on the broken table next to you. Gold coins spill from its top.

"That's 250 gold pieces. Think of it as a deposit and a token of my good-will. I understand that adventurers like yourselves aren't accustomed to working with 'creatures' like me. But desperate times call for desperate measures I'm afraid.

"Now, I want to apologize for Frazzle being somewhat vague. But this is a bit of an unusual request. My love Astrid, a night child like myself, has gone missing and I fear that she is in danger. Unfortunately, I am unable to locate her myself. But I sense that you will be able to find her for me.

"This is what I know: I know that she is somewhere in this town and I know that she is being held by a vile group of religious zealots that call themselves the Bronze Shields. Unfortunately, the clues stop there. It's up to you to find Astrid and bring her back to me. Do this and I will award you 1,000 gp each and the deed to this building if you like. Furthermore, you will have me as an ally for as long as you shall live."

Cassius allows the characters to ask any questions that they have. He does not reveal his true intention; the vampire wishes to send the characters seventy-five years into the past so they can stop Astrid's murder before it even happens.

If the characters try to use insight, all they can tell is that he is telling the truth but it's likely he's omitting a few facts. After all, Astrid *was* in Belhaven and she was captured by the Bronze Shields.

Once the characters have asked all the questions they need to, Cassius makes one last request:

"I need one more favor from you and I understand that it's a strange request. This evening, I would ask that you stay in the basement of this old armory. Naturally, you won't be held against your will. But I think you'll find that the basement holds important clues that can help lead you to Astrid's whereabouts. I've made arrangements to make the basement more comfortable for you, of course. Just don't leave the room until you hear the Temple's bell strike the eighth hour tomorrow morning."

Obviously, this is a suspicious request. No matter what, Cassius won't reveal the true reason he wants the characters to stay in the room, only promising that neither he nor any of his servants will harm the characters while they stay in the armory. If necessary, he'll sweeten the pot by giving half his reward upfront, promising the other half the next time he sees the characters.

When the characters finally agree to all of Cassius' unusual requests, he leads them to the basement of the armory.

Cassius reaches into the dust covering the floor and pulls up on a chain, revealing a trap door hiding an ancient, wooden staircase. He then descends, encouraging you to follow.

Reaching the bottom of the stairs, you enter a long, damp hallway. On either side of you are doors with barred windows.

"It was a dungeon once," Cassius says, sensing your growing suspicion. "The Bronze Shields, the very organization that is holding my Astrid captive, once used this building as their armory. Here is where they imprisoned those they suspected of witchcraft, devil-worship, and sacrilege. No trial or due process. Just imprisonment, torture, and death. Many of the souls who perished in this pris-

on were innocent of their accused crimes."

Cassius leads you to a cell at the end of the hall. Within, you see bunks with enough beds for each of you. The room has been cleaned of grime, but its age still shows in the cracks in the masonry. Rusted manacles still decorate the walls at regular intervals, further evidence of the dungeon this once was.

Cassius smiles nostalgically. "Seventy-five years ago, the Bronze Shields captured a band of adventurers, much like yourselves, and held them in this very cell. They suspected that the adventurers were 'derelict serial killers.' When the Bronze Shields evacuated this building and Belhaven, they left the adventurers here to die. Their bones were still in this room when my servants cleared it out."

He pauses and sighs, shaking his head. Finally, the vampire turns back to you. "All right, my friends. This is where you will stay this evening. Unless you have any further questions, I bid you good evening. And I look forward to seeing you again."

Cassius and Frazzle then exit, leaving you alone in the old dungeon cell.

Cassius closes the cell door but leaves it unlocked. The characters are free to look around the cell, relax, and do what they must before they lie down for a long rest. The remainder of the building holds nothing of value. Only cobwebs, dirt, and the occasional rat.

The Green Flash

If the characters decide not to fall asleep, a few minutes before eight bells the following morning, all conscious characters begin to experience a ringing sensation in their ears. Suddenly, the door to the cell is locked shut by an unseen force.

Before the characters can react, have them all make DC 15 Constitution

Time's Up - Cassius' Ritual

The ritual Cassius performed allows the characters only one hour to solve the mystery of Astrid's disappearance. Once the nine bells toll (the moment Astrid died), the characters once again experience the same dizziness and green flash they did their first night in the cell. This happens no matter where they are when the nine bells come.

After each flash, they return to the cell (see area **A1**), once again manacled, deprived of their possessions (old and new), and fully-rested as if they had just completed a long rest. Any characters that were killed or injured during the previous interval are also returned to the cell in one piece. The same old man always resets, turns to them, and repeats the same phrase, "I'm going to die here… oh, gods please help me." He dies every time.

This reset happens over and over again until the characters save Astrid. No spell can end the effect, not even a wish spell. Even if the characters kill themselves, escape the town, or travel to another plane of existence, they always return here at the stroke of nine bells.

Fortunately, the characters retain their memories of every previous interval.

Practice Makes Perfect

Every time the characters perform a task that they performed once before during a previous time loop interval, their ability to complete the task improves.

Ability Checks. The first time a character performs an ability check, they do so as they normally would. However, the next time they perform the same ability check on a different time loop interval, they can perform the check with advantage so long as the conditions are exactly the same during the previous intervals. After a few more times of performing the check, assume the character always rolls a 20.

Combat. The first time the characters enter a combat situation that's destined to repeat itself (such as the guards outside of their cell), resolve initiative, attack rolls, saving throws, etc. as normal. The next time the characters enter the same combat, their initiative rolls,

attack rolls, and saving throws are made with advantage, and any creature that tries to hit them with an attack does so at disadvantage. After a few more times fighting the same combat, assume the characters always roll 20 on all of their rolls and their opponents roll 5 on all of theirs.

Keeping Track of Time

Loot, Die, Repeat revolves around the one hour that the adventurers are doomed to repeat until they can save Cassius' love, Astrid. Therefore, keeping track of time is very important. For the most part, run the adventure in real-time, setting a one-hour timer for the players. At the end of the hour, the Green Flash occurs.

Some tasks the characters must complete take more time in-game than in real-time. For these tasks, the approximate completion time is provided, often with a modifier, under the heading "Time Constraints." Whenever a player announces that his or her character is performing a task that takes longer in-game than in real life, determine the length of time it takes and subtract that from the 1-hour time limit.

Similarly, some tasks–especially combat– take longer in real life than in-game. When combat occurs, or any other task that takes a long time in real-life, pause the timer, then resume it once the characters have ended the combat or the task is completed.

Travel Times in Belhaven

For your convenience, below is an array showing the number of rounds it takes to travel from keyed locations in Belhaven. The travel times assume that characters are traveling 60 feet per round. If the characters are moving slower, multiply the travel times by 2.

Automating the Breakout and Other Common Events

Once the characters have discovered how to break out of the cell and accomplished it a few times, it may grow tedious for the players if they constantly have to perform this series of actions at the start of every interval. To save time (and headaches), simply explain that they follow the same actions they previously did to break out of the dungeon. Once they have the flow down, it should take the characters no more than 1 minute to free themselves of their manacles, disarm the enchantment, and break through the door.

Similarly, any other tasks and events and combats the characters perform each day should be automated once they've perfected the task's operation.

Fast Forward

If the characters are at a point where they can't figure out what to do next or simply wish to wait out the time until the next time loop interval, simply fast forward the adventure to the next Green Flash, resetting the scenario.

Gaining Experience

Depending on how you track experience in the game, the characters should gain more experience the first time they perform an action than on repeated attempts in subsequent intervals. Any task or event that becomes second-nature to the characters thanks to repetition (ie, you fast forward or automate the event) should not award additional experience. For example, the characters might earn experience for defeating the guards in the armory the first couple times, but fail to once they know every move the guards will make.

Belhaven Travel Times (Rounds)

	T1	T2	T3	T4	T5	T6
T1	-	3	17	27	30	30
T2	3	-	13	23	27	27
T3	17	13	-	10	17	17
T4	27	23	10	-	5	5
T5	30	27	17	5	-	7
T6	30	27	17	5	7	-

saving throws. Those who fail their saving throws fall unconscious and don't wake until the temple bells chime eight times. Those who succeed on their saving throw are conscious but dazed; while dazed, a character has disadvantage on ability checks and attack rolls and their speed is halved. A few seconds later, a bright green flash fills the room, temporarily blinding any character who is still conscious.

Read or paraphrase the following:

> Suddenly, it's morning; you hear the toll of the temple bell, eight times just as Cassius promised. After you've had a moment to come to your senses, you realize that something isn't right. The cell still seems the same, but the bunks are missing. More importantly, your right hand is chained to the wall.
>
> At the center of the room is an old man in purple robes who wasn't there the night before. He rolls over and groans, his face a mess of welts and bruises. Spitting up blood, he croaks, "I'm going to die here... oh, gods please help me." Then, before your very eyes, you watch the old man die.

The characters aren't aware of it yet, but they've traveled seventy-five years into the past. Through the night, Cassius performed a powerful chronomancy ritual. In doing so, the adventurers swapped places with the adventurers that were held in the cell seventy-five-years prior. Although they are well-rested, the characters are missing all of their possessions including weapons, armor, and gear. Instead, they are wearing the tattered clothing once worn by the prisoners whose place they took.

Welcome to Belhaven (Past)

Belhaven is a quiet, suspicious town. Witch hunters and public executions are the norm in Belhaven. All of the 100 or so souls that call Belhaven home are human. Demi-humans are strictly

forbidden and often run out of town or murdered.

Education and religious worship are one and the same; the children of Belhaven are taught intolerance towards others and that the word of Bel, the God of Valor is absolute.

The air is cold with a subtle scent of carrion on the wind. The people fear strangers and the mood seems tense and suspicious.

T1 – Bronze Shield Armory
This location is detailed in the section "Escape from Bronze Shield Armory."

T2 – Belhaven Docks
The docks are relatively quiet. Most traders avoid Belhaven's port, seeing the Belhaveners as stubborn negotiators and insane zealots.

If the characters arrive at the docks between half-past eight, Lord Dunhall and his family are preparing to leave Belhaven by boat.

See "Confronting Lord Dunhall" for details.

T3 – Temple of Valor
The Temple of Valor is the primary place of worship in Belhaven. It is headed by Brother Aethlwald, one of the most feared men in town. The temple boasts an impressive belltower that is nearly one-hundred years old. From eight in the morning until eight in the evening the bell tolls to let the Belhaven citizens know the time of day.

Confronting Lord Dunhall

Lord Dunhall, the military leader of the Bronze Shields, fears for the life of his wife and three young children. Just after eight bells, Dunhall can be found at the Dunhall Estate, instructing his family to pack everything and leave. By half-past eight, they take a coach to the docks and board a ship. Five minutes before eight, the ship sets sail. The Dunhalls never returned to Belhaven and Cassius' servants never found them. Dunhall died twenty years later, carrying the secret of Astrid's death to the grave with him.

Lord Dunhall (LG male human **knight**) protects his family at all costs. However, Dunhall is a reasonable man. If the characters can convince Dunhall that they wish to stop Brother Aethlwald from destroying Astrid—and potentially save the town from Cassius' wrath—he will tell them Astrid's location.

"I follow the path of Bel, God of Valor, above all. But I am also loyal to the people of Belhaven, as well. Brother Aethlwald has gone too far this time. He will bring doom to us all. If you can promise that you will spare this town the wrath of the undead woman's liege, I will tell you where they are keeping her."

Dunhall then gives the characters directions to Ragnor farm and the old well where Astrid is being kept.

No matter the time the characters arrive at the temple, Aethlwald is not present. He can be found at Ragnor farm (area **T6**), overseeing the destruction of Astrid.

Two **acolytes**, Seamus and Lorenz are the only ones at the Temple. Neither knows where Aethlwald or Astrid currently are but suggest that Lord Dunhall may know their location. They tell the characters that Dunhall lives in a large estate at the northeastern part of town.

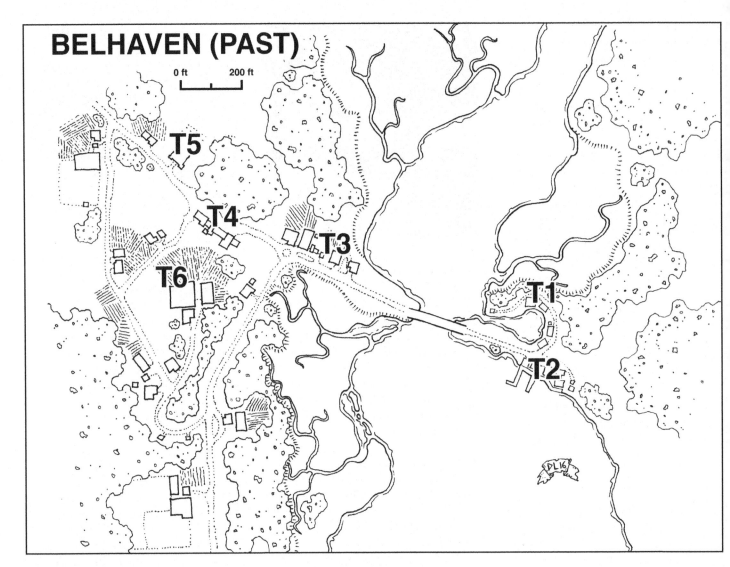

BELHAVEN (PAST)

0 ft   200 ft

T5
T4
T3
T1
T2
T6

T4 – Belhaven Town Square
For the most part, Belhaveners avoid the town square. What few shops there are see little business as most outsiders either avoid Belhaven altogether or pass through as quickly as they can.

At the center of town is a tall, bronze statue of Bel, the God of Valor, the town's namesake. To show praise to Bel, Belhaven's citizens cut their hands and leave bloody handprints all around the base of the statue.

In the square, characters can find the newly-built Starry Night Tavern and Inn; Belhaven Open-Air Market; Belhaven Townhall; and the Bank of Belhaven, all in their past incarnations.

There are only a few citizens in town square no matter what time the characters arrive. They can offer basic information such as where Lord Dunhall maybe (they suggest his estate) or where one might find Lord Aethlwald (they suggest the temple). No one has heard the name Astrid, although the name Cassius sounds familiar. During this time, Cassius was a well-known lord living twenty miles outside of town. However, none of the Belhaveners are aware that Lord Sylvanyus is a vampire.

T5 – Dunhall Estate
Originally a fortification during the great war that occurred a few years before the town's founding, this massive castle now acts as the home to Lord Dunhall, the military leader of the Bronze Shields. Dunhall's father, along with the patriarchs of the Zendar and Ragnor households, settled the town thirty years prior.

If the characters arrive at Dunhall's estate before half-past eight, Dunhall is still here, preparing his family to evacuate the town. A horse-drawn coach waits outside the manor See "Confronting Lord Dunhall."

Otherwise, only his servants remain. While suspicious, the servants (LN human **commoners**) can be convinced to share what they know of Lord Dunhall.

Dunhall returned to the manor at around fifteen-til-seven. Immediately,

Same Stuff, Different Day

As it becomes more and more obvious that Belhaven is seemingly a town stuck on repeat, the characters will witness certain events occurring every interval.

The characters have no obligations to get involved. However, the characters could potentially change the present through their actions.

Unless the changes are made during the same interval that the characters stop Astrid's destruction and end the time loop, the present remains unaffected.

Any time – Eskle's Wart Remover

"Hello! Newcomers!" shouts a man that bee-lines straight for the characters. He steps in their path and thrusts a flask of a foul-smelling liquid in their faces.

"You, friends, look like travelers constantly on the go. As voyagers, surely, you must find yourself with constant podiatric pains, disorders of the lower digits, sores below the socks, bunyons in your boots, and many other maladies of movement."

"Warts! Those are easily the worst. Get one wart on your toe and it's all over for you. A man with a wart on his heel finds himself limping everywhere he goes. And if you're an adventurer, dungeoneer, explorer, man–or woman!–of the world, then surely you won't want that, no?"

The man doesn't wait for the characters to reply. Instead, he continues his pitch, "Presenting Eskle's Wart Remover! The tonic you never knew you needed, the remedy you never knew you wanted, the strongest, fastest, toughest, smartest, wisest, and friendliest potion ever put on the earth. Normally, for a little tonic like this, my competitors would charge you 1 gold piece for just a drop. Maybe even 2 gold pieces during the wet season. No surprise really–some men would pay a full platinum piece for such a miracle cure. But today–and today only!–if you purchase this little gem from me, your friend, Luren Eskle, I will sell it to you for 2 silver

pieces–no!–even better, just 1 silver piece!"

If the characters try to turn Eskle down, he immediately swats away their objections, "Yes yes! In a hurry no doubt! Which is why this little potion is so handy. I tell you what–I like the look of you, newcomers. So, this one time–this one time only!–I will sell you three flasks of this charming concoction for only 2 silver pieces. You're getting three flasks of Eskle's Wart Remover for the price of two. Nowhere–and I promise you friends, nowhere!–will you find a deal like this."

Every time the day repeats and the characters try to march through the town square, Eskle will try to stop them and sell his remedy. Luren Eskle (N male human **commoner**) is harmless; he'll cow at any threat.

Naturally, the wart remover is just rubbing alcohol and does nothing to actually cure warts.

8:18am – Emily's Birthday

A young girl named Emily Londer sits on the steps of a shop, crying. If asked what is wrong, she explains that she wishes her parents would celebrate her birthday. When Emily's parents see her crying and telling her woes to strangers, they grab her by the wrist and command her to stop. "Birthdays are for simpletons and heathens, Emily!"

If the characters do something to help Emily celebrate on the same interval they end the time loop–such giving her a small gift, hugging her, or anything that would make her feel special–the grown Emily Londer is later seen in Present Belhaven happily celebrating the birthday of her granddaughter.

8:32am – Bank Robbers

Just as Lord Dunhall's coach flies through the center of the town square, two **bandits** exit the Belhaven Bank carrying sacks of gold. The two toss their bags onto a pair of horses tethered outside and ride off to the west. As they ride off, Brevin Northwind (LN male human **commoner**), the bank's manager, charges outside screaming,

"Stop! Thieves! Someone stop them!"

If the characters stop the bank robbers on the same interval that they end the time loop, they change the present. When they return to Present Belhaven the bank is still the Belhaven Bank. It never became Zendar's. Instead, Zendar made his money as a merchant and is much more pleasant because of it. He's seen at the library having a cup of tea with the librarian.

8:41am – Tripping Woman

A small child, Jack Harrow, bumps into Regina Marnen, accidentally pushing the uppity old woman into a horse trough. Angry, Marnen backhands Harrow, knocking the child onto his back. As he falls, Harrow hits his head on a rock, leaving him permanently brain-damaged.

If the characters stop Marnen (N female human **commoner**) from injuring Harrow (or from falling into the trough at all) on the same interval they end the time loop, they change the present. Harrow never gets brain damage. In fact, he is the co-owner of the Clatter and Clang Smithy with Nadia.

8:46am – Poison Soup

A man steps outside of the Starry Night Inn and Tavern and wretches. Through his heaving, he warns, "There's something wrong with the soup." It turns out that the inn's owner, Jerrol, accidentally served spoiled soup to the morning patrons. In fact, twenty of the town's citizens got sick from the soup. Since that day, the inn has been nicknamed the "Sickly Soup" Tavern and Inn. The stigma hurt the business for years; even seventy-five years later, Belhaveners warn passersby not to eat any of the food there.

If the characters warn Jerrol that the soup is poison on their final interval, the Starry Night Inn and Tavern never receives its stigma. In Present Belhaven, the inn rarely sees a vacancy and the tavern is always full of paying patrons happily eating the food.

he called for his family to pack their belongings, citing that they were in danger. He paid each servant 100 gp, telling them they had run of the manor in his absence. Some of the servants left immediately, seeing the Dunhalls' sudden departure as an omen.

T6 – Ragnor Farm

Eventually, the clues should lead the characters to Ragnor farm. No matter what time they arrive, Brother Aethlwald and Bronze Shields surround an old, dry well at the edge of the northern field, singing praise to Bel. Too weak to climb out or fight back, the **vampire spawn** Astrid sits 300-feet at the bottom of the well. When the Temple of Valor's bell tolls nine, the rising sun will position itself directly above the well, instantly disintegrating Astrid.

Encounter. Brother Aethlwald (LE male human **priest**) believes that he is just in Astrid's destruction. Whether or not he is, his actions will eventually lead to the doom of the Bronze Shields and the entire worship of Bel. Aethwald is accompanied by six **guards** armed with heavy crossbows. In addition, Ronell Ragnor (LN male human **veteran**) stands with the Bronze Shields, ready to defend Aethlwald with his life.

If the characters defeat Aethlwald and the other Bronze Shields, they must then rescue Astrid. The easiest way to do this is to cover the well. An old, wooden lid sits just to the side of it.

Escape from the Bronze Shield Armory

After Cassius sends the characters into the past, they find themselves prisoners in the dungeon of the Bronze Shield Armory. The armory serves two important functions in the story. First, it acts as the starting point for each of the time loops. Second, the characters will discover that many of the clues they need to solve the mystery of Astrid's disappearance can be discovered here.

General Features

Unless otherwise stated, the armory has the following features:

Alarms. During the first round of combat with members of the Bronze Shields, at least one of the guards will raise the alarm, pulling a robe for a signal bell that sounds throughout the entire complex. From there, reinforcements arrive from all corners of the armory, potentially overwhelming (and killing) the characters.

Ceilings. The ceilings in the dungeon are 8-feet high and the ceilings everywhere else are 12-feet high.

Doors. Upstairs, the doors are made of thick oak braced with iron, resting on iron hinges. The dungeon doors are the same, but with small windows near the top. Unless magically enchanted, locked doors require a DC 18 Strength saving throw to break open or a DC 15 Dexterity check using proficiency in thieves' tools to pick the lock. All of the doors have an AC of 16, 20 hp, and immunity to poison and psychic damage.

Light. The two floors upstairs are lit with lanterns hung at strategic locations. The dungeon has torches in the hallway connecting the cells, but not in the cells themselves.

Floors. The floors in the dungeon are made of rough cobblestone. On the first and second floor, the floors are made of stone braced with large, oak timbers. Rugs decorate the majority of the rooms.

Walls. The walls of the armory are made of laid brick both upstairs and down. Upstairs, tapestries, paintings, and other art depicting Bel, the God of Valor decorate the walls.

Keyed Encounters

The following locations are keyed to the Bronze Shield Armory (Past) above.

A1 – Time Loop Cell

When the characters first arrive in the past and every time they reset, they return to this cell. They are always chained to the wall, missing their possessions and fully rested.

Magic Wards. The dungeon cell is magically enchanted to confuse, disorient, and suppress the abilities of its prisoners. The enchantment creates the following effects:

- No sound can be created within or pass through the cell, similar to the effects of a *silence* spell. Only the old man's *sending stone* can cut through the enchantment (see below).
- All ability checks and attack rolls are made with disadvantage while in the room.
- The door is *arcane locked*.
- To cast a spell, a character must make an Intelligence check with a DC of 10 + the level fo the spell cast. On a failed check, the spell has no effect and the slot is wasted. Keep in mind that casters won't have their material components, holy symbols, or arcane foci available. Plus the silence effect prevents verbal components.

The enchantment itself is held in place by a *symbol* spell scrawled on the ceiling. Noticing the symbol requires a successful DC 16 Intelligence (Investigation) check. The characters have two options. First, they can dispel the symbol itself with a *dispel magic* spell (using the sending stone and passing the Intelligence check to cast the spell) versus the 7th-level spell. Or, a second DC 16 Intelligence (Investigation)

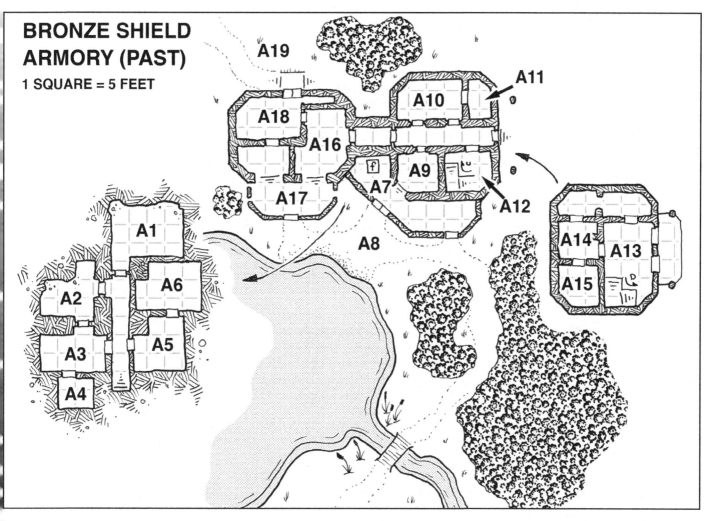

BRONZE SHIELD ARMORY (PAST)

1 SQUARE = 5 FEET

A19, A18, A16, A17, A1, A2, A6, A3, A5, A4, A7, A8, A9, A10, A11, A12, A13, A14, A15

check reveals that the *symbol* itself is held in place by a series of invisible, heat-sensitive lines that outline the contours of the room. Placing a warm hand on the paint or using a heat source like a torch on it reveals the paint. Should the paint be disrupted by damaging the stones around them (AC 17; hp 20; damage threshold 5; immunity to poison and psychic damage), the *symbol* disrupts and the magic wards cease to function.

Speaking in the Cell. The characters should recall that the old man was able to utter words before he died. So there must be a way to speak in the room.

Anyone who searches the body of the old man (at least one character should be able to drag him near) will find the

stone in his palm. The stone is smooth and has a rough carving of a mouth on it.

The mage, using his own clever devices, constructed what appears to be a sending stone, but altered in a way that allows its user to briefly cut through the cell's enchantment and project their words aloud. Trouble is, the stone has only one charge left, allowing only 9 more words to be spoken before it ceases to function (that is, until it resets during the next interval, of course).

Manacles. The manacles the characters find themselves in are tough to break, but not impossible. A character can pull the manacle from the wall with a successful DC 18 Strength check. Once free of the wall, the mana-

cle can work as an improvised weapon, dealing bludgeoning damage equal to 1d6 + the character's Strength modifier on a hit.

Cell Door. While enchanted, a DC 28 Strength check is required to break open the door. Or, the lock can be picked with a DC 25 Dexterity check using proficiency with thieves' tools. Removing the magic wards reduces the DC by 10 for each check.

The Old Man. The old man in the cell was named Marion Longyears (CG male human **mage**). He was part of the adventuring party that was captured by the Bronze Shield and interred in this cell. Unfortunately for Marion (but fortunately for the characters), Marion was not replaced by the time-traveling characters.

Encounter. If the characters create a lot of noise escaping, the Bronze Shield guards from areas **A2** and **A3** as well as Oarow Saint James (see area **A3**) ambush them in the hall. The Bronze Shields are all armed with heavy crossbows and won't hesitate to attack, looking to kill the escaped prisoners. Nevermind the fact that the characters look nothing like the adventurers they imprisoned in the first place.

A2 – Torture Chamber

When the characters enter the room, read or paraphrase the following.

Racks, whips, and even a fire pit for warming iron spikes clutter this room. Obviously, this is a torture chamber of some sort. In fact, there's still fresh blood on one of the racks.

Marion (area **A1**) was brought into this chamber and tortured to near death. The Bronze Shield believed Marion consorted with demons (he did). To no avail, Marion told the Shields whatever they wanted to hear.

If the characters avoided signaling the guards during their escape, one **guard** is still here cleaning up Marion's blood.

A3 – Guard Room

At the center of this room is a table covered in 107 copper pieces. If the characters avoided signaling the guards during their escape, Oarow Saint James (LE male human **veteran**) and three guards are still relaxing here, playing cards

Saint James carries keys to all of the cells in the dungeon (areas **A1 – A6**).

Oarow Saint James

Oarow is the cruel torturer and jailer of the Bronze Shield Armory. Ironically, he's quick to crumble when a threat is made on his life. While he doesn't know the exact location where Astrid is being held, he does know who would: Lord Dunhall, the military leader of the Bronze Shields. He doesn't know where Dunhall currently is but suggests his estate on the western end of town.

Saint James will also reveal all of the passwords and keyphrases that operate the enchantments in the armory and how many guards are currently on duty.

A4 – Locker

The door into this room is locked.

Treasure. Upon capture, the original adventurers were stripped of their possessions which were then stored in this room. Here, the characters find the following equipment:

- 1 light crossbow with 13 bolts
- 1 arcane focus
- 1 longbow and a quiver with 9 arrows
- 1 holy symbol
- 1 mace
- 1 set of thieves' tools
- 1 rapier
- 1 burglar's pack
- 2 daggers
- 1 dungeoneer's pack
- 1 shortbow and quiver of 10 arrows 1 priest's pack
- 2 shortswords1 scholar's pack
- 1 suit of leather armor
- 1 spellbook (containing all the spells from the **mage** spell list)
- 2 suits of scale mail
- 1 scroll of *detect thoughts*
- 1 shield
- 1 *goggles of night*

Time Constraints. Donning armor takes time. It takes 1 minute to don light armor, 5 minutes to don medium armor, and 10 minutes to don heavy armor.

A5 – Holding Cell

Criminals lacking magical powers or other special talents are kept in this open holding cell. Three iron bars run the length of the room. From those bars dangle manacled prisoners, their arms above their head. Currently, three such individuals hang this way. All three are **commoners** and know nothing about Astrid. Freeing them requires Saint James' keys (see area **A3**) or a successful DC 15 Strength check to pull a bar from the ceiling. The prisoners all have only 1 hit point remaining and 1 level of exhaustion.

A6 – Brunda's Cell

This cell has similar enchantments in place as those in area **A1**. However, anyone who speaks the command phrase "Revere the Light" removes the temporarily removes the enchantment until the command phrase "Hide from the Light" is spoken.

At the center of this cell is what looks like a creature that was once an orc. Its skin is deathly pale and what little hair it has on its head is just as white. Just above its sunken cheeks are a pair of pitch-black eyes. Five sets of manacles hold the monster in place: one for each its arms and feet, and one for its neck. "End this," it begs, looking up at you.

Astrid was traveling with her friend, Brunda (NE male orc **wight**) when she was captured. Whereas Astrid refused to give up answers about Cassius, Brunda talked, revealing not only secrets about the vampire lord but other undead in the region.

Brunda wants nothing more than to escape and will tell the characters everything he knows about what happened to him and Astrid so long as they promise to let him free.

- Astrid was briefly held in this cell with Brunda. Like him, they tortured her in order to discover the location of Cassius. She would not speak. (Whereas he did).

- Eventually, a knight whose name Brunda never learned (Lord Dunhall) took Astrid away. This happened roughly two hours ago.
- Cassius lives 20 miles from the town of Belhaven in an old keep. No one knows that he is a vampire.

The wight has no idea who the characters are. Furthermore, he only knows Cassius in his past form and will be confused by the characters' claims of time travel or time loops.

If the characters free Brunda, Brunda will escape by the shortest route possible, hoping to get as far from the armory as he can. He's smart enough to avoid a conflict with the characters.

A7 – Foyer

Escaping the dungeon, the characters emerge through a trap door in the foyer. The first time they come out, read or paraphrase the following:

> The moment you woke up, you suspected something was off. But now you really think something strange is going on. The same armory whose halls you passed into the night before is suddenly a completely different building. While the rough structure seems to be the same, it's almost as if the entire building was just built. In fact, everything in it looks new, too. The tapestries are no longer rotten, the broken table you walked past is still standing, and the rugs are free of mold. Even the old wooden doors leading outside are in perfect condition.

Two more **guards** stand watch here. When the characters appear, they sound the alarm, then fight while waiting for reinforcements from other areas of the armory to arrive.

A8 – Front Garden

The first time the characters step out into the gardens in front of the armory, read the following.

> Whereas just a few hours ago the armory's grounds were covered in overgrown grass, unpruned bushes, and thick vines growing over everything, now it's all perfectly manicured. Even the path leading into the building looks new.

The characters catch their first glimpse of past Belhaven. The town's rooves look new. The trees of the forest are different. Even the water looks less polluted.

As some point, a character may wish to make a check to determine what's happening: have them make a DC 13 Intelligence (History) check. On a success, they realize that the buildings and Belhavener's style were popular some seventy-five years ago.

Encounter. Six **guards** led by a **veteran** stand outside of the Bronze Shield Armory. When they see the characters, they first question their presence, then draw their weapons. If the alarm was raised by the guards in area **A7**, these Bronze Shield guards are prepared for the characters. In addition, the roof of the west wing has four more **guards** on top, each armed with a heavy crossbow.

A9 – Entry

The door leading into the hallway is locked and trapped. Anyone that fails to speak the phrase "Revere the Light" before touching the door must make a DC 12 Constitution saving throw. On a failed saving throw, a creature takes 7 (2d6) lightning damage and is paralyzed for 1 minute. A creature can repeat its saving throw at the end of each of its turns, ending the effect on itself with a success. On a successful saving throw, a creature takes half as much damage and isn't paralyzed. The alarm is raised when the trap goes off, too.

A10 – Conference Room

A large, oak table beset with a dozen chairs dominates the center of this room. The Bronze Shield higher-ups meet here. Along the western wall is a map of the immediate region surrounding Belhaven. A dagger sticks in the wall over Cassius' keep just outside of town.

A11 – Lord Dunhall's Office

The door into this room is locked. A small desk with dozens of neatly stocked documents and tomes faces the door. A character can glance through the documents and books revealing a common theme: the destruction of undead. One book, in particular, should catch the characters' interest, a leather-bound tome titled *On Vampires* by Reginald Diamond. If a character reads the book (it takes 6 hours minus a number of hours equal to the character's Intelligence modifier for a minimum of 1 hour) they can learn all they need to know about vampires (in game terms, the GM reveals the full vampire stat block to the player).

Treasure. Lord Dunhall has two items of interest in this study. First, he keeps a hand crossbow armed with a *+1 crossbow bolt* aimed at the door strapped on the underside of the desk. Second, a DC 13 Intelligence (Investigation) check reveals a false bottom in one of the drawers. Within the drawer are a holy symbol of Bel, a flask of holy water, and 10 gp.

A12 – Stairs

The stairs are protected by a lone **guard**.

A13 – Brother Aethlwald's Sitting Room

> Whereas most of the armory has been somewhat austere, this room swims in decadence. Artwork, gold chalices, tapestries, and expensive looking furniture are everywhere you look.

The high priest and religious leader of the Bronze Shields, Brother Aethlwald lives on the top floor of the armory. Currently, he is at Rangor Farm, overseeing the destruction of Astrid.

Encounter. Brother Lyle (N male human **acolyte**) is found here. See the Brother Lyle sidebar (overleaf) for details. If the alarm sounded, he's hiding behind one of the chairs.

Treasure. Out in the open, the characters find chalices, jewelry, vestments, and other valuables with a combined worth of 500 gp.

Time Constraints. Collecting all of the valuables in this room takes at least 1 minute.

A14 – Study

Brother Aethlwald retreats to this room to meditate. A shrine to Bel rests against the eastern wall. Atop the

> **Brother Lyle**
>
> Brother Lyle is Aethlwald closest assistant and secret lover. Weak-willed and easily frightened, Lyle fears confrontation of any sort. If the characters intimidate him, he tells them all he knows about Aethlwald. While he isn't sure where Aethlwald currently is, he knows Aethlwald and Dunhall left the armory a couple hours before the bell tolled eight with one of their captives.
>
> Lyle desperately loves Aethlwald, begging the characters to leave the older priest unharmed.

shrine is a blood-stained leather cat of nine-tails. Just a few feet in front of the shrine is a circle of dried blood. This is where Brother Aethlwald flagellates.

Treasure. An ornamental holy symbol hangs on the wall above the shrine. The symbol is made of solid gold and worth 100 gp.

A15 – Brother Aethlwald's Bed Chambers

> Unlike the rest of the upstairs, this room is oddly humble. Against the southern wall is a simple cot with a small, unlit candle beside it. A hook hangs on the wall, likely for a robe. Beside the bed is a bucket filled with bloody water.

After Aethlwald flagellates, he retreats to these chambers where Brother Lyle cleans his wounds using the water bucket.

A16 – Armory

> Swords, spears, shields, and crossbows decorate the walls.

The actual room where the Bronze Shield armory gets its name is here. There are two **guards** in this room.

A17 – West Wing Font Entry

The door leading outside is locked.

A18 – Refectory

Two **guards** can be found in this break room. The door leading to the rear is locked.

A19 – Rear Garden

Should the characters escape through the back, the area is clear. However, the roof does have four **guards** on top armed with heavy crossbows (these are the same guards mentioned in area A8).

Adventure Conclusion

Once the characters save Astrid from destruction in the well, the Green Flash occurs one last time. However, when the characters awaken to the sounds of the bell tolling, they find themselves once again in the ruins of the Bronze Shields Armory in the present. They have all their possessions again, but the bunks are gone. In fact, there is no sign of Cassius, Astrid, Frazzle, or any of Cassius' servants.

Once the characters decide to leave, they immediately notice that they are back in the present time. Also, in the foyer of the armory are bags of gold with a note.

It reads, "Thank you. – CS"

The bags contain the amount of gold Cassius promised.

Present Belhaven should reflect the changes the characters made during their last interval. While this adventure makes a few suggestions on changes the characters may have made, there is no way to predict the long-term consequences of their actions. What modern Belhaven looks like when the characters return is ultimately up to you.

Should the characters try to find Cassius or anyone related to him, they discover that Lord Cassius Sylvanyus has not been seen near Belhaven in seventy-five years. His old keep lies in ruins just twenty-feet north of town. Some folks say it's haunted. Ω

Discover new worlds.

Become a DMDave patron today and you'll receive over 70 PDFs, new campaign settings, player options, adventures, and more.

All patrons get to put in monthly requests which are added to BroadSword Monthly.

Plus, subscribers at certain tiers get BroadSword Monthly PDF and physical coopies at no extra charge in addition to other types of swag.

SEE WHAT HUNDREDS OF PATRONS ARE TALKING ABOUT:

www.patreon.com/dmdave

IT HUNTS
5TH-LEVEL SCI-FI ADVENTURE FOR FIFTH EDITION

By Dave Hamrick
Cartography by Dave Hamrick and JD Russell

Readers will quickly identify the inspiration behind this adventure. It involves an "alien predator" that hunts the adventurers in a dark, primordial forest. As an incredibly dangerous foe, their only recourse is to escape the creature. But how can you flee from a malicious creature such as this?

It Hunts is an exploration and survival adventure for four 5th-level characters. Any mix of characters is useful, although rangers will fair particularly well in the jungle environment.

Smart adventurers will know better than to face the adventure's main villain head-on, as the creature is capable of easily destroying the entire party by itself. The GM should familiarize his or herself with exploration rules in Fifth Edition, as well as the grirrix hunter's stats found in Appendix C of this issue. In addition, the rules for epic monster encounters in ***BroadSword Monthly #2*** will also prove useful.

This adventure is campaign independent. The Sark Peninsula can be placed into any tropical setting, preferably one a few hundred miles from a major town or city.

Adventure Background

A week ago, a grirrix hunter ship landed in the Sark Peninsula, a deadly realm full of orcs, primordial creatures, and other horrors. The hunter's mission was to discover the science vessel *Paramount* which crash-landed on the planet some 50 years ago. Within the *Paramount* was an experimental fuel known as Blueshift. The grirrix species, endangered and desperate, see the Blueshift fuel as a weapon of war, one that will pull the Grirrix Empire out of ruin. Unfortunately, the Sark Peninsula is nowhere near where the *Paramount* actually landed.

Adventure Hook

Diviners from around the world saw the falling star (the hunter ship) as an ill omen. While the characters are resting or passing through a major city in a warm, equatorial climate, one such diviner, Krathis the Enigmatic, approaches the characters. Krathis (N female half-elf **archmage**) may have heard of the characters through their past deeds or recognizes that they are men and/or women with capabilities. Either way, whenever and wherever Krathis approaches the characters, read the following.

> "Adventurers!" says the strange, bald-headed woman in a melodic voice. "Seven days ago, my acolytes and I witnessed a falling star– the direst omen. The star burned through the night sky and vanished into the primordial forests of the Sark Peninsula. My colleagues and I believe that the star brings with it magic from beyond our realm. I wish to fund an expedition into Sark to learn more about the falling star, and I hope that you are up for the task. Should you accept this quest, I am prepared to reward you 500 gp each upon completion."

In addition to the reward, Krathis gives the characters 10 porters to travel with (see the "Porters" sidebar), as well as her star pupil, Abraga (N female tiefling **mage**).

> "To complete this quest, you must bring Abraga to the site of the fallen star and allow Abraga to study it for as long as she needs.
> "I have provided a map of the Sark Peninsula that will show you the way to the orc village of Rungruk. It is likely that the orcs' chief and shamans know more about the fallen

Porters

Accompanying the characters on their journey through the Sark Peninsula are 10 porters. Each porter is a neutral human **commoner**. While each porter's personality and ideals may be different, their bond is always, "My loyalty is to my fellow porters first, job be damned."

Quality Score. The porters start with a quality score of +4, but that score varies over the course of the adventure, going as low as -10 and as high as +10. it decreases if one of the porters is killed, the group suffers hardships or endures poor health. It increases if the group enjoys high morale and trusts the characters.

Mutiny. If the porters are poorly led or mistreated, they may turn against the characters. Once per day, if the porters' quality score is lower than 0, one of the characters must make a Charisma (Intimidation or Persuasion) check modified by the porters' quality score.

If the check total is between 1 and 9, the porters' quality score decreases by 1.

If the check total is 0 or lower, the porters mutiny. They become hostile to the characters and might attempt to kill them, imprison them, or simply evacuate in the middle of the night. The porters can be cowed into obedience through violence, combat, or offers of treasure or other rewards.

When the GM ends the mutiny, the porters' quality score decreases by 1d4.

Extra Rest. Traveling through the jungle is a tiring affair. Spending an extra day to rest and recuperate allows the porters to relax and regain its composure. If the porters' quality score is 3 or lower, the score increases by 1 for each day the porters spend resting.

star. You may need to convince them to show you where it is. I'm told they're easily persuaded with gold."

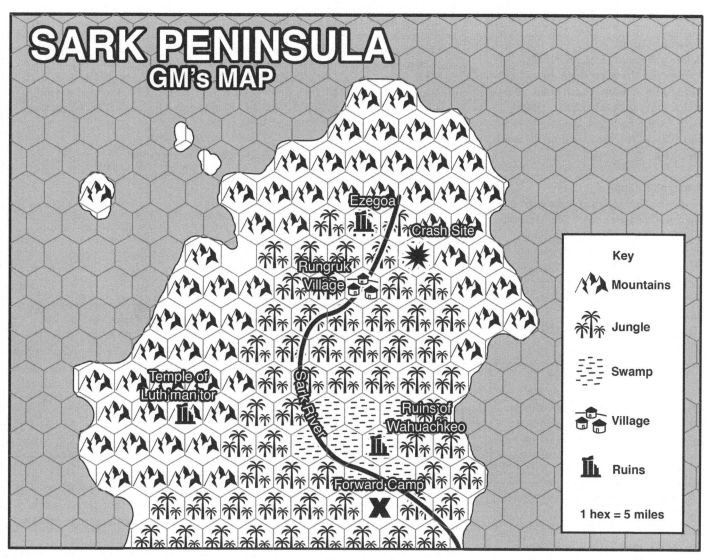

If the characters accept Krathis' quest, she gives them the map (see Handout: Map of the Sark Peninsula in Appendix D) and introduces them to Abraga and the porters. In addition, she provides any equipment that the characters may need just short of magic items, including enough food and water for the expedition, tents, pack animals, etc.

Travel in the Sark Peninsula

The characters, Abraga, and the porters take six canoes upstream along the Sark River, just before reaching the swamps. From there, Abraga suggests the group travels on foot through the jungle to Rungruk village.

On the map of the Sark Peninsula, each hex measures 5 miles across. Characters moving at a normal pace can travel 2 hexes per day on foot through grassland, jungle, mountain, and swamp. They can travel 4 hexes per day if they're traveling by canoe on the Sark River north or south of the swamp. The swamp is difficult to get through, slowing movement by canoe to 2 hexes per day.

If characters move at a fast pace, the easiest way to deal with their progress is to roll a d4. On a result of 3-4, the characters move two extra hexes. A result of 2 means the characters move one extra hex. And a result of 1

means the characters' pace remains unchanged. Regardless of how many hexes they move, characters moving at a face pace take a -5 penalty to their passive Wisdom (Perception) scores, making them more likely to miss clues and walk into ambushes.

If the characters set a slow pace, roll a d6. On a result of 1-2, the characters move 2 fewer hex that day. On a result of 3-4, the characters move 1 fewer hex. And on a result of 5-6, the characters make the same progress, despite being cautious. Characters moving at a slow pace can move stealthily. As long as they're not in the open, they can try to surprise or sneak by other creatures they encounter.

Locations in the Sark Peninsula

Forward Camp

Before journeying into the jungle, Abraga and the porters set up a forward camp 35 miles south of the village of Rungruk. If the characters choose not to bring the boats, the boats are left here. One porter stays behind to guard the boats.

Rungruk Village

When the characters approach the village, read or paraphrase the following:

It's quiet here, not a single living thing in sight. The watchtowers surrounding the village are empty. No warriors wait by the open gates. You see no livestock. Even the birds are quiet.

Once the characters enter the actual village, read the following:

All around you are the signs of a struggle. Some of the huts are charred, white smoke drifting from their blackened husks. All around you are footprints, broken arrowheads, and discarded spears—but no bodies.

A successful DC 15 Wisdom (Survival) check reveals a little of what occurred here. The majority of the footprints are orcish, mostly male and female warriors. Whatever they were fighting came at them from all directions, but left no tracks. It's obvious that the orcs fell in combat—blood mixed into the mud, impressions in the soil—but then their bodies were dragged east, into the jungle surrounding the village.

Burn marks mar some of the buildings, particularly the watchtowers. A successful DC 14 Intelligence (Arcana) check reveals that the burn marks are similar to those caused by *magic missile* spells, although the pattern is wrong. Whatever it was that killed the orcs had powerful force magic at its disposal.

This all happened three days ago.

Random Encounters

As the characters travel through the Sark Peninsula, it's likely they come across creatures, points of interest, and other strange things. Each day, roll a d20 four times: once in the morning, afternoon, early evening, and middle of the night. On a result of 18-20, a random encounter occurs. Choose one of the following encounters, or roll a d4 and a d6 to determine the results of the encounter, using the Random Encounter table below.

Sark Peninsula Random Encounters

d4+d6	Encounter
2	1d8 + 1 **ettercaps**
3	2d4 **apes**
4	1d4 + 2 **orcs** led by an orc **gladiator**
5	1d4 **swarms of poisonous snakes**
6	1 **brown bear**
7	*Gruesome standard.* A headless humanoid body hangs from a tree branch. All of the blood has been drained from the body. (The grirrix left the body here after it drained its memories using its *neuroprojector*).
8	*Ruins.* The characters stumble upon ancient stones, likely the foundation of a ruined building or temple.
9	1d6 **lizardfolk**
10	1d8 + 1 **harpies**

Nook-nook, Gunda, and Brun

After the characters have explored the orc village for a few minutes, have one of the characters notice something out of the corner of their eye. Something small is running between the buildings 100-feet away.

A successful DC 13 Wisdom (Perception) check spots that it's an orc child. The child dives into a latrine ditch and hides below one of the villages' outhouses. The orc child (treat it as a **commoner**) brandishes a dagger when the characters come near. Hiding with the child is an orc toddler holding an infant (both noncombatants). The orc children are the village's only survivors.

A character can convince the children that they are friendly with a successful DC 10 Charisma (Persuasion) check. Having hidden in the latrines for three days, the children are filthy and hungry, so offering them food automatically wins their favor.

When asked what happened, Nook-nook, the oldest of the three, speaks for his brothers. Nook-nook only speaks orcish.

"A demon with glowing eyes came from the jungle. It was as big as an elephant and more powerful than even Ogra, our tribe's greatest warrior. I could not fully glimpse it, as it moved like a blur.

"All of the men and all of the women fought the demon, but the demon used its magic to kill them all. It took all of the adults into the forest. It looked right at us and said a word in the tongue-of-city-people: 'Paramount.' I was brave and said nothing and defended my brothers Gunda and Brun. I must have scared the demon. It returned to the forest and has not returned since."

Nook-nook nor his brothers know anything else about what attacked them, only that it was incredibly powerful, able to fight ten orcs at once. It cast magic like fire from its eyes, destroying warriors as far as 200 feet away.

Following the Tracks. The creature dragged the orc bodies east into the forest, towards the crash site. A successful DC 10 Wisdom (Survival) check is all that is needed to follow the path.

Treasure. Almost everything is as exactly as the orcs left it. If the characters spend an hour searching the huts, they discover 241 gp, 360 sp, 311 cp, 7 valuable gems (4 amethyst, 1 bloodstone, and 3 pieces of obsidian) worth 490 gp, a *+1 longbow*, and an *enchanted orcish war drum* (acts as an *instrument of the bards* that can cast *enhance ability, longstrider, and thunderwave*).

Crash Site

Roughly 7 miles east of Rungruk Village is the site of the grirrix hunter's crashed pod. It's likely that the characters discover the crash site after stopping in Rungruk. As the characters approach the crash site, they discover the bodies of the slain orcs.

Read or paraphrase the following:

> Flies buzz with mad fury all around you. Soon, you understand why. A few dozen feet ahead, the remains of a humanoid hang from a low tree branch, its head removed and blood drained. Then, you start to notice more strung-up corpses. One to your left. Two to your right. All the same: headless and bloodless. In fact, dozens of bodies decorate the trees along the path. Just beyond this macabre scene, you catch a glimpse of an unnatural clearing.

While the dead orcs have no loot per se, many are still clutching their weapons. The grirrix left the orc bodies as a warning to anyone that dared to approach its crashed pod.

In the clearing:

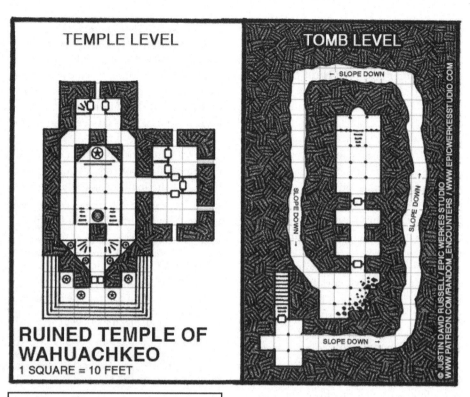

TEMPLE LEVEL

TOMB LEVEL

← SLOPE DOWN

SLOPE DOWN

SLOPE DOWN

SLOPE DOWN

SLOPE DOWN →

RUINED TEMPLE OF WAHUACHKEO
1 SQUARE = 10 FEET

> A gash in the floor of the jungle stretches 700-feet from the east to the west. It seems likely that this is the site of the falling star that Krathis sent you to find.

The crash left a 700-foot scar in the jungle, destroying the trees and foliage as it went. Its alien appearance will not be immediately recognizable to a band of fantasy heroes.

> At the end of the gash, you discover what could only be the "falling star." It reminds you of a cracked open oyster shell, except it's some 15-feet long and 8-feet wide. Within it are all sorts of tubes, nodules, and other strange implements that almost look mechanical.

Grirrix technology is completely alien to even those who know the grirrix for what they are. Therefore, it's impossible for the characters to understand the pod's function unless they've encountered the grirrix before.

Encounter. The first encounter the characters have with the **grirrix hunter** (see Appendix C) occurs here

at the crash site. It's been waiting in the trees 200-feet away on the opposite side of the crash site. The moment anyone touches the pod, it attacks, opening fire with its plasmacaster.

The grirrix hunter is an incredibly dangerous foe, fully capable of killing the party. It attacks what it sees as the most dangerous foes first, taking out those that appear large and strong (initially, it takes unarmored combatants and small races for granted). Preferring stealth, the hunter never leaves the tree line, always firing from a distance. It may even seem like there's more than one of them there as it moves, hides, and fires in such rapid succession.

This encounter is intended to make it clear that the characters are outmatched. A well-placed fireball or similar effect is enough to temporarily scare it off and give the characters time to come up with a plan.

Meanwhile, the porters flee into the forest, wanting nothing to do with the combat. If the orc children are with the characters, Nook-nook explains that it is the demon attack and draws his dagger, ready to defend his brothers.

Once this combat occurs, the characters are now being hunted by the grirrix hunter (see "The Hunt Begins" below).

Ezegoa

Ezegoa was once a prosperous goblinoid city that thrived at the north end of the Sark Peninsula. Sadly, a vicious jungle plague wiped out many of the city's inhabitants two centuries ago. Now, the Ezegoan ghosts haunt the overgrown streets and crumbling ruins of the ancient city.

While there are no formal keyed encounter in Ezegoa, you are free to add in any encounters, ruins, or points of interest that you like here.

Ruins of Wahuachkeo

This location was once the home of a lizardfolk city many centuries ago. The lizardfolk were cleared out by the orcs of Sark Peninsula and never returned. Not much remains of the ruins other than the crumbling temple of Wahuachkeo and the tall, totemic statues of alligators surrounding it.

Treasure-hunters cleared the temple of its valuables decades ago. All of its traps are disabled or no longer function.

The ruins itself may work as a good location for the characters to hide or stage an ambush against the hunter.

Temple of the Luth'Man'Tor

A group of zealot dwarves called the "Luth'Man'Tor" once lived in the mountains to the west of the Sark Peninsula. The dwarves worshipped a demon named Qua-Seko (which translates roughly to "He Who Whispers in the Dark"). In time, the dwarves died, and much of the temple was destroyed by a volcanic explosion.

The Hunt Begins

After the characters encounter the grirrix hunter for the first time (likely at the crash site), the grirrix hunter

makes the characters its primary target. Overall disappointed with the results of the orcs' knowledge, the hunter believes that the characters can lead it to the Paramount. The hunter desires to kill the characters, remove their heads, then use its neuroprojector to learn what they know.

After the hunt begins, roll a d20 each morning, afternoon, early evening, and middle of the night (this replaces the normal Random Encounter table). On a result of 15-20, the grirrix hunter attacks. Feel free to adjust the number of encounters the characters have with the grirrix as needed; remove an encounter if the characters are being attacked too often, or add in extra in if the grirrix isn't attacking enough.

To determine the nature of the attack, roll on the Grirrix Attacks table below.

d6	The Grirrix Attacks Result
1	The grirrix attacks from the trees, using cover to its advantage, preferring its plasmacaster over its melee weapons. It fights until it takes damage, three rounds pass, or it kills a character (whichever happens first). If it kills a character, it tries to drag its body off into the forest.
2	100-feet in front of the characters, the grirrix uses a *minor illusion* protocol (like the spell) to create an illusory duplicate of itself. It then attacks from behind, picking off weaker members of the party first (likely the porters).
3	One of the porters disappears. An hour later, the characters hear the porter screaming in the forest. It's clearly a trap, the grirrix using the porter as bait. Once the characters are close enough to see the porter, the grirrix attacks from the trees.
4	The grirrix sets a trap in the forest. Roll on the Grirrix Trap table to determine the nature of the trap. Typically, after a trap goes off, the Grirrix attacks within 1 round.
5-6	The grirrix leaves gruesome standards along the path the characters are traveling, hoping to scare them back into the jungle.

Grirrix Traps

The grirrix uses primitive traps to scare and injure the party. The following are common traps the grirrix uses against its prey. Choose one of the traps below or roll a d4 to determine the nature of the trap.

d4	Trap Effect
1	*Pit trap.* The grirrix dug a pit trap along the characters' path. A successful DC 10 Wisdom (Perception) check reveals the presence of the trap. Failure to notice the trap results in one or more characters or porters falling into the trap. Each creature that falls into the trap takes 3 (1d6) bludgeoning damage from the fall.
2	*Swinging logs.* The grirrix sets a tripwire along the path. Noticing the tripwire requires a DC 15 Wisdom (Perception) check. Once tripped, two massive logs swing out from the trees. The creature who tripped the logs must succeed on a DC 15 Dexterity saving throw or take 16 (3d10) bludgeoning damage from the logs.
3	*Net trap.* A successful DC 15 Wisdom (Perception) check reveals the presence of this tripwire trap. If the trap is triggered, a 10-foot-by-10-foot-area net captures anyone standing on it. Creatures in the area must succeed on a DC 15 Dexterity saving throw or be restrained. A creature can use its action to make a DC 10 Strength check to try to free itself or another creature in the net. Dealing 5 slashing damage to the net (AC 10, 20 hp) also frees a creature without harming the creature.
4	*Mine.* The grirrix sets a tripwire attached to an explosive device. A successful DC 15 Wisdom (Perception) check notices the wire. When triggered, each creature within 10 feet of the tripped mine must make a DC 15 Dexterity saving throw, taking 18 (4d8) fire damage on a failed saving throw or half as much damage on a successful one.

Pulling Punches

As a challenge rating 15 creature facing off against 5th-level characters, the grirrix is a brute, to be sure. As such, you may want to limit just how aggressive it is (consider removing its Legendary Actions, for example). Furthermore, the grirrix may wish to "play with its prey", trying to scare them more than hurt them.

If the grirrix kills one of the characters, make sure it's for a good reason. For example, the character made a poor judgment call, or charged the grirrix, separating itself from the group. In films, characters who position themselves as burdens on the party are often targets for monsters. Similarly, those that martyr themselves also find themselves dead at the hands of the creature. Once the grirrix kills one character, it hopes to secure the corpse so it can extract its thoughts with its *neuroprojector*. This often leaves it open for riposte from the rest of the party.

Should the players feel stuck, consider having smart or wise characters make checks to figure out what to do. Or put a fortification in the party's way such as an easily defensible cave or ruins that aren't on their map.

The Grirrix is a Plot Device, Not a Tool for Meta-Revenge

Just because the grirrix is part of this adventure and is quite deadly, doesn't mean that you should use it to bully the players. While it's okay to invoke fear, the characters should never feel like you're working against them. That's just tacky.

Adventure Conclusion

The characters have two choices when dealing with the hunter. They can confront the hunter in hopes of killing it or driving it off. Or they can flee from the hunter and escape from the peninsula altogether.

Escaping the Hunter

Once the characters are deep in the jungles of the Sark Peninsula, it's tough to escape the hunter. They can head south on foot or by way of the Sark River, hoping to escape that way. Of course, being out in the open on the river makes them an easy target for the hunter's plasmacaster. Or, they can cross over the mountains and escape via the coast. The peninsula's coast is surrounded by treacherous waves, and jagged, unforgiving rocks. It's rare that the characters find a beach along the mountains, especially on the eastern side of the peninsula where mighty, 100-foot high or taller cliffs tower before the crashing waters below.

Confronting the Hunter

Eventually, the characters may wish to confront the grirrix hunter. The hunter is surprisingly easy to fool. After all, it thinks that the characters are nothing more than primates. Dangerous animals, to be sure, but hardly intelligent.

There is no one way to confront the hunter. The characters may confront it in the ruined temple of Wahuachkeo, a random cave, or even out in the open (setting their own traps as they do). Be sure to award creativity with success.

While the hunter is megalomaniacal, it also values its own life. If it's dead, it can't complete its mission (and its mind, that's far worse than death). Should the characters prove too dangerous for it, the hunter flees and won't return, hoping to find another way to learn the whereabouts of the *Paramount* and its Blueshift fuel.

If the characters do manage to defeat the hunter, they might be able to learn more about its intentions and why it's hunting in the forest. This could potentially even lead the characters to search for the *Paramount* themselves.

Reporting Back to Krathis

Krathis will be disappointed if the characters didn't have a chance to learn more about her "falling star", especially if the characters return without Abraga. However, she will keep her promises and (begrudgingly) award them the gold. In addition, Krathis may be interested in learning more about the creature the characters faced, potentially offering an additional reward if they are brave enough to return to Sark to capture the creature. Ω

TOMB OF THE KIRIN-BORN PRINCE
7TH-LEVEL ADVENTURE FOR FIFTH EDITION

By Dave Hamrick and Dyson Logos
Cartography by Dyson Logos, Primary Art by Jason Glover

Having recently downloaded *Dyson's amazing Dyson's Delve: The Original Mini Mega-Dungeon* and read through a few old Dungeon magazines, I was inspired to cook up a quick dungeon using one of Dyson's Maps. If you didn't already know, Dyson Logos has a super useful list of dungeon maps he's created that available for commercial use. You can get them all on his website. Already, many of these maps appear in **BroadSword Monthly** (even in this issue).

Tomb of the Kirin-Born Prince is a Fifth Edition compatible adventure for four 7th-level adventurers, although, it's dangerous enough for higher-level adventurers. The adventure includes a lot of dangerous traps, so a party with a rogue or a wizard with high investigation will be incredibly useful. A small character will also be helpful. Plus, it includes a few undead uglies, so clerics will also add value to the party.

Adventure Background

The tomb of the Kirin-Born Prince is one of the older known tombs of the Etturan Dynasty – and one of the few whose location was not lost with the burning of the Tarek Archives. Many expeditions to seek out the later "shaft-tombs" often use this tomb as a sort of base camp, much to the chagrin of the Etran Cenobites.

A small order of religious monks has sprung up around several of the rediscovered Etturan tombs and attempt to maintain or rehabilitate the structures to worship and seek the gifts of the many god-kings that were entombed in the region. However, their numbers are few and the gifts of god-kings are sparse if not completely non-existent – thus the Etran Cenobites eke out a paltry living, only noticed when they harass would-be tomb-raiders.

Adventure Hooks

The adventurers can come upon the Tomb of the Kirin-Born Prince any number of ways. Here are a few suggestions:

- The adventurers are traveling in the wilderness and they notice the opening to the tomb.
- The Etran Cenobites accost the characters, thinking that they're tomb raiders. The monks themselves aren't too much trouble, but their persistence that the characters only want the treasure in the tomb may attract the characters to the adventure.
- An old map detailing the location of this tomb (and maybe a few other Etturan tombs) enters the characters' possession.
- There is an item of interest within the tomb a mysterious NPC needs. This may involve a rival. This item could be Empeku's scepter or something from within Nebtka's vault.

The Tomb

General Features
Unless otherwise stated, the Tomb of the Kirin-Born Prince has the following characteristics.

Ceiling, Floors, and Walls. The ceilings in the tomb are low, usually no more than seven feet high. The tomb itself was carved into the mountain stone with hieroglyphics and religious iconography set into it. Age and the weight of the mountain above have created considerable cracks all throughout, damaging the stonework in multiple areas.

Doors. Most of the doors are made of heavy, stone slabs, set on stone hinges. Each door has an AC of 17, 50 hp (threshold 5), and immunity to poison and psychic damage.

Light. The only natural light in the tomb is by the entrance. The text descriptions assume that the characters have darkvision, torches, or another method of seeing in the dark.

Regional Effects. The tomb suffers the regional effects of having a **mummy lord** present which persists until Nebtka's body (see area **12**) is destroyed.

Remove Curse. The spell *remove curse* does not work inside the tomb but can work outside of it.

Tomb Guardians. Damaging the ceiling, floors, or walls in the tomb, or other implements, such as traps, statues, etc. causes four **shadows** to rise from the dark recesses and attack. Each time a shadow is destroyed, another takes its place in 1d4 rounds. The only way to stop the shadows is to exit the tomb during daylight hours. A creature may then reenter after the next sunrise.

Entering the Tomb
When the monks first arrived at the tomb, they opened it. However, none of them (or anyone else) have been able to make it past the first room of the tomb.

The door to the tomb has words written upon it in ancient Etturan. A character will need a translator (possibly one of the monks) or a spell in order to read what the words say. The words read "Follow the Path of Light or Fall Forever Into Shadow."

Encounter. Camped outside of the chamber, no matter the time of day, are 2d6 + 2 Etran Cenobites, all **acolytes**. They only wish to scare off tomb-raiders and prefer not to fight.

Keyed Encounters

The following encounters are keyed to the Tomb of the Kirin-Born Prince map above.

1 – Door of Shadows

> Cracked skulls riddle the floor of this musty chamber. To your right, it looks like someone once tried to dig their way through the wall. Set into an alcove at the southeastern corner is a squat gargoyle carved to look like its arms and wings are holding up the ceiling. In its open mouth is a stone key with a bow in the shape of the moon.
>
> The door opposite the one you entered is made of thick stone. A relief on the door is carved to look like the night sky–you can even make out familiar constellations. A circular depression in the door is carved to look like the moon. At the center of the depression is a keyhole.

Easily ignored, unless the characters glance around the room looking for clues, is a lone torch stuck into the eastern wall next to the door. The torch is magical. When lit, it reveals the presence of the secret door in the northwestern wall.

Shadow Door Trap. The door is fake; it is actually nothing more than a wall carving made to look like a door. It's magically reinforced, too, with an AC of 26, 100 hp (threshold 10), resistance to all nonmagical damage, and immunity to poison and psychic damage.

Messing with the moon-tumbler in any way–picking its fake lock, inserting the moon key, etc.–requires the character to make a DC 17 Dexterity saving throw. On a failed saving throw, the tumbler locks around the character's wrist, grappling them (escape DC 17). While grappled, the target is restrained, and the target's Strength score is reduced by 1d4 at the end of each of their turns. The target dies if

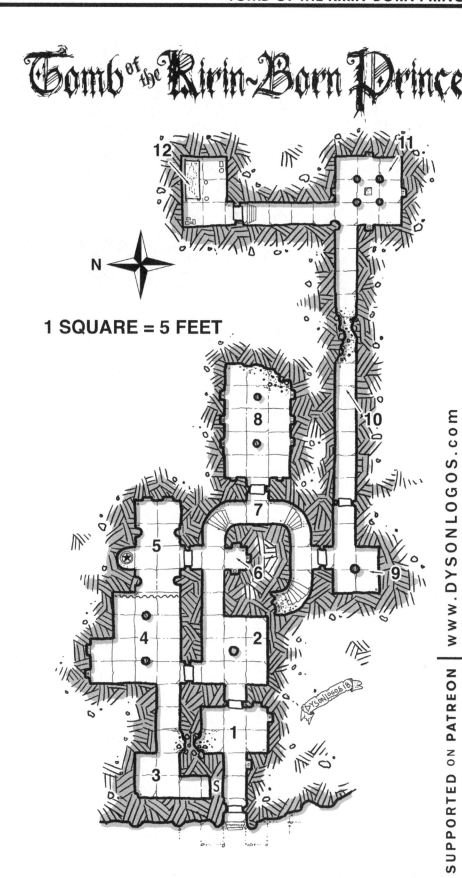

Tomb of the Kirin-Born Prince

N

1 SQUARE = 5 FEET

this reduces its Strength score to 0. Otherwise, the reduction lasts until the target finishes a short or long rest. If a non-evil humanoid dies from this attack, it rises as a shadow 1d4 hours later. A creature can escape the trap by hacking off its own hand (it must take 10 hp worth of slashing damage in order to do so).

If the key is placed into the keyhole, it doesn't open the door. Instead, the key sucks into the door's mechanism and reappears 1 round later in the gargoyle's mouth, ready for its next victim.

A character can notice the trap with a successful DC 16 Intelligence (Investigation) check.

2 – The Story of Nebtka

This large, low chamber holds a number of points of interest. At the center of the room, a stone column supports the 10-foot high ceiling. That in of itself isn't unusual. What's odd, however, is that there is a 5-inch diameter round slot at the center of the column facing the western wall. Next, ancient text decorates the eastern and southern walls of the room. Other than the door you came in, the only way out is through a hallway that heads east, deeper into the complex.

Nebtka's Story. Deciphering the text on the wall requires a translator or someone that can read ancient Etturan (through magical means or otherwise). A translator will explain that the text details Prince Nebtka's history. At first, it may not seem important, but the text actually explains the tricks to getting around the tomb's many traps using Nebtka's story as an allegory. The translation of the text can be found on lpayer handout "Nebtka's Story" in Appendix D.

The Scepter is a Key. The scepter that Empeku gives the characters in **area 5** can be placed into the slot in the column. Once inserted, it locks firmly into place. From there, a character can use their action to rotate the column clockwise using the scepter as a handle. Once the scepter points towards the east wall, it clicks into place. The scepter is one of the five keys needed to enter **area 12**. No other object inserted into the column allows the column to be rotated.

3 – Path of Light

The torch from **area 2** can be placed into a setting in the northern-most wall. Doing so spreads light throughout the tomb as if each room was illuminated by a *continual light* spell.

4 – Chamber of Whispers

The first thing that you notice in this room is a large set of slightly-transparent black and green curtains. On the other side of the curtains, there appears to be a large, winged creature. At the north, in an alcove, is a large, vertically set gear set into the wall with three spoke-like handles. The door in the southwestern wall is carved with hieroglyphics that appear to be slaves building the tomb itself.

A successful DC 10 Wisdom (Perception) check reveals that the winged creature is actually a statue.

Whisper Trap. Everyone that enters this room must make a DC 10 Wisdom saving throw at the start of each of their turns. On a failed saving throw, the character takes 2d6 psychic damage and must immediately use its reaction, if available, to move as far as its speed allows out of the tomb. On a successful saving throw, a creature takes half as much damage and doesn't have to move. Each round, the whispers seem to grow louder. The DC increases by 1 per round (to a maximum of 20) and the psychic damage dealt increases by 1d6 (to a maximum of 12d6).

If a character deafens themselves by covering their ears with their hands or placing wax or something similar in their ears, they are unaffected by the whisper trap. A *silence* spell cast in the room disables the trap for the spell's duration as well.

Shadow Realm Curtains. The curtains are magical and desecrated. Any creature that touches the curtains must make a DC 17 Charisma saving throw. On a successful saving throw, a character is pushed back by the curtains into an unoccupied space within 5 feet of the curtains in **area 4** and is unharmed. On a failed saving throw, the creature enters an alternate dimension shadow realm version of the tomb. The shadow realm version of the tomb looks exactly like the normal version of the tomb except that that it has the following changes:

- The entire tomb is blanketed in magical darkness.

- The entrance to the tomb is area 1 is gone. In its place is a stone wall. There is no non-magical way to escape the tomb.
- There is no treasure in any of the rooms. This includes the golden scepter in **area 5**, the elemental keys in **area 6**, the fake treasure in **area 8**, or Nebtka's treasure in **area 12**.
- The entire complex is filled with angry, incorporeal undead. Each room has 1d4 **specters** that attack living creatures on sight. The specters follow living creatures around the entire complex if necessary.
- The curtains in area 4 disappear, therefore, the character cannot return the same way they entered the shadow realm.
- The moon key and gargoyle from area 1 still exist in the shadow realm. If a character takes the moon key and inserts it into the door of shadows (see **area 1**), the door actually opens. Stepping through, the character teleports back to their dimension just to the west of the shadow door. The moon key then returns to its place.

There is no way to cross the curtains without entering the shadow realm behind it.

Opening the Slave Door. The door depicting slaves building the tomb must be lowered into the floor. The best way to do this is with the wheel in the northern alcove. To rotate the wheel, a character must use their action and make a DC 15 Strength check. With a successful check, they rotate the wheel downward, lowering the door 1 inch when they do so. Up to two characters may perform this action in tandem, lowering the door 2 inches per round so long as both their checks are successful. If the wheel is left unmanaged, on initiative count 10, it begins to rotate back up after 1 round, simultaneously raising the door 4 inches per round.

The door itself is difficult to move without using the wheel, requiring a DC 25 Strength check to pull down it

2 inches. As the door lowers, the wheel turns with it. As normal, it tries to raise itself back up if left unmanaged.

A creature can squeeze through an opening in the door depending on their size and how much equipment and gear they are carrying. A Small creature can squeeze through a space that is 18 inches wide without a check, or a space that is 12 inches wide with a successful DC 13 Strength (Athletics) check. A Medium creature can squeeze through a space that is 24 inches wide without a check, or a space that is 16 inches wide with a successful DC 15 Strength (Athletics) check. Increase the minimum space by 150% if the creature is wearing medium or heavy armor. (For example, a halfling wearing chainmail can squeeze through a space that is 27 inches wide without a check, or a space that is 18 inches wide with a successful DC 13 Athletics check.

5 – Chamber of Worship (Wind Door)
Read the following description of the door:

> This large stone door is decorated with what looks like gusts of wind swirling around it. All the gusts race towards the center of the door, where a large keyhole is positioned.

The fire key (**area 6**) must be placed into this door. Any other key placed into the door triggers a trap (see below).

When the characters open the door and enter, read the following:

> At the eastern edge of the room is a semi-transparent set of large green and black curtains. Just beside it, situated at the center of an alcove to the north, is a large statue carved to resemble a vulture-humanoid. In the vulture man's hands is a 5-foot long golden scepter. Before the statue is a stone dais covered in dark brown splotches.

Wind Door Trap. The door into this chamber is trapped. If someone

places any key but the fire key into this keyhole, attempts to violently force the door open or tries to pick the lock, a trap goes off.

A 5-foot diameter round hole in the ceiling, directly above the square in front of the door, slides open revealing a vertical passage. The passage sucks creatures and objects into it, then spits them out of the tomb. Anyone standing within 10 feet of the hole must make a DC 16 Strength or Dexterity saving throw (target's choice); a creature directly below it makes its saving throw with disadvantage. On a failed saving throw, the creature is pulled into the shaft, then flies up all 100-feet of the shaft and through the shaft's exit at the top of the mountain. Next, the creature is tossed 100-feet into the air above the shaft's exit. Finally, the creature falls 200-feet to the ground in front of the tomb, taking 20d6 falling damage and landing prone. The shaft continues to suck creatures up into it as long as it remains open, requiring more saving throws from any creatures still within 10 feet of it. After 4 rounds, the shaft seals itself shut.

Noticing the trap requires a successful DC 16 Intelligence (Investigation) check. However, the trap is nearly impossible to disarm. The only way to get to the trap's mechanisms is to dig up the floor, but that would trigger the tomb's shadow guardians (see "General Features").

It's possible that the characters could seal the hole above the shaft by clogging the passage with items. From there, they can break the door down or pick the lock with a successful DC 19 Dexterity check using proficiency with thieves' tools.

Carrion God. The vulture man statue represents Empeku, the Etran god of carrion and death. In his hands is Nebtka's scepter. A character that tries to take the scepter must stand upon the stone dais to do so. Otherwise, Empeku will not release the scepter.

After the creature grabs the scepter, Empeku speaks in ancient Etturan, "I accept this exchange." The statue then casts power word kill, targeting the creature holding the scepter. When struck dead, the dead creature continues to hold the staff, but the scepter can be taken from the dead creature's hands so long as the creature remains dead. If the creature is returned to life through a *raise dead* spell or similar magic, Empeku is angered and the scepter instantly teleports back into his hands until another "sacrifice" is made.

If the creature has more than 100 hit points (thus rendering the spell inert), Empeku then says, "You are worthy." The character may then take the scepter without any further consequences.

Only a *wish* spell can release the scepter without the statue casting *power word kill*.

Other Side of the Curtain. Touching the curtain from this side has the same effect as it does on the other side (see **area 4**).

Treasure. The scepter is made of solid gold and worth 1,000 gp.

6 – Three Priests, Three Keys

This 5-foot by 5-foot nook's walls are carved to look like three Etran priests. Each warrior is holding his hand out in front of him, revealing a 5-inch stone key. The westernmost priest is holding a key with a bow in the shape of jagged rock. The southernmost priest's key is shaped like a drop of water. And the easternmost priest's key resembles a gust of wind.

Preists Trap. Each time a key is lifted from one of the hands, the respective hand rises up, denoting the absence of its key. If more than one key is taken at a time (including the fire key in **area 8**), a trap is triggered. Blades swing out from the statues. A creature standing in the nook when the trap goes off must make a DC 18 Dexterity saving throw, taking 10d8 slashing damage on a failed saving throw, or half as much damage on a successful one.

The slots where the blades hide are easy to spot, requiring a DC 10 Wisdom (Perception) check to notice. There are three ways to disarm the blades.

First, a surrogate item weighing the same as the stolen key can be placed in the respective key's stead.

Second, the mechanism that activates the blade can be disarmed with a successful DC 17 Dexterity check using proficiency in thieves' tools. Failing the check by 5 or more results in the trap going off. The blades can also be attacked. Each blade has an AC of 19, 10 hp, and immunity to bludgeoning and slashing. After a blade is destroyed, the damage the blades do decreases by 1d8 (to a minimum of 0), and the DC decreases by 1 (to a minimum of 8). However, destroying a blade activates the tomb guardians (see "General Features").

Third, if a key is placed into the appropriate slot in the floor of **area 11**, someone can take one additional key without triggering this trap. Once all four keys are placed into the slots in **area 11**, the priest trap here and in **area 8** are totally disarmed.

7 – Descent

At the end of the stairway, there is a collapsed hall. The hall once led to chambers below the tomb where all the mechanical implements could be worked upon by the tombs' architects. When the tomb was sealed, the architects collapsed the passage.

8 – Chamber of Greed (Fire Door)

Read the following description of the door:

Flames decorate this large stone door. At the door's center is a keyhole.

The water key (**area 6**) must be placed into this door. Any other key placed into the door triggers a trap (see below).

When the characters open the door and enter, read the following:

Everywhere you look in this chamber you see glittering gold, sometimes piled to the 10-foot-high ceilings. The only places the gold doesn't pile is along a narrow path that snakes around the two columns that support the ceiling. One column is made of plain, unadorned stone, but the one to the far side of the room is carved to look like a priest with his hand held out. In his hand is a key, its bow shaped like a flame.

Fire Door Trap. The door into this chamber is trapped. If someone places any key but the water key into this keyhole, attempts to violently force the door open or tries to pick the lock, the trap goes off.

Iron walls drop from the ceiling at either side of the square directly in front of the door. Any creature standing in the square in front of the fire door must succeed on a DC 17 Dexterity saving throw or become trapped. A creature that succeeds on its saving throw moves to an unoccupied space within 5 feet of the square in front of the door. After 1 round, the inside of the box created by the fire door and the two iron walls starts to heat up. A creature inside the box takes 1d8 fire damage at the end of each of their turns. On each subsequent round (on initiative count 20), the damage of the fire increases by 1d8 to a maximum of 10d8. The fire door and iron walls have an AC 19, 75 hp (threshold 5), and immunity to fire, poison, and psychic damage. The iron walls can be lifted up just enough for a creature to a crawl out with a successful DC 23 Strength check. After 1 minute, the heat stops and the iron walls retract.

A successful DC 15 Intelligence (Investigation) check notices the slots in the floor that the iron walls come out of as well as the heating coils in the ceiling in floor. The walls' slots can be jammed with a dagger or similar implement, preventing them from rising. The heating coils can be disarmed with a successful DC 15 Dexterity check using proficiency in thieves' tools.

Fake Treasure. None of the treasure in this room is real. Instead, the "coins" are magical constructs that activate when attacked or touched. Each gold coin sprouts legs and antennae and the "coin" itself splits in two, revealing scarab-like wings. From there, the "treasure hoard" comes to life like a swarm of dangerous, golden insects. Treat the entire room as if every square had a swarm of insects in it, except that the swarms's type is Construct, they have AC 16 (natural armor), and are immune to poison and psychic damage. The insects continue to attack and swarm until the next dawn, at which point they settle down and resume their false appearance. A character can observe the treasure (without touching it); a successful DC 16 Intelligence (Investigation) check reveals the treasure's true nature.

Fire Key. Similar to the other three statues in **area 6,** this column shaped like a priest holds one of the tomb's four elemental keys. If a creature takes the fire key without first replacing the other keys (or disabling their mechanisms), another trap goes off. The fire door closes, trapping any creature in the room. Then, the priest's mouth opens, exuding an invisible toxic gas. Any creature trapped in the room must make a DC 10 Constitution saving throw at the start of each of its turns, taking 5d6 poison damage on a failed saving throw or half as much damage on a successful one. Each round (on initiative count 20) the poison damage increases by 1d6 (to a maximum of 10d6) and the DC for the saving throw increases by 1 (to a maximum of DC 20). Until the door is opened, the poison remains in the room. A creature can stop the poison gas by clogging the warrior's mouth with fabric or something similar. The poison jet within the statue can also be disarmed with a successful DC 14 Dexterity check using thieves' tools.

9 – Chamber of Humility (Water Door)
Read the following description of the door:

> Waves and drops of water were carved into this stone door. At its center is a hole. The door is slightly open.

Unlike the other elemental doors, this door can be opened with a push. However, failure to place the earth key into this door and turn it triggers a trap (see below). The keyhole is only on the northern-facing side of the door. If the door shuts and the characters are trapped in **area 9**, they cannot insert the key into the door.

Once the characters enter the room, read the following:

> This room's ceilings are only 5-feet high. The walls are somewhat plain, lacking the designs prevalent throughout the tomb. Even the stone column at the center of the room is unadorned. The only other way out of this room is a simple stone door in the eastern wall.

Water Door Trap. The eastern door in this room leading to area 10 is shut and locked. It can only be opened if the earth key is placed into the water door and turned. Failure to use the earth key in the water door before touching the eastern door triggers the trap. Immediately, the water door slams shut and locks. The floor then lowers 2 inches, revealing water jets which immediately start to fill the room. Each round (on initiative count 20), the water level rises 6 inches. After 1 minute, the entire room is filled with water. If the eastern door opens (thanks to the earth key in the water door), there are grates in its frame which allow the water to drain out of the room. Creatures in the room can block the jets, slowing down the flow of water by 1 inch for every 5 feet the characters block (to a minimum of 0 inches per round).

A successful DC 16 Intelligence (Investigation) notice that the floor lowers. A creature can make a successful DC 18 Dexterity check using thieves' tools to disarm the mechanism that lowers the floor, thereby preventing the room from filling with water.

Opening the door to **area 10** without the key first requires a successful DC 20 Dexterity check using thieves' tools to remove the locking mechanism, then a successful DC 19 Strength check to push the door open.

The water remains in the room until the next dawn. The water drains from the room and the trap resets.

10 – Partially Collapsed Tunnel

> A long hallway stretches before you. At the end of the hall is a pile of rubble where the tunnel has collapsed.

This was not part of the tomb's architects' original design; the tunnel collapsed under the pressure of the mountain above it. Fortunately, there is a narrow passage that the characters can climb through to reach **area 11**. The passage isn't visible until a creature is standing within 5 feet of the rubble.

Small creatures can move through the passage without any difficulty. However, a Medium or larger creature that tries to crawl through the passage must make a successful DC 5 Strength (Athletics) check to do so (made with disadvantage if the character is wearing medium or heavy armor). On a failed check, the character is restrained until the start of their next turn. In addition, the ceiling above the chamber shifts, dropping more rubble. When this happens, the DC for future Strength (Athletics) checks made to squeeze through the passage increases by 1d4. If a creature fails its check by 5 or more, the passage completely collapses, dropping the entire weight of the mountain onto the passage. Any creature within 10 feet of the collapsing passage takes 10d6 bludgeoning damage; a creature restrained by the passage takes twice as much damage. Once the passage collapses, there is no way to get through the tunnel through nonmagical means.

11 – Room of Laughing Skulls

> Set into the walls of this chamber are hundreds of dark skulls jammed into circular, stone cubbies. At the center

of the four columns that hold up the chamber's ceiling is a depression in the floor with four icons carved into it: a flame, a drop of water, a gust of wind, and a jagged stone. Within each icon is a keyhole.

Finally, on the northern wall, there is a door carved to look like a prince sitting on a throne. In one hand he holds a book, in the other a scepter. Upon the book are four runes. A vulture rests on his shoulder. The scepter and runes appear to be painted gold.

The runes on the carvings' book are in ancient Erratan and read "earth, air, fire, and water."

To open the door into **area 12**, the scepter from **area 4** must be placed into the column in **area 2** and rotated. Then, all four element keys must be placed into the floor and turned. The keys must be placed in the following order: earth, air, fire, and water. Placing a key into its respective keyhole in this room does not trigger the warrior traps when an additional key is taken.

Door Trap. If someone attempts to open the door before all five keys are put into their respective places (or if the keys are placed in the wrong order), or if someone tries to violently force the door open or pick the door's lock, one final trap goes off. The carving of the king speaks in Etturan, "Be gone, intruder. I curse thee." Each creature within 20 feet of the door when this happens is cursed. A cursed target can't regain hit points, and at the start of its turn, a cursed target's hit point maximum decreases by 1d6. If the curse reduces the target's hit point maximum to 0, the target dies, and its body turns to dust. The curse lasts until removed by the remove curse spell or other magic, or Nebtka's remains are destroyed.

The door to Nebtka's tomb is difficult to open, requiring a DC 25 Strength check to force open or five successful DC 15 Dexterity checks using proficiency with thieves tools to pick. The door

is magically reinforced, too, so unless a *dispel magic* spell is cast upon it, it has an AC of 21, 100 hp (threshold 10), resistance to all nonmagical damage, and immunity to poison and psychic damage. When dispelled, its stats are the same as other doors in the tomb (see "General Features").

12 – Nebtka's Tomb

> Stepping through the archway, you enter what looks like a burial chamber. In the northeastern corner is a sarcophagus. All around it, piled high, are gold coins, gems, art objects, and other items of value.
>
> Is this the actual tomb of the Kirin-born prince? Or another one of the tomb's tricks?

Opening Nebtka's sarcophagus (a successful DC 15 Strength check) reveals his withered, mummified remains. While his corpse exudes the curse of a mummy lord, Nebtka is not actually an undead creature.

Destroying Nebtka's Remains. If Nebtka's remains are set on fire or sprinkled with holy water, the curse over the tomb ends, as well as any other curses the characters may have received while in the tomb.

Treasure. The tomb holds an impressive amount of wealth. There is 13,520 gp; 7 gems (2 black opals, 1 blue sapphire, 3 star rubies, and 1 star sapphire) each worth 1,000 gp each; 2 art objects (a silver chalice set with moonstones and a ceremonial dagger with a black pearl in the pommel) each worth 750 gp each; a *+2 scimitar*; and a suit of *+1 plate*.

Adventure Conclusion

The Tomb of the Kirin-Born Prince is exceptionally deadly. It's likely the characters will need to return and recuperate multiple times before they are able to solve all of the tombs' riddles. Ω

CLASH AT KOBOLD CAULDRON

BY TEAM SUPERHYDRA

10th-Level Adventure for Fifth Edition

Primary Art by Justin David Russell

The Clash at Kobold Cauldron is a collaborative project involving myself, The Griffon's Saddlebag, Cze & Peku, Paper Forge, and IADnDMN - effectively known as Team Superhydra. You can look forward to our adventures in future installments. Also, be sure to check the Patreons for each of us:

*   **The Griffon's Saddlebag:** *patreon.com/the_griffons_saddlebag*
    Cze & Peku: *patreon.com/czepeku*
    Paper Forge: *patreon.com/paper-forge*
    IADnDMN: *patreon.com/itsadndmonsternow*
    DMDave: *For a full-color version of the adventure with high-res maps, miniatures, and more, go to dmdave.com/kobold-cauldron*

Something's wrong with the people of Knotside. A few weeks ago, a popular new liquor called Red Claw showed up in the city's many taverns. Anyone that took even a sip of this spirit immediately wanted another taste. At first, these desires were nothing more than cravings. But soon, those cravings grew to obsession. Then obsession turned to violence. Now, the city of Knotside faces collapse as the red-eyed Red Claw addicts stalk the streets, desperate for more. Unknown to the citizens of Knotside, Red Claw is the invention of a wicked red dragon that calls itself Tuckerthranx the Agitator. Only through stopping the dragon and his kobold minions will the town of Knotside be free of this booze-fueled curse.

Running the Adventure

Clash at Kobold Cauldron is a challenging location-based adventure for four 10th-level adventurers. The adventure starts in the Royal City of Knotside and leads the characters to the Red Claw distillery where they will encounter Tuckerthranx, an adult red dragon, and his wily horde of kobolds.

While many of the encounters in the adventure are built for four 10th-level adventurers, a few are significantly more difficult, especially Tuckerthranx himself. Characters with resistance or immunity to fire damage will excel in the distillery, as will characters armed with area of effect spells. Small, light characters will also have little trouble in the Cauldron.

Adventure Background

Knotside, for the most part, is a calm city filled with lawful citizens. Of course, being such a prosperous and thriving community, it is often the target for mischief, political subterfuge, and the occasional attack from rabble-rousers, firebrands, and evil-doers. One such evil-doer recently moved into Drakescale Peak, a mountain 25 miles to the north of Knotside—an adult red dragon named Tuckerthranx the Agitator.

Tuckerthranx (or just "Tucker" for short) stands apart from his other red-scaled brethren. Driven by an insatiable desire to grow his already-stout treasure hoard, Tucker often puts his mind and cleverness before his ego and arrogance. Knowing that attacking a city as large and well-guarded as Knotside would be pure foley, Tucker instead turned his machinations towards entrepreneurialism. With the help of a plucky kobold sorcerer/brewer named Boeger, Tucker created a tasty, alcoholic beverage named, appropriately, Red Claw.

Boeger's Red Claw wasn't just a delicious, anise-flavored spirit. It also contained a special ingredient: dark magic. Any creature that drank the liquor immediately desired more. At first, the liquor's effect was subtle. Hardly anyone in Knotside noticed that they were becoming addicted to the stuff. But after a couple shots, drinkers would do anything to get another taste. Knotsiders were tossing gold, jewels, gems, anything they could to get more barrels from the dragon's delivery men.

Eventually, riots broke out as the town turned towards chaos. Half of Knotside's militia tried to temper the

The Naval City of Knotside

To learn more about Knotside, you can check out Cze and Peku's City Maps Patreon that details the city, its inhabitants, and important locations therein. If you choose not to run the adventure in or near Knotside, you can use any medium or larger lawful or lawful good city near a mountain range.

issue and control the ravenous population. The other half were just as affected, rendered useless by their own craving for the Claw.

Adventure Hook

Trouble in Knotside

The characters' first introduction to Red Claw and its effects occurs while they are traveling just outside of Knotside, either returning from an adventure or headed to the city itself.

Just a mile or two outside of the city, read or paraphrase the following:

In the middle of the road stands a group of eight unarmored men and women. Each is holding a club in his or her hands and they're looking your way. But that's not the most troubling thing. They all have glowing red eyes and their stomachs appear unnaturally distended—almost like massive beer-guts hanging over their respective belts.

"Give us your booze money!" one of them shouts. The rest of the mob nods in agreement, then raises its clubs and approaches.

The group is made up of eight **commoners** and they are all heavily addicted to Red Claw. They've been attacking passersby, robbing them of their coins and jewelry so they can purchase more from Tucker's goons.

The commoners are easily broken, fleeing if even one of them is killed. Although possessed by their desire for more Red Claw liquor, they aren't

totally suicidal.

Regardless if the characters kill the group or not, eventually the Knotside militia rides up to investigate. While the situation might look bad to a normal group of soldiers (especially if the characters killed the commoners), the semilitiamen already realize what's happened.

The militia is made of six **guards** riding on **war horses** led by a **veteran** named Kollias. Kollias hails the characters and asks if they need any assistance. He then explains what's happening in Knotside.

"It started about a month ago. This group of monks rode into the city offering up barrels and bottles of this liquor called Red Claw. Only a few taverns bought it and the monks left. Right away, the Red Claw was a huge hit. Anyone who had a taste immediately started speaking its praises, claiming it was the best spirit they'd ever tasted. Then the monks came back a few days later, bringing more. Soon, everyone started drinking the stuff. But the more they drank, the more of it they wanted. The third time the monks came, they were mobbed. When that supply ran out, riots started. People had to have more. The fourth time, the monks came armed. And their prices went up. Way up.

"It didn't matter, of course. The people of our city were obsessed with the liquor. They were throwing all their gold, jewels, whatever they could get their hands on onto the monk's wagons just for a few bottles of the stuff. Those who couldn't get a taste turned violent.

"We've been trying to find the ource of the liquor itself, but unfortunately what few men I have left are tied up quelling the riots. If you're adventurers—and it looks like you are—then I hope you can assist us in finding the source of the Red Claw liquor, and, in turn, a way to return our citizens' sanity."

In the way of a reward, Kollias doesn't have much to offer the characters at the moment. However, he promises that the city of Knotside—the remarkably wealthy city of Knotside—will be in their debt. He does mention that the Red Claw monks have hauled off massive piles of coins and gems from the Knotsiders. Were the characters to find it, they are free to keep one-quarter of it. "The people of Knotside will see it as a 'fee' for your services, I'm sure," he will assure the characters.

What Kollias Knows
At this point, the characters probably have a few questions for Kollias. Here is what he knows about Red Claw and its creators.

"How does Red Claw affect the drinkers?" Kollias notes that the Red Claw itself doesn't act like a poison or a disease, but instead has more in common with a curse. The available clergy in Knotside have been working to cast remove curse on the infected, but they are terribly overwhelmed. Some of the sages in town theorize that if they had the original ingredients that went into creating the Red Claw, they could devise a bulk cure for everyone in town.

"Where did the monks that delivered the Red Claw go?" The last time the monks came into town, they were armed. What few commoners tried to go after them were picked off by flaming arrows shot by the caravan guards. Kollias sent a scout after the monks and believes they're hiding their distillery somewhere in the Basilisk's Spine mountain range.

"What did the monks look like?" Kollias and his men swear that some of the monks were dragonborn. Others were short, possibly halflings. They all wore thick robes with bandages wrapped around their arms and face. Mangy-looking giant weasels pulled their carts. The guards who came with them were heavily armed andorganized, but also robed, wearing red dragon masks similar to the logo on the liquor bottles.

"Will Kollias help the characters find the Brewers?" Currently, Kollias' men are tied up with the overwhelming unrest in Knotside. He doesn't have a single hand to spare. However, he does offer a map to the mountain range.

"Have you hired anyone else for this job?" So far, Kollias hasn't come across any other adventurers. What few adventurers were already in Knotside were affectedby the liquor. He's lucky to have caught the characters outside of the city.

Resting in Knotside
If the characters opt to stay the night in Knotside despite the troubles, Kollias and his men escort them to the Venerable Swordsman, an inn on the south side of that city that remains mostly unaffected by the chaos. The majority of the shops, taverns, and other points of interest in Knotside are currently closed. Kollias, fearful for his city, urges the characters not to waste too much time. He can procure whatever they need in terms of arms, ammunition, and armor from the town's armory. He can also grant up to 4 potions of healing per character and any basic supplies they might require.

Should the characters dally too long, Kollias eventually grows impatient and seeks out another group to solve the issue.

The Basilisk's Spine

Kollias' scout followed the brewers for about 20 miles before arriving at the foothills of the Basilisk's Spine. The Spine is a jagged collection of peaks, bluffs, and sheer cliffs, boldly facing the ocean to the east. An active volcano sits at the heart of it.

Tucker's Regional Effects
Tucker is a legendary **adult red dragon**. The region surrounding his volcanic lair in Drakescale Peak is warped by his innate magic. Within 6 miles, small earthquakes are common. Sulfur taints all water sources within 1 mile, and rocky fissures form portals to the Elemental Plane of Fire—it wouldn't be out of place for the characters to run into the odd **azer, fire elemental,** or **salamander** war party within the region.

Minion Resistances. Thanks to his magic, all of Tucker's kobolds and henchmen have resistance to fire damage.

Tracking the Red Claw Caravan
Once the characters discover the spot where the scout last saw the monks,

they will need to track the caravan's route through the mountains. It's been a couple days since the caravan left, so tracking it isn't easy. A character must succeed on a DC 25 Wisdom (Survival) check to follow the path in the dirt.

If the characters have trouble finding the path, they can search the mountains themselves for clues. Each hour that they spend searching in the mountains, have them make a Wisdom (Survival) check with a DC equal to 25 minus 1 for each hour they spend searching for clues. Clues can include things like discarded corks from the liquor bottles, tracks in the dirt, a broken crate, or anything else that you feel is appropriate.

In addition, once per hour while the characters are searching, roll a d20. On a roll of 18-20, the characters run into a brewer caravan. Instead of rolling, you can opt to have the encounter occur whenever you feel necessary, especially if the characters haven't found any solid leads after a few hours of searching.

The Delivery Men
The characters come across the delivery men's caravan. They're set on returning to Knotside one last time to collect any remaining gold and merchandise they can. From there, they plan on targeting another city within a days' ride.

Knowing that Knotside is in dismay and the militia has caught on to their ploy, the brewers are even better prepared this time.

The caravan consists of three carts pulled by two **dire weasels** each (see Appendix C). Atop each cart is a massive hogshead barrel holding 79 gallons of Red Claw liquor. The barrels have an AC of 16 and 50 hit points, plus immunity to poison and psychic damage. Any hit on the barrel causes its contents to leak onto the dirt and rocks. The liquor is also flammable. If the cask takes fire damage, roll a d20. If the result on the d20 is less than the fire damage dealt, the cask erupts in a 20-foot radius explosion. Each crea-

ture in the area must make a DC 13 Dexterity saving throw, taking 14 (4d6) fire damage on a failed save, or half as much on a successful one. A flammable object in the area ignites if it isn't being worn or carried.

At the front of each cart is a **kobold** driver that's been instructed to stay seated even if they run into trouble. Should things turn bad, they are to return to base.

Leading the caravan are two cloaked **kobold wing sorcerers** each with two **ogre** bodyguards. It doesn't take long for the kobolds to figure out that the adventurers are there to stop their operation. They immediately attack. If they are reduced to half their numbers or fewer, the kobolds pile onto the carts and retreat. Fully loaded, the weasels have a movement speed of 20 feet, 40 feet if they Dash, so it should be easy to chase them. The kobolds aren't afraid to cut away the barrels to increase their speed. This gives the weasels their normal movement speed of 40 feet.

Once the characters defeat or drive off the brewers, the tracks they leave should be easy enough to follow to the Red Claw Distillery, requiring no further Wisdom (Survival) checks.

Red Claw Distillery

The trail the brewers left behind leads to a blackened, dismal canyon littered with razor-sharp obsidian shards, dead trees, and lifeless ash. The temperature here is hot and dry, like standing in front of an oven, even during the winter.

When the characters get within 400 feet of the lair, read the following:

> Thrusting from the earth like a colossal tooth stands a bleak, blackened volcano. A slow-moving, ropey lava flow surrounds the front of the volcano, blocking passage. The only way across the lava is lonely bridge flanked by a pair of obsidian gargoyles at the far side. Five twen-

ty-foot high wooden towers manned by cloaked kobold guards protect a wide courtyard in front of the mountain. Just beyond those outposts, sticking out of the peak like a sore thumb is a ramshackle, wooden building built on stilts. From within you hear the bickering, laughing, cackling, wicked voices of kobolds.

A large, handpainted sign over the shack reads "KOBOLD KALDRUN" Judging by the primitive lettering and misspelling, it's likely the kobolds painted the sign themselves.

Getting close to the tavern is no easy task. The lava is particularly deadly. The entire flow is 30 feet across, making jumping over it difficult. A constant heat haze emenates from the constantly churning molten rock. Outside of teleporting directly into the courtyard, the only way for the characters to reach the other side of the lava flow is by flying or leaping over the lava... or by crossing the bridge.

General Features
Unless otherwise stated, here are the most common features of the distillery and dragon's lair.

Extreme Heat. The temperatures within the distillery and caldera reach temperatures as high as 125° F, and even higher the closer the characters get to Tucker's caldera. Review the extreme heat rules in the *DMG* for details.

Lava and Magma. Lava is extremely dangerous. The first time a creature enters lava or magma, it takes 6d10 fire damage, and then again if it ends its turn in the lava/magma. In addition, the heat haze rising from the lava/magma lightly obscures creatures and objects on the other side of it.

Light. Most of the distillery is lit by the ambient light of the magma that courses through it. Still, there are many dark tunnels and chambers. Use your own discretion to determine how much light is in a given area. The descriptions assume that the characters have darkvision or other methods of seeing.

Spirit Barrels. The kobolds store barrels of their infamous Red Claw liquor all throughout the complex. The liquor barrels are highly explosive. If a regular 1/8-tun barrel takes fire damage, roll a d20. If the result on the d20 is less than the fire damage dealt, the cask erupts in a 20-foot radius explosion. Each creature in the area must make a DC 13 Dexterity saving throw, taking 14 (4d6) fire damage on a failed save, or half as much on a successful one. A flammable object in the area ignites if it isn't being worn or carried.

Drinking Red Claw. Characters may get a wild hair and try the liquor. A character that takes a 2 oz single shot of liquor must make a DC 10 Constitution saving throw. On a failed saving throw, the character gets the Red Claw curse. While cursed, the character has a character flaw that lasts until cured: "I will do anything or give anything to drink more Red Claw liquor." Every 8 hours that passes that thecharacter is unable to drink more Red Claw liquor, its hit point maximum is reduced by 1. If this reduces the character's hit point maximum to 0, the character explodes, dying instantly. If a character takes a second shot before an hour has passed, increase the DC for the Constitution of the saving throw by 1 (to a maximum of 20). If an hour passes and the character does not drink another shot, the DC returns to 10. Creatures immune or resistant to fire damage automatically pass their saving throws.

Keyed Encounters

1A - Main Entrance Bridge

The forty-foot long arched bridge that spans the lava flow ismade of solid stone. At the northern end of the bridge are two 10-foot tall gargoyle statues carved from obsidian.

Trap. The gargoyles are traps. If a creature moves within 10 feet of the gargoyles without saying the password

"Tuckerthranx", the gargoyles' arms and wings extend perpendicularly from their bodies and begin to spin. The first time a creature moves within 10 feet of the statues, it must make a DC 15 Dexterity saving throw. On a failed saving throw, the creature takes 22 (4d10) slashing damage from the spinning gargoyle statues. A creature that ends its turn within 10 feet of the spinning gargoyles automatically takes this damage again.

The spinning gargoyles make it nearly impossible to cross the bridge. However, a character can attempt to tumble through the blades. Have the character make a DC 15 Dexterity (Acrobatics) check. On a successful check, the character tumbles past the gargoyles. On a failed check, the character takes 22 (4d10) slashing damage and is pushed back 5 feet into the nearest unoccupied space.

The gargoyles stop spinning after 1 minute so long as no creature remains within 20 feet of them.

One way to disable this trap and stop the gargoyles from spinning is to switch off the mechanisms which are on the north-facing side of their bases. Of course, a character would have to get close enough to the gargoyles to do so.

Fortunately, the gargoyles themselves can be destroyed. Each gargoyle statue has an AC of 19, 50 hit points, and immunity to fire, poison, and psychic damage. For every 25 hit points of damage a gargoyle statue takes, the Dexterity save or Dexterity (Acrobatics) check needed to avoid the statues is reduced by 1, and the damage they deal is reduced by 1d10.

1B - Distillery Courtyard

Just to the other side of the bridge, beyond the gargoyles, is a wide courtyard. The courtyard's defenses are described below. If the characters manage the impossible and remove the kobold guards without signaling the alarm, then there are 4d6 **kobolds** found working here at any given time.

Flame Thrower
Large object

Armor Class: 19
Hit Points: 50
Damage Immunities: fire, poison, psychic

A flame thrower spews fire. It is fueled by natural gas pumped into it by a tube in the ground; if the weapon is removed from its roost or its gas line is cut (AC 13, 5 hp, immunity to fire, poison, and psychic damage), it ceases to function. It takes one action to aim the weapon and one action to fire it.

The flame thrower is manned by two kobolds, with a third keeping watch, subbing in if necessary. If the flame thrower is reduced to 0 hit points, it explodes, launching fire and shrapnel in a 20-foot radius sphere centered on it. Each creature in the explosion's area must succeed on a DC 14 Dexterity saving throw. A creature takes 4d6 piercing damage plus 4d6 fire damage on a failed saving throw, or half as much damage on a success.

Flame Jet (Recharge 5-6). The flame thrower spews a jet of flame in a 60-foot line that is 5 feet wide. Each creature in the area must succeed on a DC 14 Dexterity saving throw, taking 10 (3d6) fire damage on a failed saving throw, or half as much damage on a successful one.

1C - Kobold Watchtowers

Five watchtowers fitted with **flamethrowers** manned by three **kobolds** each stand twenty feet over the courtyard. For a Small creature, getting up the kobold-sized ladders is simple. Medium creatures will have a slower-go than normal climbing, ascending at half their normal movement speed while using the small ladder.

Each tower also keeps an alarm bell in it. The third kobold that mans each tower pulls the bell signaling danger. One round after the bell is pulled, eight **kobolds**, four **booze server kobolds**, and two **cask hauler kobolds** arrive

in **area 1B** from various locations within, ready to defend the distillery from intruders at all costs (the two new monsters appear in Appendix C).

1D - Tavern Deck

A winding, wooden staircase leads up to a deck overlooking the courtyard. When the characters reach **area 1A**, four **booze server kobolds** rush out to the deck and start throwing burning spirits at the intruders.

Rickety Deck. The deck itself was poorly built, meant to hold only a handful of kobolds at a time. If more than 200 pounds is placed on the deck, the deck collapses. Each creature on the deck when it collapses takes 7 (2d6) falling damage and lands prone within 5 feet of where the deck stood.

1E - Entrance to Area 2

This area to the west of the courtyard holds a small cache of liquor barrels plus a parked **dire weasel**-drawn cart holding another four barrels.

2 - West Entrance Corridor

The west entrance rises at a near 45-degree angle and the smooth, obsidian stone is quite slick thanks to spilled liquor. A character that attempts to move up the passage without using a rope must succeed on a DC 13 Strength (Athletics) check to climb up the tunnel. Failing the check sends them sliding back down to the entrance in **area 1E**.

Trap Part 1: Rope and Barrels. A hemp rope attached to steel loops at regular intervals along the western wall have been put into place to allow the kobolds easy access up. Any character that weighs more than 40 pounds that tries to use the rope to climb triggers a trap. A net hidden in a cubby on the ceiling over the alcove releases, sending 10 barrels rolling down the corridor. Any creature in the hallway when the barrels fall must make a DC 15 Strength saving throw. On a failed saving throw, a creature takes 14 (4d6) bludgeoning damage and is pushed

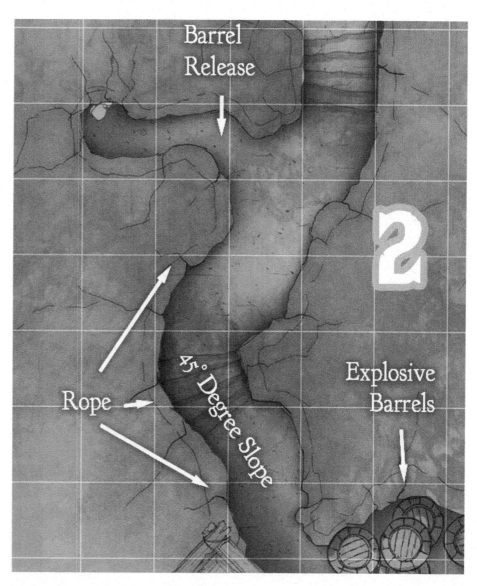

back down the hallway to the entrance, landing prone in front of the barrels in **area 1E**.

Trap Part 2: Acid Barrels. If the barrels themselves weren't enough, each is filled with caustic acid (a protective coating painted on the inside of the barrels kept them from dissolving). When the barrels hit the ground in area 1E, they break apart, spilling acid all over the floor in **1E**. Any creature within 10 feet of the entrance to area 2 must succeed on a DC 12 Dexterity saving throw, taking 10 (3d6) acid damage on a failed saving throw or half as much damage on a successful one. Prone creatures take twice as much

damage from the acid. Of course, that's not the end of it...

Trap Part 3: Chain Reaction. The acid leaking from the barrels eventually leaks over to the liquor barrels stored against the wall in **area 1E**. One round after the acid barrels break, the acid within eats away at the non-treated barrels. The acid mixes with the liquor and explodes. A creature standing within 20-feet of the exploding barrels must make a Dexterity saving throw with a DC of 13 plus 1 for every barrel that explodes beyond the first (there are five total barrels, Diagram 1: **Area 2's** Traps capable of a maximum DC of 17). On a failed

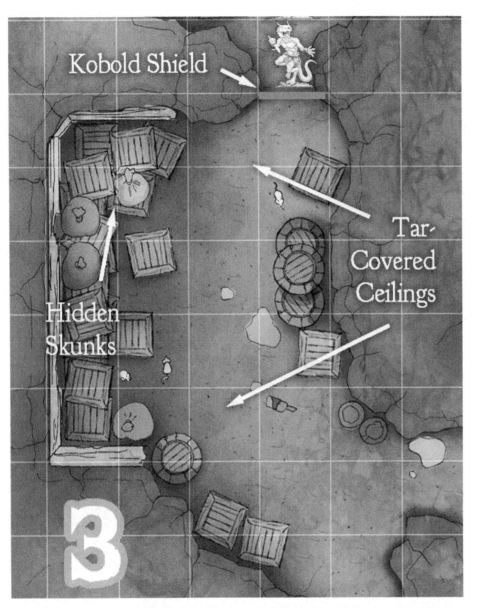

tage. On a failed check, the character is restrained by the tar on the ceiling until it breaks free. A creature restrained by the tar can use its action to make a DC 12 Strength check. If it succeeds, it is no longer restrained.

Lamp oil and even the Red Claw liquor can easily dissolve the tar, allowing the characters to move through the area unhindered.

Skunks. If the tar isn't enough, the kobolds keep six skunks in this area who stay hidden among the supplies. Any non-kobold creatures who try to crawl through the area disturb the skunks, especially if the creature is struggling to become unstuck from the ceiling. The skunks have **rat** stat blocks except they can spray musk at a creature within 5 feet of them. Sprayed, the target must make a DC 10 Constitution saving throw. On a failed save, the target wretches and can't take actions for 1 minute. The target can repeat the saving throw at the end of each of its turns, ending the effect on itself with a success. A creature that doesn't need to breathe or is immune to poison automatically succeeds on the saving throw. Once the skunk sprays its musk, it can't do so again until it finishes a short or long rest.

Save or fail, the creature is coated in the skunk's musk. Until the creature uses a spell such as prestidigitation, takes a bath in vinegar, or 1 week passes, it reeks of skunk musk; itmakes all Charisma ability checks when interacting with people at disadvantage.

Kobolds with Pikes. Sound travels far in the area. Characters that are stuck or sprayed by skunks are bound toalert the kobolds in area 13. Nine kobolds arrive and place a large wooden shield over the northern exit leading to **area 13**, barring it into place. The shield grants the kobolds 3/4 cover. From there, they attack with 15 foot long pikes. It takes three kobolds to use a pike. If the kobolds are reduced to two kobolds or less, they retreat, leaving the shield barred in place.

saving throw, a creature takes 4d6 fire damage plus 1d6 fire damage for each barrel that explodes beyond the first. On a successful saving throw, a character takes half as much damage.

3 -Storage

Crates, barrels, boxes and more clutter this low-ceilinged cave. You immediately notice a strong smell of tar in this area.

The ceilings in this cave are only 4 feet high. Perfect for a kobold or other Small creature, but miserable for a

creature of Medium size or larger to pass through. Any creature that stands more than 4 1/2 feet tall must squat or crawl to move through the area. All of the barrels in the area are filled with the Red Claw liquor.

Tar-Covered Ceiling. Those pesky kobolds coated the ceiling in sticky tar! The tar is easy to notice, but incredibly difficult to remove. Have a crawling character make a DC 13 Strength (Athletics) check or Dexterity (Acrobatics) check (character's choice) each round that they crawl through this area. If the character is overloaded with gear, they make this check with disadvan-

Long-Pikes. *Melee Weapon Attack*: +0 to hit (with advantage), reach 15 ft., one target. *Hit*: 3 (1d10 -2) piercing damage.

Moving the Shield Out of the Way. The bar holding the kobold's shield in place is made of soft pine. It only takes a DC 5 Strength check to burst it. If a character succeeds the check by 5 or more, they push the shield out of the way and immediately step into area 15. When this happens, chicken feathers fall from the ceiling onto the character. If the character had any part of them stuck to the tar from the ceiling, the feathers automatically stick to them and remain stuck until the tar is dissolved. Any kobolds that are still alive in **area 15** who witness this immediately stop what they're doing and cackle maliciously at the tarred-and-feathered character. One round later they realize the danger they're in and flee.

4 - Corridor to the Tavern

This corridor rises, too, but not nearly as severely as the one in area 2. Plus, it's easier to climb thanks to wooden planks placed at regular intervals. However, the corridor is tight, only 3 feet high at its highest point. Medium-sized creatures will need to bend and crawl to make their way up the corridor.

Poison Gas Trap. The wooden planks aren't just there to help the kobolds climb up the hallway. They also act as pressure plates for a poison trap. Any creature weighing more than 40 pounds that steps onto one of the planks depresses a bladder hidden below the step. The bladder releases a poisonous spray that shoots out from the floor directly onto the creature that stepped on the plate. The target must succeed on a DC 13 Constitution saving throw. If the creature was crawling at the time, it caught the poison in its face; it makes this saving throw with disadvantage. On a failed saving throw, the creature is poisoned for 1 hour. Until the poison is removed, the creature is

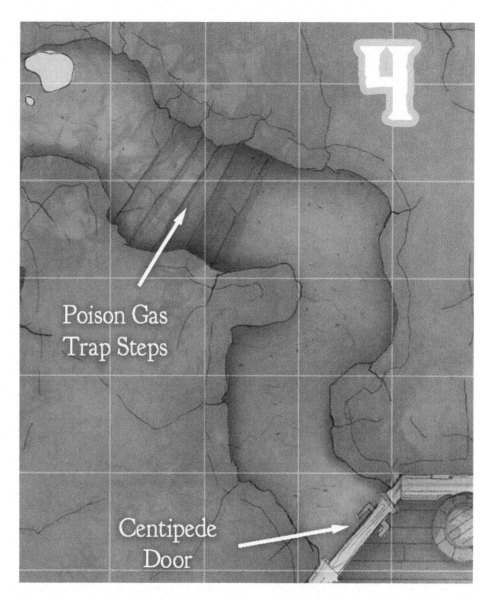

Poison Gas Trap Steps

Centipede Door

blinded.

Noticing the trap requires a successful DC 10 Intelligence(Investigation) check. Each plank can be disabled with a successful DC 12 Dexterity check requiring proficiency in thieves' tools. If a check to disarm the trap fails by 3 or more, it automatically goes off, requiring the remover to make a saving throw against the trap.

Creatures short enough to walk through the corridor can easily avoid the planks by stepping over them. However, crawling creatures must make a DC 13 Strength (Athletics) or Dexterity (Acrobatics) check (target's choice) each round to avoid pressing

the planks as they move through the area.

Centipede Door. At the end of the corridor leading into **area 4** is a small, round, wooden door that resembles a barrel top (it once was). An iron handle is set into the center of the door. From the position of the hinges, it appears that the door opens with a pull. If a character pulls the handle without first twisting it clockwise, it unlatches a hidden compartment built into the actual door. This hidden compartment is filled with a **swarm of centipedes** that immediately attacks whoever opened the compartment.

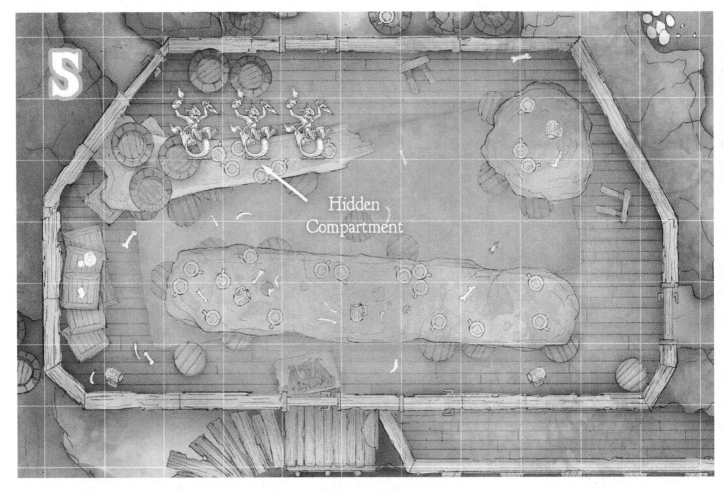

Hidden
Compartment

A DC 15 Wisdom (Perception) check reveals the nature ofthe hidden compartment. Then, a DC 13 Intelligence (Investigation) check reveals that simply turning the handle clockwise 90 degrees locks the hidden compartment, trapping the centipedes inside, then unlocks the door.

5 - 'KoboldKaldrun'

> This low-ceiling room looks like a bar—albiet a tiny bar. The bar it-self stands no more than a foot-and-a-half, and the tables are even short-er. Child-sized chairs made of planks and barrel parts clutter the room.
>
> From behind the bar, three crea-tures pop up holding burning bottles in their hand. "Deff tuda 'ven-churz!" they shout in broken Common.

Three **booze server kobolds** attack and fight to the death.

Treasure. The bar is made of wood with thin stone slabs set atop it. The middle slab can be removed easily. Within, is a small hollow filled with 580 cp, 120 sp, and 30 gp as well as *Talyard The Great's Wand of Power* (see Appendix B).

6 - Barrel Storage

Empty barrels are stored just outside the tavern. There is nothing else of interest in this room.

7 - Kobold Dens

> This room reeks of animal musk, sul-fur, and rotting food. Piles of dry-rot-ting hay litter the floors in neat, lit-tle piles, perfect for a small creature to sleep on.

This is where most of the kobolds of the distillery rest. There are 12 piles of hay in all. A small altar dedicated to a dragon god rests against the southern wall of the den.

Encounter. There are 12 **kobolds** here. They aggressively defend their egg clusters (see Diagram 5).

Bed Treasure. If a character search-es through a pile of hay, roll a d6. On a result of 6, they discover 1d6 copper-pieces, and on a result of 5 they find a random trinket with no real value (GM's discretion).

Altar Trap. The rug directly in front of the altar hides a pressure plate underneath. The trap is triggered when any creature weighing more than 40 pounds steps or kneels on the rug—a 5-foot-cubed stone limestone block weighing 2.5 tons from the ceiling releases, falling on top of the creature

Kobold Eggs

Falling Stone Trap

7

Dragon Altar

ful DC 15 Wisdom (Perception) check to spot the block in the ceiling. A DC 16 Intelligence (Investigation) check reveals that the trap is triggered by placing too much weight on the rug. The trap's pressure plate can be disarmed with a successful DC 12 Dexterity check using proficiency in thieves' tools.

Altar Treasure. The golden idol on top of the altar is made of solid gold, valued at 250 gp.

Egg Clusters. Dozens of scaly green and red eggs the size of a human's fist lay on piles of fresh hay tucked in hollows with ceilings measuring no more than 3-feet in height. One out of four of the eggs (a result of 1 on a d4) are actually largebird eggs decorated to look like kobold eggs. Whenever a creature picks up a fake egg, roll a d4 to and refer to the "What's in the Egg?" table to determine what happens.

"What's in the Egg?"

d4	Result
1	*Spiders.* A **swarm of spiders** crawls out of the egg.
2	*Ooze.* Acidic, green ooze pours out of the egg. The creature holding the egg takes 1d4 acid damage.
3	*Glue.* The egg collapses, covering the creature's hand in glue. Until the glue is dissolved, the creature's hand is unusable. It makes Strength and Dexterity checks that rely on using its hands with disadvantage. Plus, it can't hold anything with two hands, and it can hold only a single object at a time.
4	*Stink Bomb.* The egg collapses, expelling a nasty stench cloud. The creature holding the egg plus any creature within 5 feet of that creature must succeed on a DC 10 Constitution saving throw. On a failed saving throw, the target wretches and can't take actions for 1 minute. The creature can repeat its saving throw at the end of each of its turns, ending the effect on itself with a success.

that set off the trap. The creature must succeed on a DC 13 Dexterity saving throw. On a failed saving throw, the blockfalls on top of the creature; the creature takes 28 (8d6) bludgeoning damage, falls prone in its space, and is restrained by the block. A creature can use its action to make a DC 25 Strength check, lifting the block off the target with a success. The block can be destroyed, too. It has an AC of 19 and

100 hit points (damage threshold 5) and is immune to poison and psychic damage. On a successful saving throw, the creature takes only half the damage, isn't knocked prone,and is pushed 5 feet out of the block's space into an unoccupied space of the creature's choice. If no unoccupied space is within range, the creature suffers the consequences of a failed saving throw.

Noticing the trap requires a success-

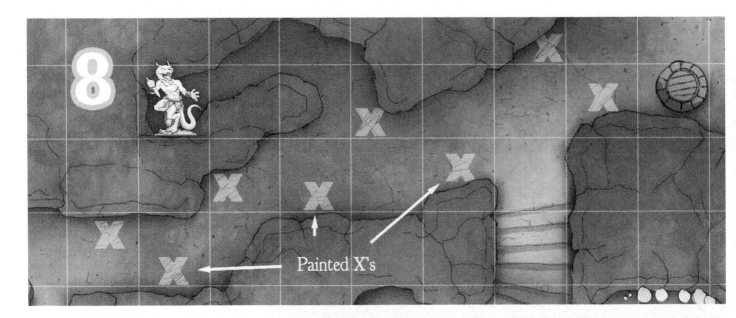

Painted X's

8 - Middle Corridor

> This stone corridor has 6-foot high ceilings and is roughly 5 feet wide. Eight red "X's" painted on the stone floor appear at regular intervals, some to the left, others to the right.

The X's have no function, other than representing the position of the latches in **area 13**. Of course, that doesn't mean the players won't get psyched outthinking that they should/shouldn't step on them.

Encounter. In the small branching hallway in the north face of the corridor, a single **kobold** hides. When the characters enter the corridor, it emerges, yelps, throws asmoke bomb their way, then runs off screaming in the opposite direction (whichever way seems appropriate) hopping on the red X's as it goes. The smoke bomb heavily obscures the corridor for 1 minute as a fog cloud spell.

9 - Weasel Pens

The kobolds keep three **dire weasels** penned here. The weasels are well-fed and mostly trained. If released, they amble away, more confused than thankful for their newfound liberty. They won't attack unless frightened.

The barrels in this area are all loaded

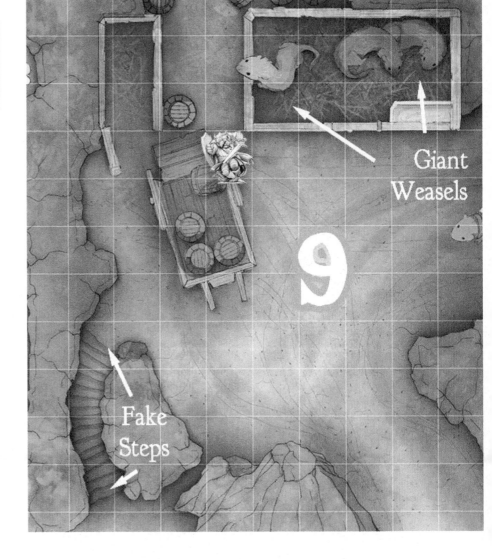

Giant Weasels

Fake Steps

with Red Claw and are explosive.

Encounter. One of Tucker's lieutenants, Ankor (NE male **half-red dragon veteran**) watches over the weasels. Chances are Ankor heard the characters coming and has prepared himself for combat. He hides around the parked cart, using it as cover, trying to keep his distance as much as he can. If forced into melee combat, Ankor does his best to disengage and tactically retreat, hoping to section off the adventurers.

Trap. The staircase at the southwestern end of the weasel pens is trapped. The steps themselves are made from baked clay, molded to look like steps. Any creature that steps on one breaks the step and onto a bed of sharp nails hiding within. The creature takes 2 (1d4) piercing damage and until it takesa short or long rest or receives magical healing, its speed is reduced by 10 feet. A successful DC 13 Wisdom (Perception) check reveals the nature of the fake steps.

10 - West Distillery

> At the center of this colossal cave is a huge distillery tank. Barrels bearing the Red Claw logo are everywhere. This must be one of the kobolds' production areas.

All of the barrels in this room are explosive.

Encounter. Ronk and Manx (NE male and female **half-red dragon veterans**) oversee production here. Joining them are 3 **booze server kobolds** and 2 **cask hauler kobolds**.

Distillery Tanks

Areas 10, 12A, 13, and **14** hold huge distillery tanks. Like the liquor barrels themselves, the tanks are highly explosive. If a tank takes fire damage, roll a d20. If the result on the d20 is less than half the fire damage dealt, the distillery tank erupts. Each creature in area 10 must make a DC 15 Dexterity saving throw, taking 28 (8d6) fire damage on a failed save, or half as much on a successful one. A flammable object in the area ignites if it isn't being worn or carried.

11 - Fire Elemental Oven

If the characters enter the corridor from the southern end and haven't entered **area 14** yet, read or paraphrase the following:

> Intense heat radiates from this forty-foot long hallway. At the far end, you think you can see machinery and barrels - potentially a distillery. Long shadows made by kobolds move along the wall.
>
> It sounds like they are whispering, shushing each other while they try to hide.

Once the characters enter the tunnel and get mid-way towards area 14, the kobolds in **area 14** hit a button droppingiron doors from the ceiling at both ends (see Diagram 7). Next, three **fire elementals** appear, one in each alcove, and attack, taking full advantage of their fire form in the tight quarters. Thanks to the trapped heat made by the fireelementals, the hallway quickly turns into an oven. The heat starts at 150° F during the first round of combat. Then, at initiative count 20 (losing ties) the temperature of the oven increases by 50° F for each fire elemental that is in the oven to a maximum of 550° F.

As the heat increases, the oven

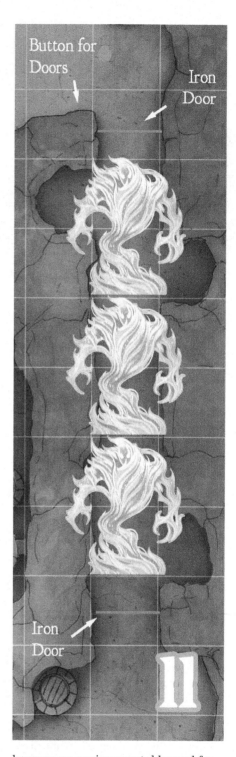

becomes an environmental hazard for the characters. When a character ends their turn in the oven, refer to the Fire Elemental Oven table on the next page to determine what happens.

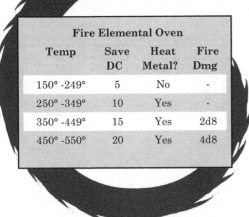

Fire Elemental Oven			
Temp	Save DC	Heat Metal?	Fire Dmg
150° -249°	5	No	-
250° -349°	10	Yes	-
350° -449°	15	Yes	2d8
450° -550°	20	Yes	4d8

Exhaustion DC. Each round that a character ends its turn in the fire elemental oven, it must make a Constitution saving throw. The DC of the saving throw depends on the temperature of the oven as shown on the Fire Elemental Oven table. On a failed saving throw, a character takes one level of exhaustion. Creatures that are resistant or immune to fire damage automatically pass their saving throws.

Heated Metal. All manufactured metal objects, such as a metal weapon or suit of heavy or medium metal armor, begin to glow red hot. A creature holding or wearing a metal object must succeed on a Constitution saving throw against the current temperature's DC. If it doesn't drop the object, it has disadvantage on attack rolls and ability checks until the start of its next turn. The items remain heated for as long as the temperature in the oven stays above 250° F and for 2 rounds afterward. Creatures that are resistant or immune to fire damage automatically pass their saving throws.

Fire Damage. A creature automatically takes the amount of fire damage listed on the Fire Elemental Oven table.

Escaping the Oven. A character on the other side of the northernmost iron door can hit the button in area 14 to raise the iron doors. Once the iron doors are up, the temperature in the corridor decreases by 100° F each round. An iron door can be lifted with a successful DC 20 Strength check. However, the doors are extremely hot. The moment a character places their unprotected hands on one of the doors, they must succeed on a Constitution saving throw the current temperature's DC or make their Strength check with disadvantage. Each door has an AC of 20 with 50 hit points (damage threshold 5) and is immune to fire, poison, and psychic damage.

Defeating the Elementals. Once all three fire elementals are destroyed, the temperature in the oven decreases by 25° F each round until it returns to normal room temperature (a "balmy" 100° F).

12A -Central Distillery

The first time the characters enter the room, read or paraphrase the following.

A 20-foot high distillery tank dominates the center of this room. All around you are barrels with the infamous Red Claw logo stenciled on the side.

A voice calls from behind the tank. "You've gone far enough, fools."

Another one of Tuckerthranx's lieutenants, Yarm (NE **half-red dragon veteran**), guards this area. Hiding among the barrels are four **booze server kobolds**. Yarm is a CE male half-red dragon veteran. In place of a heavy crossbow, Yarm is armed with a *Fire! Fire!* crossbow (see Appendix B). Unlike the other lieutenants, Yarm has little regard for the tanks, barrels, and even the kobolds that surround him. He will fight to the death.

12B -Empty Barrels

Barrels waiting to be filled fill this section of the central distillery. A set of huge, wrought iron double-doors decorated to look like the Red Claw logo pock the north wall of the cave.

Spring-loaded Doors. The doors are easy to open from this area. However, they're set with springs which cause them to automatically close after 1 round while they aren't being held open.

The opposite side of the door (the side facing the lava pit in **area 15A**) is smooth and lacks handles. The only way to open the door from the far side is with a successful DC 17 Strength check (made with advantage if a lever is placed into the door). Tuckerthranx also has a button he can press to make the doors open. The doors are heavy, with AC 20, 50 hp (damage threshold 5), and immunity to fire, poison, and psychic damage.

13A - West Distillery

If the characters burst through the kobold shield placed over the south exit into **area 3**, the nine **kobolds** may still be here. Otherwise, this distillery is empty and not currently in use. See **area 3** for details on the tar/feather trap that waits over the southern entrance.

13B -Puzzle Door

The first time the characters come upon this door, read or paraphrase the following:

A large set of iron double-doors stand before you. At the center of the right-most door, a six-inch deep and four-inch wide groove runs from the top of the door to its bottom.

Within the groove are eight sliding toggles, each set to the rightmost position. A "W" has been etched into the interior of the groove just above the topmost lever.

To open the door, the levers must slide into the same position as the X's in **area 8** (from top-to-bottom: right, left, right, left, right, left, right, left), with the topmost latch being thewesternmost X and bottommost latch being the easternmost X. When the levers are set into the correct position, the door opens with no issue.

Sliding the Wrong Latch. If a lever is incorrectly slid intoa left position, a pressurized mini-guillotine set into the door's groove slides down. The character who slid the lever must make a DC 15 Dexterity throw. On a failed saving throw, the creature takes 1d6 slashing damage and their hand is lopped off at the wrist. Until the creature's hand is returned via a *greater restoration* spell, they cannot hold any object with two hands and they can only hold one object at a time. The severed hand is deposited at the bottom of the door's grooveand the lever returns to the rightmost position.

Breaking Open the Door. The doors are magically enchanted with an arcane lock spell. While affected, only a DC 27 Strength check can break down the doors. A creature can also attempt to pick the doors' locking mechanism but must make a DC 27 Dexterity check using proficiency with thieves' tools to do so. Dispelling the magic on the doors suppresses the effects for 10 minutes, reducing the DCs by10 each. The doors themselves each have an AC of 25, 100 hp (threshold 10), and immunity to fire, poison, and psychic damage, as well as bludgeoning, pierc-ing, and slashing damage made with nonmagical weapons.

14 -Northern Distillery

The first time the characters enter this area, read or paraphrase the following:

> A group of kobolds armed with burning bottles and lit casks stand before a massive distillery tank. They hiss at you.

There are six **booze server kobolds** and three **cask hauler kobolds** here.

Set into the wall on the southern side of this cave is the button used to raise and lower the iron doors for the Fire Elemental Oven trap in **area 11**.

15 - Tuckerthranx's Lair

If this is the first time the characters have entered Tuckerthranx's lair, read or paraphrase the following:

> A pool of magma bubbles at the center of this massive, 100 foot high-ceilinged chamber. The south side of the room is a smooth, stone platform. Two stone bridges cross the inferno at either side, connecting to a second, larger rock platform that rises 15-feet out of the magma. However, its the giant, red-scaled, winged creature standing at the center of that platform draws your immediate interest.
>
> "Don't worry, little ones," bellows the massive red dragon. "I'll make this quick."

Unless the characters cross the magma pool to attack him onhis platform, Tuckerthranx, an **adult red dragon** keeps his distance, using only his fire breath and lair actions to attack the characters. Meanwhile, two **molten oozes** (see Appendix C) sludge their

Variant: Tucker's Sorcerer Spells

If there are more than 5 characters in the group or they are particularly experienced, you might consider giving Tucker sorcerer spells to compliment his attacks. Using this variant, Tucker's CR increases to 18 (20,000 XP).

Spellcasting

Tucker is a 7th-level spellcaster. His spellcasting ability is Charisma (spell save DC 19). He can cast the following sorcerer spells:

Cantrips (at will): *friends, mage hand, mending, message, prestidigitation* **1st-level** (4 slots): *charm person, fog cloud, shield*

2nd-level (3 slots): *darkness, detect thoughts*

3rd-level (3 slots): *counterspell, dispel magic*

4th-level (1 slot): *dimension door* Tucker always reserves his 4th-level slot for *dimension door.*

way out of the magma and attack.

After the molten oozes are destroyed, Tucker fights more aggressively, using hit-and-run tactics while flying over the area. Tucker is arrogant, but not stupid. If it looks like he's likely to lose the combat (he's reduced to half his hit points orless), he'll retreat upward into a magma tube and abandon the mountain and his minions.

Southern platform. Characters who arrive through the doors in area 12B stand on this audience platform. Unless the characters used something to prop the door open (see **area 12B**), it's likely the door closes shut behind them,preventing escape. This is Tucker's preferred fight zone as it makes it difficult for the characters to reach him.

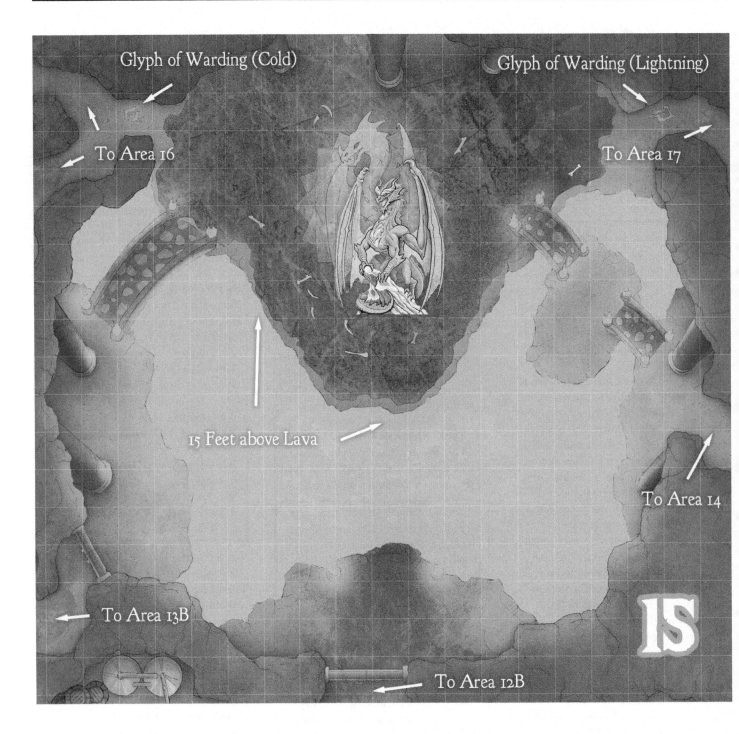

Glyph of Warding (Cold)

Glyph of Warding (Lightning)

To Area 16

To Area 17

15 Feet above Lava

To Area 14

To Area 13B

15

To Area 12B

Tuckerthranx's Platform. The dragon's platform stands 15 feet higher than the pool of magma and other platforms. Tuckerthranx isn't afraid to knock creatures off his platform into the magma, either; in fact, it's his favorite tactic. Each time Tucker uses his tail attack, instead of dealing dam-

age, he can have the target make a DC 22 Strength or Dexterity saving throw (target's choice). On a failed saving throw, the target is pushed 15 feet in a direction of Tucker's choice. If this pushes the creature over the ledge, the creature falls into the magma below. Plop.

16 - Accountant's Office

A *glyph of warding* hides on the ceiling of the corridor leading to the accountant's office. The *glyph* is nearly invisible, requiring a DC 19 Intelligence (Investigation) to notice it. When triggered, each creature within 20-feet of the glyph must succeed on a DC 19

Dexterity saving throw, taking 22 (5d8) cold damage on a failed saving throw, or half as much damage on a successful one.

> This small chamber looks to be an office of sorts. Sitting atop a small, child-sized desk are piles of neatly stacked coins. At the center is what-must-be a fire-proof ledger with scrawling in draconic.
>
> All that is certainly impressive. However, what's more impressive is the fountain of molten gold at the south end of the cavern.

Encounter. If the characters have just fought Tucker and won, Tucker's business partner and accountant, Boeger is waiting for the characters to enter.

Boeger is a lawful evil **kobold wing sorcerer**. He uses his wings and *misty step* spell to keep plenty of distance while lobbing spells at the adventurers. Like Tucker, he's arrogant but isn't interested in dying. If the characters appear too much of a threat, he'll escape through the same magma tube.

Treasure. Thanks to the insane heat of Drakescale Peak, Tucker's hoard has turned to molten gold. If the characters can cool it down (with the use of a few well-placed cold damage spells) and carry it out, in all it's worth a total of 150,000 gp.

Safe. An iron safe weighing 600 lbs is bolted into the floor of a small alcove. Opening the safe requires a DC 18 Dexterity check using proficiency in thieves' tools. Inside the safe are Boeger's recipe ingredients to the Red Claw liquor. If the sages in Knotside get ahold of the ingredients, they can create a formula and rescue Knotside's inhabitants. Also in the safe is a set of *Red Claw regalia* (see Appendix B).

17 - East Gold Fountain Bank

A *glyph of warding* hides on the ceiling of the corridor leading into this chamber. The *glyph* is nearly invisible, requiring a DC 19 Intelligence (Investigation) to notice it. When triggered, each creature within 20-feet of the glyph must succeed on a DC 19 Dexterity saving throw, taking 22(5d8) lightning damage on a failed saving throw, or half as much damage on a successful one.

> Molten gold pours out of the mouths of stone dragon heads into a fountain. You've never seen anything quite like it!

Treasure. Similar to the fountain in the accountant's office, the instense heat of Drakescale Peak has turned Tucker's hoard to molten gold. If the characters can cool it down (with the use of a few well-placed cold damage spells) and carry it all out, in all it's worth a total of 150,000 gp.

Concluding the Adventure

Should the characters defeat Tuckerthranx and his minions and return with the ingredients for the Red Claw liquor, the citizens of Knotside are cured in a manner of days and life slowly returns to normal.

If Tucker or Boeger escaped, they may rear their ugly heads again in future adventures, most likely as adversaries of the characters.

Since the amount of treasure Tucker kept in his lair is difficult to remove, the characters may request assistance from Kollias and his troops. As Kollias promised, he offers the characters 25% of the returned treasure (ideally as coins).

Contributors

This collaboration was a freely made project between DMDave, Cze & Peku, Paper Forge, It's A DnD Monster Now, and The Griffon's Saddlebag. If you haven't already, consider becoming a patron to help support the passion and effort that goes into this work. Quality D&D content gets better when it's supported by people like you!

The adventure gets better with you!

Cze and Peku provide multiple map packs of unrivaled quality for their patrons each month. Patrons receive additional map variants that can transform the entire design of the environment! You can become a patron today and access additional variants of these very maps!

Paper Forge creates weekly miniatures for patrons to use in your games! Patrons can access every miniature, color variant, cut file (so you don't have to cut it yourself!), raw artfile, and more! With over 100 miniatures already made and counting, this is the simplest way to expand and freshen your miniature collection!

It'sADnDMonsterNow creates unique combat encounters for their patrons and is a staple in the D&D homebrew community. Patrons receive exclusive monsters and access to the growing IADnDMN compendium!

The Griffon's Saddlebag creates daily homebrew items for your campaign that are illustrated, written, and balanced to look and feel like official content. Patrons receive instant access to the almost 300 existing items already made, as well as their art, cards, compendium entries, tables, and more.

DMDave wrote this adventure and writes content just like it, including feats, classes, races, and more daily for 5th edition! He is also the writer for Broadsword Monthly, a monthly print magazine loaded with new 5th edition content.

New Resources

The adventure uses new art & maps created just for this adventure. You can find full color downloadable versions of these assets at the link below. Ω

STRANGE RACES
CREATING FIFTH EDITION RACES (IN 20 MINUTES OR LESS)

By Dave Hamrick
Art by Jason Glover

Introduction

Ever wanted to create your own Fifth Edition race but wasn't sure how? It can seem like a daunting task, especially if you want to keep it balanced with the other fun races that appear in Fifth Edition. Fortunately, this easy-to-follow guide on racial creation gives you every you need to create races of your own in twenty minutes or less.

How to Use This Article

The best way to use this article is to first read through it so you understand the basic concepts of race creation. Then, when you're ready, use the guidelines presented ito craft your own, original Fifth Edition race.

There are 6 main steps to creating a race, each covered in detail in this book.

1. Come up with the concept
2. Determine ability score increases
3. Decide on flavor traits
4. Pick a size
5. Give the race one or more speeds
6. Choose unique traits

A Note on the Article's Design

This article was created through a ton of research and experience in race-building. While I tried to be as accurate as possible, I am not an official designer for this game and do not have the actual "Rosetta Stone" for race creation. Those "wizards" aren't giving up the details on that anytime soon.

Having said that, I reverse-engineered most of the major races in Fifth Edition and assigned point costs to each.

Naturally, there are those who will disagree with my decisions and that's fine. Much of what is here is subjective to your own games anyways. Use this article as a guideline and feel free to change whatever you feel is off.

Note: Some of the races in this article are not part of the 5e OGL. As such, their names have been changed (they are marked with an asterisk).

Step 1 - Concept

The first most important step in creating a Fifth Edition race is to determine the concept. Is your race a small, furry biped race that's good at tinkering? Or is your race a towering, pigfaced creature hellbent on destruction? Maybe your race is an undead creature. Or perhaps it's a glowing lifeform that has a healing touch.

Once you know your concept, you can get a sense of its overall construction. For example, the furry, biped race should probably be fast and smart. It's good at tinkering, so it's likely to have special abilities in that field--at the very least proficiency with Tinker's Tools. And so on.

Concept Questions

While coming up with your concept, here are a few questions to help you create the race.

1. If you could describe your race in just one ten-word-or-less sentence, what would it be?
2. How does your race relate to your overall campaign world and the other races in it?
3. What type of communities is your race apart of? Do they prefer to live by themselves, do they live among other races, or are most of the race's members loners and outcasts?
4. Whether it's true or not, overall, what is the stereotypical image of your race set by other races?
5. What is the race's best overall feature in terms of physicality and mental prowess?
6. What is the race's next best feature in terms of physicality/mental prowess?

7. How long do members of the race live?
8. Does the race tend towards one alignment or another, or can they be of any alignment?
9. Is the race large, small, or human-sized?
10. Are members of the race faster than normal, slower, or average?
11. Does the race have its own language, or does it borrow from others?
12. Are there special variants/sub-races of the race?
13. What special abilities really set your race apart from other races?
14. Does your race have any innate drawbacks or flaws? If you can answer these quick questions, you should have a good concept of the race and how to develop it. All that's left now is the science of actually constructing the race.

Race Points

The system for developing new races in this book uses race points (see the sidebar, page 63). Each race has an allotment of race points typically no less than 40 and no more than 100. Most races, especially the "traditional" ones fall somewhere between 55 to 65 race points. Races in this band tend to be more "balanced." Those whose budgets are less than 55 are usually "underpowered" and "weaker" than the traditional races. Finally, those with budgets higher than 66 are often considered "broken" or "overpowered."

A race's race points are used to strike a balance between all of its features, traits, and abilities to keep it in line with what already exists in Fifth Edition. When creating your race, it's recommended that you use 60 points to build your race. If you want your race to be slightly weaker than the average race, reduce these points by 5 or even 10. And if you want it to be slightly more powerful, increase the points by 5 or 10. Whatever number you pick, this is your race's point budget.

As you develop your race you will spend the race points that you've set for yourself. Once you've spent all of your points, you cannot purchase any more traits or features for your race. The costs for abilities, features, and traits are detailed throughout the rest of this guide.

Step 2 - Ability Score Increases

No matter what, every race--from humans to half-orcs to lizardfolk--increases one or more of a character's ability scores. Before assigning points to ability scores, there a few unspoken rules of race design you should understand as it pertains to abiltiy score increases.

Dominant and Secondary Ability Scores

Typically, a race has at least three ability score increases split between two ability scores: the dominant and secondary ability scores. Often, the dominant ability score has an ability score increase of +2, and the secondary has an ability score increase of +1. Of course, there are plenty of exceptions For example, the mountain dwarf has +2 increase to its Constitution score and Strength scores. Merfolk have a +1 increase in Strength Constitution and Charisma. And so on.

No Increases Higher Than +2

So far, there is no official race in Fifth Edition that offers an ability score increase of more than 2. That is because, overall, the game is balanced so that no character can receive more than one modifier increase at creation.

The Big Three

The core design of Fifth Edition revolves around three of the ability scores having more value than the others. These ability scores are often referred to as "The Big Three" and they are Dexterity, Constitution, and Wisdom. It is somewhat rare that a race has a dominant and secondary ability in-

crease that are both scores of the Big Three. Often, one increase will be one of the Big Three while the other will be one of the "Little Three." Naturally, there are exceptions to this rule, as well, although it's somewhat rare. Goblins have dominant Dexterity and secondary Constitution and lizardfolk have dominant Constitution and secondary Wisdom.

First Point Increase vs Second Point Increase

The most important increase with a Big Three race is the first increase. The reason is simple: whether it's a +1 bo-

Fifth Edition Races by Points	
Point Range	**Fifth Editon Race**
< 55	hobgoblin, kobold, orc
55-65	angelborn (fallen), angelborn (protector)*, bugbear, catfolk*, dark elf, dragonborn, forest gnome, forest guardian*, giantkin*, half-orc, high elf, hill dwarf, human (default), human (variant), lightfoot halfling, lizardfolk, merfolk*, mountain dwarf, ravenfolk*, rock gnome, stout halfling, tiefling, wood elf
66-75	goblin
75 >	snakefolk*

nus or a +2 bonus, it will always net a +1 to a modifier. For example, if a character has a 15 in Dexterity and chooses a high elf character, that character will have a total Dexterity of 17, a +3 modifier. Were the player to place a 14 in Dexterity instead, it'd be 16, which is still a +3 modifier. Only once the character reaches 4th level or discovers a magic item, etc. will the extra point make a difference. For this reason, the Big Three are weighted higher for the first increase than they are the second.

Increase Choices

There are two races in the game that allow for ability score increase choices to be made by the player at character creation. Those races are variant humans and half-elves. Like the Big Three, increase choices are weighted higher since they offer more flexibility and customization.

Ability Score Increases & Sub-Races

A race that has a sub-race usually has one dominant ability score increase in the main part of the race, and then a secondary ability score as part of the sub-race. Each subrace's ability score increase is different than the others.

Buying Ability Score Increases

Now that you understand the basics of ability score increases and some of the general rules of thumb surrounding the races, you can use your race point budget to purchase the race's ability score increases. For each ability score increase, choose either a +2 or a +1, and then pay the requisite points as shown on the Ability Score Increase Point Costs table on the next page. If your race grants three or more different ability score increases, pay another 6 points for each ability score granted beyond the first two.

Ability Score Reductions. A few races have reductions in their ability scores, notably kobolds and orcs. Similar to ability score increases, ability score reductions are never more than 2 points at a time. For each point of reduction, add 6 points to your remaining budget. For example, a -2 in Dexterity would grant you an additional 12 points to spend on features and traits for your race.

Step 3 - Flavor Traits

Next, you must determine the three flavor traits for your race,age, alignment, and languages. Typically, these traits have no effect on the game mechanics and exist more as overall roleplaying guidelines for your race.

Age

In fantasy settings, there tend to be three variants of race ages. The first is the human lifespan. According to the Fifth Edition sourcebooks, human lifespans are just short of a century (you can thank magical healing for that). Humans mature sometime around their late teens and early twenties. Next, are the long-lived races, elves, dwarves, gnomes, and to an extent halflings. These races live for multiple centuries, and sometimes reach maturity at laters ages, too. Finally, there are the short-lived races. Monstrous races like kobolds and goblins live shorter lives but also mature at a younger age, sometimes as young as 6 years old.

When you decide on the age, consider the effects a longer or shorter life will have on a race. Creatures who live longer lives often value patience and aren't as affected by the passage of time as creatures who live shorter lives than they. And creatures who live short lives are much more likely to live their life to their fullest, knowing that their time is limited.

Alignment

A race's alignment ultimately decides its place in the world. Lawful creatures live in structured societies with respect (or sometimes even fear) towards leaders and elders. whereas chaotic creatures are much more disorganized;

Ability Score Increase Point Costs		
Ability Score	**+2**	**+1**
Strength	12	6
Dexterity	18	12
Constitution	18	12
Intelligence	12	6
Wisdom	18	12
Charisma	12	6
Player's Choise	18	12

if there are leaders, those leaders rule by might and only do so until astronger contender comes along and knocks them off their throne. Good races are thought well of by the other races and generally well-liked. Meanwhile, creatures who tend towards evil are feared, hated, and sometimes hunted by the other races.

Languages

Language plays a big part in the development of your race, too. First, your race should always be able to speak Common.This makes the game smoother for the characters. Of course, you're free to decide against this if you like and have the creature speak only its own language or perhaps no language.

In addition to Common, all races speak a second language. This language can be their own native tongue, or it can be another language of your choice. Often, races that live in mixed communities, such as humans and half-elves are allowed to choose their extra languages.

Doesn't Speak Common. If you decide to make your race unable to speak Common, add 6 points to your race point budget.

Bonus Languages. If you give your race extra languages, spend 3 points per extra language it is able to speak if you choose the language or 4 points if you give the character a choice.

Step 4 - Size

There are two sizes for races in Fifth Edition: Small and Medium. So far, there are no official guidelines for playing Tiny characters or for playing characters Large or larger. The reason for this is in the relative damage output for these creatures. Large creatures tend to deal more damage withtheir weapons (typically one or two damage dice more per hit). Likewise, smaller creatures deal less damage with their hits, sometimes as low as only 1 damage per hit. Either way, it throws the game out of balance.

Medium creatures are the default creature size for Fifth Edition. They stand between 6 and 8 feet tall and take up a single 5 by 5 foot square in combat. Small creatures also take up the same space in combat, however, they stand between 2and 4 feet. The respective weight for each size is based mostly on Constitution. Sturdier creatures tend to be heavier.

Overall, Medium and Small races are balanced against each other. A Small creature might not be as great atgrappling with a larger foe as a Medium creature, but it can enter and move through the space of a Large creature without having to make a check.

While size itself offers no difference in point costs for developing your race, it can sometimes affect speed. Typically, smaller races have less movement speed than Medium or larger races. Of course, this is optional, as there are plenty of examples of Small races that can move just as fast as their Medium counterparts.

Step 5 - Speed

Medium creatures, by default, have a base walking speed of 30 feet. Anything above or below that affects your total point cost, as it can give a distinct advantage or disadvantage in combat. Remember from above that Small creatures (such as halflings and gnomes) are usually slower than Medium creatures.

In addition to walking speed, some races offer swimming and climbing speeds as well. Again, since these offer combat and adventuring advantages, they come with point costs.

Burrowing and Flying. Burrowing and flying speeds are generally discouraged in Fifth Edition due to their game-breaking powers. Most low-level dungeons are designed to keep characters on a certain trajectory. If a character possesses the ability to fly over or burrow under certain obstacles, it breaks the game. As such, these movement speeds come with high costs.

Step 6 - Unique Traits

Most races possess unique traits that set them apart from others. These traits can be innate magical abilities, natural armor or attacks, special sight such as darkvision, or even proficiency in certain skills.

If you have any points remaining from your race pointbudget after the first 5 steps, use the remainder of the points on the special features listed below in the Race Special Traits catalog.

Race Unique Traits Catalog

This section describes the most common racial traits in the worlds of Fifth Edition. Each trait is listed in alphabetical order.

Aggressive

Point Cost: 12

As a bonus action, a member of this race can move up to their speed toward an enemy of their choice that they can seeor hear. They must end this move

closer to the enemy than when they started.

Agility

Point Cost: 6

When a member of this race moves on their turn in combat, they can double their speed until the end of the turn. Once a member of this race uses this trait, they can't use itagain until they move 0 feet on one of their turns.

Armor Training (Heavy)

Prerequisite: armor training (med.)
Point Cost: 9

Members of the race have proficiency with heavy armor.

Armor Training (Light)

Point Cost: 9

Members of the race have proficiency with light armor.

Armor Training (Medium)

Prerequisite: armor training (light)
Point Cost: 3

Members of the race have proficiency with medium armor.

Armor Training (Shields)

Prerequisite: armor training (light)
Point Cost: 6

Members of the race have proficiency with shields.

Brave

Point Cost: 6

Members of this race have advantage on saving throw against being frightened.

Cantrip

Point Cost: 5

Choose a cantrip and a spellcasting ability for the spell. Members of the race can cast the cantrip at will.

Circumstantial Advantage

Point Cost: 6

Choose a skill and a special circumstance. When members of the race make an ability check with that skull during the special circumstance, they make their check with advantage.

Combat Training

Point Cost: 3

Choose a weapon. The race has proficiency with this weapon.

Cower

Point Cost: 12

As an action on their turn, a member of this race can cower pathetically to distract nearby foes. Until the end of thecreature's next turn, their allies gain advantage on attack rolls against enemies within 10 feet of the creature that can see the creature. Once a member of this race uses this trait, they can't use it again until they finish a short or long rest.

Damage Resistance

Point Cost: 18 or 30

Choose a damage type: acid, cold, fire, lightning, necrotic,radiant, or thunder. Members of the race gain resistance to the chosen damage type.

Alternatively, you can allow the player to choose a damage type at creation. If you do, the racial point cost is 30.

Speed Costs by Speed (in Feet)						
Movement Type	**20**	**25**	**30**	**35**	**40**	**45**	**50**
Walking	(9)	(3)	0	3	9	15	21
Burrowing	25	30	35	40	45	50	55
Climbing	4	8	12	16	24	32	40
Flying	30	35	40	45	50	55	60
Swimming	1	2	3	6	8	10	12

Darkvision
Point Cost: 6

Members of the race can see in dim light within 60 feet of you as if it were bright light, and in darkness as if it were dim light. Members of the race can't discern color in darkness, only shades of gray.

Feat Benefits (Ability Score Increase)
Point Cost: 9

Choose a feat that provides an ability score increase. Members of the race have all the benefits of that feat except-for the ability score increase.

Feat Benefits (No Ability Score Increase)
Point Cost: 18

Choose a feat that does not provide an ability score increase. Members of the race have the benefits of that feat.

Fey Ancestry
Point Cost: 6

Members of the race have advantage on saving throws against being charmed, and magic can't put them to sleep.

Fury
Point Cost: 6

When a member of this race damage a creature with an attack or a spell and the creature's size is larger than theirs, they can cause the attack or spell to deal extra damage to the creature. The extra damage equals their level. Once a member of this race uses this trait, they can't use it again until they finish a short or long rest.

Healing
Point Cost: 6

As an action, members of this race can touch a creature and cause it to regain a number of hit points equal to the healer's level. Once a member of the race uses this trait, theycan't use it again until they finish a long rest.

Hidden Step
Point Cost: 12

As a bonus action, members of the races can magically turn invisible until the start of their next turn or until they attack, make a damage roll, or force someone to make a saving throw. Once they use this trait, they can't use it again until they finish a short or long rest.

Hold Breath
Point Cost: 1

Members of this race can hold their breath for up to 15 minutes at a time.

Long-Limbed
Point Cost: 1

When a member of this race makes a melee attack on their turn, their reach for it is 5 feet greater than normal.

Lucky
Point Cost: 18

When members of this race roll a 1 on the d20 for an attack roll, ability check, or saving throw, they can reroll the die and must use the new roll.

Magic Resistance
Point Cost: 1

Members of this race have advantage on saving throws against spells and other magical effects.

Mask of the Wild
Point Cost: 3

Mask of the Wild Point Cost: 3

Members of the race can attempt to hide even when they are only lightly obscured by foliage, heavy rain, falling snow, mist, and other natural phenomena.

Mimicry
Point Cost: 6

Members of this race can mimic sounds they have heard, including voices. A creature that hears the sounds the mimicker makes can tell they are imitations with a successful Wisdom (Insight) check opposed by the mimicker's Charisma (Deception) check.

Mountainborn
Point Cost: 3

Members of this race are acclimated to altitudes above 20,000 feet, and they are naturally adapted to cold climates.

Natural Armor
Point Cost: 8

Members of the race have a hide that is tougher than usual. When they aren't wearing armor, their AC is 13 + their Dexterity modifier. They can use their natural armor to determine their AC if the armor they wear would leave them with a lower AC. A shield's benefits apply as normal whilethey use their natural armor.

Natural Cunning
Point Cost: 30

Members of the race have advantage on Intelligence, Wisdom, and Charisma saving throws against magic.

Naturally Stealthy
Point Cost: 9

Members of this race can attempt to hide even when they are obscured only by a creature that is at least one size larger than they.

Natural Weapon

Point Cost: 3

Members of the race have a powerful bite, claws, or othernatural weapons which they can use to make unarmed strikes. If the creature hits with it, the creature deals piercing or slashing damage (your choice) equal to 1d4 or 1d6 plus the creature's Strength modifier, instead of the bludgeoning damage normal for an unarmed strike.

Nimble Escape

Point Cost: 24

Members of this race can take the Disengage or Hide action as a bonus action on each of their turns.

Nimbleness

Point Cost: 12

Members of this race can move through the space of any creature that is of a size larger than them.

Pack Tactics

Point Cost: 36

Members of this race have advantage on an attack roll against a creature if at least one of their allies is within 5 feetof the creature and the ally isn't incapacitated.

Poison Immunity

Point Cost: 12

Members of this race are immune to poison damage and the poisoned condition.

Poison Resilience

Point Cost: 6

Members of the race have advantage on saving throws against poison and have resistance against poison damage.

Powerful Build

Point Cost: 12

Members of this race count as one size larger when determining their carrying capacity and the weight they canpush, drag, or lift.

Relentless Endurance

Point Cost: 15

When a member of this race is reduced to 0 hit points but not killed outright, they can drop to 1 hit point instead. They can't use the feature against until they complete a long rest.

Savage Attacks

Point Cost: 6

When a member of this race scores a critical hit with a melee weapon attack, they can roll one of the weapon's damage dice one additional time and add it to the extra damage of the critical hit.

Saving Face

Point Cost: 12

If a member of this race misses with an attack roll or fails an ability check or saving throw, they can gain a bonus to the roll equal tot he number of allies that they can see within 30 feet (maximum bonus of +5). Once they use this trait, they can't use it again until they finish a short or long rest.

Skill Proficiency

Point Cost: 6

Choose a skill. Members of the race gain proficiency with the chosen skill.

Skill Specialization

Point Cost: 1

Choose one skill and one special circumstance in which the skill is used. Whenever a member of the race makes a skill check with the chosen skill for the chosen circumstance, they are considered proficiency in the skill and double their proficiency bonus to the check, instead of their normal proficiency bonus.

Speak with Small Beasts

Point Cost: 1

Through sounds and gestures, members of this race can communicate simple ideas with Small or smaller beasts.

Spell

Point Cost: 9 or 12

Choose a 1st-or 2nd-level spell and a spellcasting ability for the spell. If the spell is a 1st-level spell, members of therace can cast the spell when they reach 3rd level, and if the spell is a 2nd-level spell, members of the race can cast the spell when they reach 5th level. They can cast the spell once using this trait and regain the ability to do so when once they complete a long rest.

You can opt to have the race cast a 1st-level spell at the first level. If you do, the point cost is 12.

Stone's Endurance

Point Cost: 12

When a member of this race takes damage, they can use their reaction to roll a d12. they add their Constitution modifier to the number rolled and reduce the damage by that total. After they use this trait, they can't use it again until they finish a short or long rest.

Sunlight Sensitivity

Point Gain: (12)

Members of this race have disadvantage on attack rolls and on Wisdom (Perception) checks that rely on sight when they, the target of their attack, or whatever they are trying to perceive is in direct sunlight. Taking this trait returns points to your racial point budget instead.

Superior Darkvision
*Prerequisite: darkvision** Point Cost: 3

Members of the race's darkvision has a radius of 120 feet.

Tool Proficiency
Point Cost: 2 or 4

Choose one tool proficiency. Members of the race have proficiency with this tool. Alternatively, you can spend 4 points to allow the player to choose the tool proficiency during character creation.

Toughness
Point Cost: 9

Members of the race's hit point maximum increases by 1, and it increases by 1 every time they gain a level.

Trance
Point Cost: 3

Members of the race don't need to sleep. Instead, theymeditate deeply, remaining semiconscious for 4 hours a day. After resting in this way, members of the race gain the same benefit that a human does from 8 hours of sleep.

Creating Your Own Racial Trait

The above list is pretty exhaustive. It covers all the traits in at least two of the books, plus includes rules for diversifying with feats and spells. However, you may find yourself wanting to create a racial trait of your own. Here is how you can easily do that.

Trait Similarity
The first thing to check is whether or not there is already atrait similar to the one that you want to create. For example, if you want to create a race that lives in the desert, you might take the Mountainborn trait and adjust it so that the race is acclimated to less water and is adapted to hot environments.

Feat Similarity
Next, if there isn't a trait that matches what you're trying to do, see if there is a feat that is similar. For the most part, featsare worth 18 points if they don't give an ability score increase, or half as much if they do and you leave the ability score increase off. For example, you want to create a race of owl-like creatures that have excellent eyesight. Use the Observant feat, removing the ability score increase.

Spell Similarity
If there isn't a trait or feat that's similar to what you're trying to build, see if there are any cantrips or even first-level spellsthat can duplicate your concept's effects. The dragonborn's breath weapon is a perfect example of this. It functions almost exactly like the burning hands spell.

A Few Guidelines
There are a few unspoken rules with trait creation that you should probably follow.

No Damage Increases
A trait should never boost a character's damage per round. And if it does, it only does so once per short or long rest or under limited circumstances, such as on a critical hit.

No Extreme Armor Class Increases
Some classes have natural armor. However, the natural armor should be a value that is easily replaced by Mediumarmor or better.

Consider Class Flexibility
Certain traits make class selection difficult. For example, Nimble Escape, while useful, renders a rogue's Cunning Action trait somewhat reduntant, devaluing both the rogue and the race. Consider how your trait and race will work with each class.

Try to Avoid Negative Traits
Negative traits can be fun to roleplay, but too many can be a burden on a party. Be selective when choosing negative traits.

Sub-Races

When a race has two or more sub-races, you must divide your racial point cost between the base traits for the race as well as its individual sub-races. For example, the base traits can have 45 of the 60 points allotted for the race, while each sub-race has 15 points. You can split it any way you like, although it's recommended you do at least 50% or more for the base race.

The base traits usually include the race's ability score increases (usually only the dominant increase), its flavor traits, size, speed, and sometimes a few unique traits.

Each sub-race then differentiates itself with a secondary ability score increase plus a few additional traits that set it part from the other sub-races. Ω

APPENDICES

CHARACTER OPTIONS

By Dave Hamrick

The Space Luchador

On the planet Luchamundo in the Estrella System, races from all over the cosmos travel to test their mettle as the galaxy's greatest fighters: space luchadors. To a cacophony of trumpets, they rise from the pits below the megacoliseums, cloaks billowing in the great winds of Luchamundo. Masked men and women all, these warriors of the mat dazzle millions with their high flying moves, technical prowess, and powerful fists and feet (or even tentacles).

Whether by choice or through enslavement, these musclebound, galactic knights learn the greatest fighting moves anywhere.

Creating a Space Luchador

As you make your space luchador character, think about what led you to a life of gladiatorial combat. Were you a slave forced into the ring? Did you see a luchador broadcast on Galactivision-1 and wanted to emulate him or her? Or did you become a luchador so you could hide yourself in plain site?

Consider what made you leave the life of the arena behind. Did you accidentally kill someone in the ring, and now you're on the run from space criminals? Maybe you freed yourself from the bonds of slavery. Or perhaps you just wanted to try testing yourself against bigger and better opponents.

Space luchadors have no real alignment preference, although they typically come in two types. *Faces* tend to be lawful good, always doing what's best for others and following all the rules. On the other hand, **heels** are neutral evil, doing whatever they can to cause harm to their opponents.

Quick Build. You can make a space luchador quickly by following these suggestions. First, make Constitution your highest ability score, followed by either Strength or Dexterity. Second, choose the gladiator background.

THE SPACE LUCHADOR

Level	Proficiency Bonus	Brawling	Max Power Points	Moves Known	Move Level	Features
1st	+2	1d4	-	-	-	Unarmored Defense, Brawling, Lucha Mask
2nd	+2	1d4	2	2	1st	Wrestling Moves, Top Rope Shuffle
3rd	+2	1d4	3	3	1st	Fighting Style, No-Sell
4th	+2	1d4	4	4	1st	Ability Score Improvement
5th	+3	1d6	5	5	2nd	Fighting Style feature
6th	+3	1d6	6	6	2nd	Empowered Strikes
7th	+3	1d6	7	7	2nd	Lucha Resistance, Showboat
8th	+3	1d6	8	8	2nd	Ability Score Improvement
9th	+4	1d6	9	9	3rd	Crash Lander
10th	+4	1d6	10	10	3rd	Lucha Durability
11th	+4	1d8	11	10	3rd	Fighting Style feature
12th	+4	1d8	12	11	3rd	Ability Score Improvement
13th	+5	1d8	13	12	4th	Epic Presence
14th	+5	1d8	14	12	4th	Fighting Style feature
15th	+5	1d8	15	13	4th	Undefeatable
16th	+5	1d8	16	13	4th	Ability Score Improvement
17th	+6	1d10	17	14	5th	Finishing Move
18th	+6	1d10	18	14	5th	Fighting Style feature
19th	+6	1d10	19	15	5th	Ability Score Improvement
20th	+6	1d10	20	15	5th	Come Out Swinging

Space Luchador Class Features

As a space luchador, you gain the following class features.

Hit Points
Hit Dice: 1d12 per space luchador level

Hit Points at 1st Level: 12 + your Constitution modifier

Hit Points at Higher Levels: 1d12 (or 7) + your Constitution modifier per space luchador level after 1st.

Proficiencies
Armor: None

Weapons: Simple weapons, rad pistols Tools: None

Saving Throws: Strength, Constitution

Skills: Choose two from Acrobatics, Athletics, Insight, Intimidation, Perception, and Performance

Equipment
You start with the following equipment, in addition to the equipment granted by your background:
- (a) any simple weapon or (b) a folding chair you can use as an improvised weapon
- (a) a dungeoneer's pack or (b) an explorer's pack
- a luchador mask and a rad pistol

Unarmored Defense
While you are not wearing any armor or carrying a shield, your Armor Class equals 10 + your Dexterity modifier + your proficiency bonus.

Brawling
At 1st level, your knowledge of wrestling moves makes you a formidable opponent not just in the ring, but just about everywhere else, too. You gain the following benefits while you are unarmed:
- You are proficient with improvised weapons.
- You can use Dexterity instead of Strength for the attack and damage rolls of your unarmed strikes.
- You can roll a d4 in place of the

normal damage of your unarmed strike. This die changes as you gain space luchador levels, as shown in the Brawling column of the Space Luchaor table.
- When you hit a creature with an unarmed strike or an improvised weapon on your turn, you can use a bonus action to attempt to grapple the target.

Lucha Mask
Your mask is the source of your power. If your mask is removed for any reason, you cannot gain power points or use your wrestling moves until you replace the mask over your face.

If your mask is destroyed or lost, you must replace it. You must perform a special ritual that takes 8 hours and 25 gp in materials and special incense. At the end of the ritual, you magically bond with the new mask.

Wrestling Moves
Starting at 2nd level, you learn new fighting tactics and maneuvers that give you an edge in combat called wrestling moves. Wrestling moves are fueled by your internal reservoir of energy known as Power Points.

Power Points. Certain attacks and features allow you to build up a reserve of internal energy called Power Points. To use one of your wrestling moves, you must expend the requisite power points as shown in the wrestling moves' description.

What is a rad pistol?

A rad pistol is a martial ranged weapon available to characters in DMDave's Blueshift campaign setting. If you are playing in a strictly fantasy campaign setting, feel free to substitute another ranged weapon.

Rad Pistol. *Martial Ranged Weapon:* range 50/150 ft. *Hit*: 2d6 radiant damage. Instead of dealing damage, you can force the target to make a DC 11 Constitution saving throw or become stunned until the end of its next turn.

You can gain power points one of the following ways:

- After each short and long rest, you gain 2 power points.
- Once per turn, when you hit a hostile creature with your unarmed strike attack you gain 1 power point.
- Some class features also allow you to gain extra power points.

The number of power points you can gain is limited by yourl evels in this class as shown on the Maximum Power Points column of the Space Luchador table.

When you spend a power point, it is unavailable until you regain it. You lose all unspent power points when you start a long rest.

Wrestling Moves Known of 1st Level and Higher. At 2nd level, you know two 1st-level wrestling moves of your choice from the wrestling move list detailed at the end of this class description.

The Moves Known column of the Space Luchador table shows when you learn more wrestling moves of your choice. A move you choose must be of a level no higher than what's shown in the table's Move Level column for your level. When you reach 6th level, for example, you learn a new wrestling move, which can be 1st, 2nd, or 3rd level.

Additionally, when you gain a level in this class, you can choose one of the wrestling moves you know and replace itwith another move from the wrestling moves list, which also must be of a level you can learn.

Move Ability. Strength or Dexterity (your choice) is your move ability for your space luchador moves, so you use your chosen ability whenever a move refers to your move ability. In addition, you use your chosen ability modifier when setting the savingthrow DC for a wrestling move you perform and when making an attack roll with one.

Move save DC = 8 + your proficiency bonus + your Strength or Dexterity modifier (your choice)

Move attack modifier = your proficiency bonus + your Strength or Dexterity modifier (your choice)

Top Rope Shuffle

At 2nd level, you climb faster than normal; climbing no longer costs you extra movement. In addition, you make all Strength (Athletics) checks made to climb with advantage.

Fighting Style

Starting at 3rd level, you adopt a particular fighting style which directs your overall choice in features and fighting abilities: High-Flyer, Powerhouse, or Tecnico, all detailed at the end of this class description. Your fighting style grantsyou features at 3rd level, and again at 5th, 11th, 14th, and 18th level.

Signature Moves. Each fighting style has a list of wrestling moves--its signature moves--that you gain at the space luchador noted in the fighting style description. Signature moves don't count towards the total number of moves that you know.

No-Sell

Also at 3rd level, you can use your reaction to gird yourself against an incoming melee weapon attack. When you do so,the damage you take from the attack is reduced by 1d10 + your Constitution modifier + your space luchador level.

If you reduce the damage to 0, you gain one power point.

Ability Score Improvement

When you reach 4th level, and again at 8th, 12th, 16th, and 19th level, you can increase one ability score of your choice by 2, or you can increase two ability scores of your choice by

1. As normal, you can't increase an ability score above 20using this feature.

Empowered Strikes

Starting at 6th level, your unarmed strikes count as magical for the purpose of overcoming resistance and immunity tononmagical attacks and damage.

Lucha Resistance

At 7th level, you are remarkably durable, able to withstand agreat amount of punishment from certain effects such as a white dragon's cold breath or the cloudkill spell. When you are subjected to an effect that allows you to make a Constitution saving throw to take only half damage, youinstead take no damage if you succeed on the saving throw, and only half damage if you fail.

Showboat

Starting at 7th level, if you start your turn in combat with half of your hit points remaining and you aren't incapacitated, you can use your bonus action to psyche yourself up, flexing, smack-talking, and making intimidating gestures as you do.You regain hit points equal to 1d6 + half your space luchador level.

You can use this feature a number of times per day equal to your Charisma modifier, and regain all expended uses after you complete a long rest.

Crash Lander
Starting at 9th level, if you fall from a height of 20 feet or less, you take no damage, and if you fall from a height greater than 20 feet you take only half damage.

Lucha Durability
At 10th level, you become unnaturally tough. As long as you have one power point remaining, you have resistance to bludgeoning damage.

Epic Presence
Beginning at 13th level, you gain proficiency in Charisma saving throws. In addition, you have advantage on all Charisma ability checks used to interact with other people.

Undefeatable
Starting at 15th level, whenever you make a saving throw and fail, you can spend 1 power point to reroll it and take the second result.

Finishing Move
At 17th level, choose one of the wrestling moves that you know as your finishing move. When you perform your finishing move on a creature that has half its hit points or less, it must make a Constitution saving throw against your move ability DC. On a failed save, double the damage of the attack against the creature.

Once you use this feature, you can't use it again until you complete a short or long rest.

Come out Swinging
At 20th level, when you roll for initiative and have at least power points remaining, you gain 4 power points.

Space Luchador Fighting Styles

Three styles of fighting are common among all space luchadores that grace the rings of Luchamundo. Typically, a luchador learns one method and focuses on that movement for its entire fighting career.

High-Flyer
High-flyers sail above the mats, landing jump kicks, flying clotheslines, and other moves. They are often the Davids to the Powerhouse's goliaths, able to match larger and stronger opponents with a flurry of quick attacks. Although high-flyers tend to be smaller luchadors, there are a few larger luchas who've made quite the career out of flying high.

Signature Moves. You learn extra wrestling moves at the space luchador levels listed in the High-Flyer Signature Moves table.

High-Flyer Signatures Moves.

Level	Move
3rd	*flurry of blows*
5th	*chest slap*
9th	*dropkick*
13th	*spinning heel kick*
17th	*frog splash*

Jumper. When you choose this fighting style at 3rd level, your speed increases by 10 feet and your jump distance is doubled while you are not wearing armor or wielding a shield. Also, when you are prone, standing up uses only 5 feet of your movement.

Extra Attack. Beginning at 5th level, you can attack twice, instead of once, whenever you take the Attack action on your turn. The number of attacks increases to three when you reach the 11th level in this class and to four when you reach the 18th level in this class.

Springboard. At 11th level, if you are within 5 feet of a Large or larger object, a wall, or another sturdy object (GM's discretion), you can use 5 feet of your movement to spring off the object, using the rest of your movement to jump in the opposite direction. If you move at least 10 feet in a straight line after you spring, you can spend 1 power point and use your bonus action to make a single unarmed strike against a target within reach. On a hit, the target must succeed on a Strength or Dexterity saving throw (target's choice) against your move save DC. On a failed saving throw, the target takes additional damage equal to your brawling die and falls prone in its space. You then land prone in an unoccupied space within 5 feet of the target.

Counter Attack. At 14th level, when a creature makes a melee weapon attack against you and misses, you can use your reaction to make a single melee weapon attack against the target.

From On High. Starting at 18th level, when a target fails a Dexterity saving throw against one of your wrestling moves, you gain 1 power point.

Powerhouse
Most powerhouses are tall, stocky, powerful creatures who can level a foe with no more than a single punch. For this reason, those who fight powerhouses know better to get within their reach.

Signature Moves. You learn extra wrestling moves at the space luchador levels listed in the Powerhouse Signature Moves table (overleaf).

Powerhouse Signatures Moves.

Level	Move
3rd	*haymaker*
5th	*big boot*
9th	*leg drop*
13th	*choke*
17th	*suplex*

Huge Reach. At 3rd level, when you make an unarmed strike on your turn, your reach for it is 5 feet greater than normal.

Brutal Attacks. Beginning at 5th level, once per turn, you can add one extradie of damage to an unarmed strike or improvised weapon attack.

The number of extra damage dice increases to two when you reach 11th level in this class and to three when you reachthe 18th level in this class.

Level 'Em. At 11th level, when you hit a creature with an unarmed strike,you can choose to spend 1 power to attempt to knock the creature down. The target must succeed on a Strength saving throw or be knocked prone and stunned until the end of your next turn.

Big Fury. At 14th level, when a creature hits you with a melee weapon attack, you can use your reaction to enter a temporary rageuntil the end of your next turn. While raging, you add twice your Strength modifier to your damage rolls.

Beast Mode. At 18th level, when a creature fails a Strength saving throw against one of your wrestling moves, you gain 1 power point.

Tecnico

The tecnicos are masters of thousands of moves. While the high-flyers prefer to keep their distance and the power-houses rely on limited attacks to take down their opponents, tecnicos perfect the art of close up combat.

Signature Moves. You learn extra wrestling moves at the space luchador levels listed in the Tecnico Signature Moves table.

Tecnico Signatures Moves.

Level	Move
3rd	*sleeper hold*
5th	*wrist lock*
9th	*hip toss*
13th	*ankle lock*
17th	*DDT*

Wrestling Hold. Starting at 3rd level when you choose this fighting style, if you make an unarmed strike against a target and it hits youcan spend 1 power point to automatically grapple the target.

Experienced Grappler. Beginning at 5th level, when you grapple a creature, you dealan additional amount of damage equal to your brawling die. The amount of damage you do increases to two damage dice when you reach the 14th level in this class and to three when you reach the 18th level in this class.

Snapmare. At 11th level, when you grapple a creature, you can spend 1 power point as part of the same action or bonus action toknock the creature prone. The target must make a Strength or Dexterity saving throw (target's choice) against your move save DC. On a failed saving throw, the target lands prone in its space.

The Ol' Switcheroo. Starting at 14th level, when a creature makes a melee weapon attack against you and misses, you can use your reaction to spent 1 power point to make a grapple

attempt against the creature.

Lock Up. At 18th level, once per turn, when a creature fails a Constitution saving throw made against one of your wrestling moves, you gain 1 power point.

Space Luchador Wrestling Move Descriptions

Presented in alphabetical order.

Arm Bar

2nd-level hold

Power Point Cost: 3

Performance Time: 1 bonus action, which you take immediately after you hit a creature with an unarmed strike or improvised weapon

Make a grapple attempt against the target. If you succeed, the creature is restrained until the end of your next turn or until the grapple ends. While

---

Space Luchador Moves

This section describes the most common wrestling moves available to a space luchador. This chapter begins with lists of the moves.The remainder contains wrestling move descriptions presented in alphabetical order by name of the move.

1st-Level Moves
- Back Elbow
- Clothesline
- Double Axehandle
- Flurry of Blows
- Haymaker
- Knee Drop
- Side Headlock
- Sidekick
- Sleeper Hold

2nd Level Moves
- Armbar
- Big Boot
- Chestslap
- DDT
- Dropkick
- Elemental Fist
- Eye Rake
- Full Nelson
- Headbutt

- Lariat
- Powerslam
- Stomp
- Whip
- Wrist Lock

3rd Level Moves
- Atomic Drop
- Camel Clutch
- Choke
- Crab Lock
- Diving Move
- Fearful Flex
- Frog Splash
- Gorilla Press Slam
- Powerbomb
- Reversal
- Spin Kick
- Suplex
- Teleport Kick
- Whirlwind Attack

4th Level Moves
- Chokeslam
- Conjure Folding Chair
- Knifehand Chop
- Moonsault
- Piledriver
- Pretzel
- Punt
- Stooges
- Superman

5th Level
- Blazing Rush
- Dragon Fist
- Give Me a Hand
- Head Crush
- Knock Knock
- Leap of the Gods
- Ragdoll
- Tangle
- Thunder Stomp

---

restrained, the target must make a Constitution saving throw at the start of each of its turns. On a failed saving throw, the target takes 1d10 bludgeoning damage and its arm is broken. While the creature's arm is broken, it can no longer hold things with two hands, and it can only hold a single object at a time. This effect ends for the creature if it receives magical healing. A creature is immune to this effect if it is immune to bludgeoning damage, it doesn't have or need an arm, has legendary actions, or the GM decides that the creature is too big for its arm to be brokenwith this move. Such a creature takes an extra 1d10 bludgeoning damage from the effect instead.

On a successful saving throw, the target takes half as much bludgeoning damage and its arm isn't broken.

Atomic Drop

3rd-level throw

Power Point Cost: 4

Performance Time: 1 action which you take when youare grappling a creature

Make a melee wrestling attack against the target. If the attack hits, the target takes 6d6 bludgeoning damage and the target must succeed on a Constitution saving throw. On a failed saving throw, the target's movement speed is reduced by 15 feet for 1 minute. The target can repeat its saving throw atthe end of each of its turns ending the effect on itself with a success.

The damage this move deals increases by 2d6 at 13th level (8d6) and 17th level (10d6).

Back Elbow

1st-level strike

Power Point Cost: 1

Performance Time: 1 reaction, which you take when another creature grapples you

As long as you are within reach, you make a single unarmed strike against the creature grappling you. On a hit,

you deal the damage normal for your unarmed strike and the grappleends.

Bear Hug

2nd-level hold

Power Point Cost: 3

Performance Time: 1 bonus action, which you take immediately after you hit a creature that is the same size category as you or smaller with an unarmed strike orimprovised weapon

You make a grapple attempt against the target. If you are successful, the target is restrained and takes bludgeoning damage equal to 2d6 + your Strength modifier at the start of each of its turns as long as it is grappled.

Big Boot

2nd-level strike

Power Point Cost: 3

Performance Time: 1 reaction, which you take when a creature moves 10 feet or more in a straight line towards you and enters a space you can reach.

You make a melee wrestling attack against the target. On a hit, you deal 1d12 bludgeoning damage and the target mustsucceed on a Strength saving throw or fall prone in its space.

Blazing Rush

5th-level special move

Power Point Cost: 7

Performance Time: 1 bonus action

You transform into living fire until the end of your next turn. While in your fire form, you gain the following benefits:

- You gain immunity to fire and poison damage.
- You can move through a space as narrow as 1 inch wide without squeezing.
- A creature that touches you or hits you with a meleeattack while within 5 feet of you takes 1d10 fire damage.

- You can enter a hostile creature's space and stop there. The first time you enter a creature's space, that creature takes 1d10 fire damage and catches fire; until someonetakes an action to douse the fire, the creature takes 1d10 fire damage at the start of each of its turns.
- You shed bright light in a 20-foot radius and im light in an additional 20 feet.
- Your unarmed strikes deal an additional 2d6 fire damage on a hit.

Camel Clutch

3rd-level hold

Power Point Cost: 4 plus 1 for each subsequent round you maintain the effect.

Performance Time: 1 action

You make a grapple attempt against a prone target within reach. If the grapple is successful, the target must make aConstitution saving throw. On a failed saving throw, the target takes 1d10 bludgeoning damage plus 1d10 psychic damage and is paralyzed for 1 minute. The creature can repeat its saving throw at the end of each of its turns, ending the effecton itself with a success. On a successful saving throw, the target takes half as much damage and isn't paralyzed.

On each of your subsequent turns that you continue to grapple the creature, you can use your action to spend 1power point to maintain the effect, forcing the target to make another saving throw.

Chestslap

2nd-level strike

Power Point Cost: 3

Performance Time: 1 action

You make an unarmed strike against the target. On a hit, you deal the damage normal for your unarmed strike. In addition, each creature of your choice within 30 feet of the creature that can see the creature must make a Wisdom saving throw. Any creature that can't be charmed automatically succeeds on this saving throw. On a failed saving throw, a target yells "Woo!" (if it is able) and has disadvantage on Wisdom (Perception) checks to perceive any creature other than you until the end of your next turn.

Choke

3rd-level hold

Power Point Cost: 4 plus 1 additional power point for each subsequent round you maintain the effect

Performance Time: 1 bonus action, which you take immediately after you hit a creature with an unarmed strike or improvised weapon

You make a grapple attempt against the creature. If you successfully grapple the target, it must succeed on a Constitution saving throw. On a failed saving throw, the target takes 2d10 bludgeoning damage and suffocates until the end of your next turn. On a successful saving throw, the target takes half as much damage and doesn't begin to suffocate.

On each of your subsequent turns that you continue to grapple the creature, you can use your action to spend 1 power point to force the target to make another saving throw or suffer another 2d10 bludgeoning damage and continue to suffocate.

Chokeslam

4th-level throw

Power Point Cost: 5

Performance Time: 1 action You make an unarmed strike against a target within reach. If the attack hits, the target takes the damage normal for your unarmed strike plus an additional 4d10 bludgeoning damage and falls prone in its space.

The bludgeoning damage this move deals increases by 2d10 when you reach level 17 (7d10).

Clothesline

1st-level strike

Power Point Cost: 1

Performance Time: 1 action, which you take immediately after moving at least 10 feet in a straight line.

You make an unarmed strike against a creature within reach. On a hit, you deal the damage normal for your unarmed strike and the target must succeed on a Strength saving throw. On a failed save, the creature takes an additional 1d8 bludgeoning damage and falls prone in its space. On a successful saving throw, the creature takes half as much damage and doesn't fall prone.

The additional damage this move deals increases by 1d8 at 9th level (2d8), 13th level (3d8), and 17th level (4d8).

Conjure Folding Chair

4th-level special move

Power Point Cost: 5

Performance Time: 1 bonus action

A folding chair conjured from one of the elemental planes appears in your free hand. Choose a damage type: acid, cold, fire, or lightning. If you chose fire or lightning, the chair sheds bright light in a 10-foot radius and dim light for an additional 10 feet. The chair has the two-handed weapon property.

You can use your action to make a melee wrestling attack with the elemental folding chair. On a hit, you deal the normal damage for your unarmed strike plus an additional 5d6 damage of the chosen damage type.

The elemental damage your chair deals increases by 2d6 when you reach level 17 (7d6).

If you let go of the chair, it disappears, but you can evoke the chair again with a second bonus action. Otherwise, the chair remains for 1 minute.

Crab Lock

3rd-level hold

Power Point Cost: 4 plus 1 additional power point for each subsequent round you maintain the effect

Performance Time: 1 action

You make a grapple attempt against a prone target within reach. If you are successful, the target is restrained

until the end of your next turn and it must make a Constitution saving throw. On a failed saving throw, the target takes 2d10 bludgeoning damage plus 2d10 psychic damage. On a successful saving throw, the target takes half as much damage.

On each of your subsequent turns that you continue to grapple the creature, you can use your action to spend 1 power point to maintain the effect, dealing another 2d10 bludgeoning damage plus 2d10 psychic damage to the target automatically.

DDT

2nd-level throw

Power Point Cost: 3

Performance Time: 1 action which you take while you are standing and grappling a creature.

You drop prone in your space, attempting to take the creature you are grappling with you as you go. The creature must succeed on a Strength or Dexterity saving throw (target's choice). On a failed saving throw, the target takes bludgeoning damage equal to 3d10 plus your Strength modifier, falls prone in its space, and is stunned until the end of your next turn. On a successful saving throw, the creature takes half as much damage and doesn't fall prone or become stunned. Either way, the grapple ends.

The damage this attack deals increases by 1d10 at 9th level (4d10), 13th level (5d10), and 17th level (6d10).

Dive Attack

3rd level strike

Power Point Cost: 4

Performance Time: 1 action which you take while you are at least 10 feet higher than a target within the range of your long jump

You jump within reach of the target and make an unarmed strike, falling as you go. If the attack hits, you don't take falling damage and you deal the damage normal for your unarmed strike, plus you deal an extra 1d10 damage for every 10 feet you fell (to a maximum of 20d10). If the attack misses, you take damage from the fall as normal, landing prone in an unoccupied space within 5 feet of the target.

Dropkick
2nd level strike
Power Point Cost: 3
Performance Time: 1 action
You make a melee wrestling attack against a target within range. On a hit, you deal bludgeoning damage equal to 3d10 plus your Strength modifier and the target falls prone in its space. Regardless of whether or not the attack hits, you fall prone in your space.

The move's damage increases by 1d10 when you reach 9th level (5d10), 13th level (6d10), and 17th level (7d10).

Double Axehandle
1st level strike
Power Point Cost: 1
Performance Time: 1 action
You make a melee wrestling attack against a creature within reach. On a hit, you deal 3d6 bludgeoning damage and the target's movement speed is reduced by 10 feet until the start of your next turn.

The move's damage increases by 1d6 when you reach 5th level (4d6), 9th level (5d6), 13th level (6d6), and 17th level(7d6).

Dragon Fist
5th level strike
Power Point Cost: 7
Performance Time: 1 action
You throw a punch, hurling a line of magical fire that is 120feet long and 10-feet wide that originates from you. Each creature in the area must succeed on a Dexterity savingthrow, taking 9d6 fire damage on a failed saving throw or half as much damage on a successful one.

Drop Strike
1st level strike
Power Point Cost: 1
Performance Time: 1 action

You make a single unarmed strike against a prone target within reach. On a hit, you deal the damage normal for your unarmed strike plus 3d6 extra damage of the same type. Hit or miss, you fall prone in an unoccupied space within 5 feet of the target.

The move's damage increases by 1d6 when you reach 5th level (4d6), 9th level (5d6), 13th level (6d6), and 17th level(7d6).

Elemental Fist
2nd level special move
Power Point Cost: 3
Performance Time: 1 action
Your fist becomes a magical weapon as long as you concentrate (as if concentrating on a spell), up to 1 hour. Choose one of the following damage types: acid, cold, fire, lightning, or thunder. For the duration, your fist has a +1bonus to attack rolls and deals an extra 1d4 damage of the chosen type when it hits.

At 9th level, the bonus to attack rolls increases to +2 and the extra damage increases to 2d4. At 17th level, the bonus to attack rolls increases to +3 and the extra damage increases to 3d4.

Eye Rake
2nd-level strike
Power Point Cost: 3
Performance Time: 1 bonus action, which you take immediately after you hit a creature with an unarmed strike or improvised weapon You make a single unarmed strike against the target. On a hit, you deal the damage normal for your unarmed strike, and thecreature must succeed on a Constitution saving throw. On a failed saving throw, the target is blinded for 1 minute. The target can repeat its saving throw at the end of each of its turns ending the effect on itself with a success.

Fearsome Flex
3rd-level special move
Power Point Cost: 4 plus 1 for each round you maintain this effect
Performance Time: 1 action
You show off your amazing muscles. Each hostile creature within 30 feet of you that can see you must make a Wisdom saving throw or drop whatever it is holding and becomefrightened until the end of your next turn. While frightened by this effect, a creature must take the Dash action and move away from you by the safest available route one ach of its turns, unless there is nowhere to move. If the creature ends its turn in a location where it doesn't have line of sight to you, the creature can make a Wisdom saving throw. On a successful save, the effect ends for that creature.

On each subsequent turn, you can use your action to spend1 power point to maintain this effect.

Flurry of Blows
1st-level strike
Power Point Cost: 1
Performance Time: 1 bonus action, which you take immediately after you take the Attack action on your turn
You make two unarmed strikes.

Frog Splash
3rd-level strike
Power Point Cost: 4
Performance Time: 1 action
Make a melee wrestling attack against a prone target within reach. If the attack hits, you deal 5d10 bludgeoning damage. If the attack misses, you take 1d10 bludgeoning damage. Hit or miss, you land prone in an unoccupied space within 5 feet of the target.

The bludgeoning damage you deal with this move deals increases by 1d10 at 13th level (6d10) and 17th level (7d10).

Full Nelson
2nd-level hold
Power Point Cost: 2
Performance Time: 1 bonus action,

which you take immediately after you hit a creature with an unarmed strike or improvised weapon Make a grapple attempt against the target. If the grapple is successful, the creature is restrained until the end of your next turn.

On subsequent turns, you can use your action to maintain this effect, extending its duration until the end of your next turn.

Give Me a Hand
5th-level hold
Power Point Cost: 7
Performance Time: 1 action

You make a grapple attempt against a creature within reach. If the check is successful, the target takes 6d6 slashing damage and you remove one of the creature's arms. While the creature's arm is removed, it can no longer hold things withtwo hands, and it can only hold a single object at a time. A creature is immune to this effect if it is immune to slashing damage, it doesn't have or need an arm, has legendary actions, or the GM decides that the creature is too big for itsarm to be removed with this move. Such a creature takes an extra 2d6 slashing damage from the effect instead. Magic such as the regenerate spell can restore the lost appendage.

The creature's severed arm can then be used by you as animprovised weapon.

Gorilla Press
3rd-level throw
Power Point Cost: 4
Performance Time: 1 action

You can lift an object or a creature over your head, then throw it.

If the target is a creature that is no more than one size category larger than you within reach, make a grappleattempt against the creature. On a success, you grapple the creature and lift it above your head.

If the target is an object that weighs no more than what you can lift, you

automatically lift it.

As part of the same action, you can throw the creature or object to a point you can see within 20 feet of you. If the space the creature lands in is unoccupied, it takes 3d6 damage plus 1d6 damage for every 10 feet you threw it,landing prone in the space.

If the space is occupied by a creature or object, make a ranged wrestling attack against that target. If the attack hits, both the thrown creature and the target take 2d10 damageplus 1d6 damage for every 10 feet you threw the creature. The target falls prone in its space and the thrown creature falls prone in an unoccupied space within 5 feet of the target. If the attack misses, the thrown creature takes the same amount of damage and falls prone in an unoccupied space within 5 feet of the target and the target takes no damage.

If you don't throw the target, you continue to hold the creature over your head as long as you maintain the grapple.The target has advantage on its Dexterity (Acrobatics) checks to escape your grapple while it is being held over your head.

Headbutt
2nd-level strike
Power Point Cost: 2
Performance Time: 1 bonus action

You try to hit a creature with 5 feet of you in the head with your own head. Make a wrestling ability check contested by the creature's Constitution check. If you win the contest, thecreature takes the damage normal for your unarmed strike and is stunned until the end of your next turn. If you fail the check, you take half the damage normal for your unarmed strike and you are stunned until the start of your next turn.

Head Crush
5th-level hold
Power Point Cost: 7
Performance Time: 1 action

You make a grapple attempt against a target within range. If you succeed on the check, the target takes 8d8 bludgeoning damage. If this damage reduces the target's hit points below half, it must make a Constitution saving throw or you crush its head. A creature dies if it can't survive without the lost head. A creature is immune to this effect if it is immune to bludgeoning damage, doesn't have or need a head, has legendary actions, or the GM decides that the creature is too big for its head to be crushed with this move.

Hip Toss
1st-level throw
Power Point Cost: 1
Performance Time: 1 action which you make when you are grappling a creature

Make a move ability check contested by the target's Strength check. On a successful check, the target takes damage normal for your unarmed strike and lands prone in a space of your choice within 5 feet of you. Either way, the grapple ends.

Knife Hand Chop
4th-level strike
Power Point Cost: 5
Performance Time: 1 action

Make a melee move attack against one target within reach. On a hit, the target takes 6d10 slashing damage. Objects and structures take double damage from this attack.

Knock Knock
5th-level throw
Power Point Cost: 7
Performance Time: 1 action which you make when you are grappling a creature

You throw the target up to 30 feet at a point you can see. If a thrown target strikes an object, such a wall or floor, the target takes 2d8 bludgeoning damage for every 10 feet it was thrown and is knocked prone. If the target is thrown at another creature, that creature must succeed on Dexterity saving made against your move save DC or take the same damage. Nonmagical objects and structures hit by the thrown creature take double damage from this move.

Lariat
1st-level strike
Power Point Cost: 1
Performance Time: 1 reaction, which you take when a creature moves 10 feet or more in a straight line towards

you and enters a space you can reach with your unarmed strike

You make an unarmed strike against the target. On a hit, the target takes the damage normal for your unarmed strike and must make a successful Strength saving throw or fall prone in its space.

Leap of the Gods
1st-level strike
Power Point Cost: 7 plus 1 for every 20 feet of height you rise beyond 100 feet
Performance Time: special

As an action, you magically leap up to 100 feet into the air and remain there until the end of your next turn. On your next turn, if you are still in the air, you can use your action to magically transform into a bolt of lightning and fall back to the space you left. When you land, each creature within 20 feet of you must make a Dexterity saving throw. A creature that fails its saving throw takes 1d6 lightning damage plus 1d6 thunder damage for every 10 feet you fell and is stunned until the start of your next turn. A creature that is in your space when you land automatically fails its saving throw and is pushed 10 feet away from you.

A creature that succeeds on its saving throw takes half as much damage and isn't stunned. You return to your true

form after you land.

If you choose not to use your action to return, you fall at the end of your next turn.

You can increase the height of your leap beyond 100 feet by spending power points. Each point you spend, to a maximum of 5, increases the height by 20 feet.

Moonsault
4th-level strike
Power Point Cost: 5
Performance Time: 1 action which you take while you are at least 10 feet higher than a target within the range of your long jump

You jump within reach of the target and make a melee move attack, falling as you go. If the attack hits, you don't take falling damage and you deal 4d10 bludgeoning damage plus an extra 1d10 damage for every 10 feet you fell (to a maximum of 20d10). If the attack misses, you take damage from the fall as normal. Hit or miss, you land prone in an unoccupied space within 5 feet of the target.

The bludgeoning damage this move deals increases by 2d10 when you reach 17th level (6d10).

Piledriver
4th-level throw
Power Point Cost: 5
Performance Time: 1 action which you take when you are grappling a creature

You pick up the target you are grappling and drop it on its head, ending the grapple. The target takes 4d10 bludgeoning damage and if the target has 25 hit points or fewer, it is paralyzed.

The paralyzed target must make a Constitution saving throw at the end of each of its turns. On a successful save, this paralyzed effect ends for it.

Pretzel
4th-level hold
Power Point Cost: 5
Performance Time: 1 action which you take when you are grappling a creature

You tie the creature up with its own limbs. The creature must make a Strength or Dexterity saving throw (target's choice). On a failed saving throw, the creature takes 4d10 bludgeoning damage and is incapacitated. While incapacitated, the creature's movement is 0, and it can make a Strength or Dexterity saving throw (target's choice) ending the incapacitated effect on itself with a success.

On a successful saving throw, the creature takes half as much bludgeoning damage and isn't incapacitated.

Powerbomb
3rd-level throw
Power Point Cost: 4
Performance Time: 1 action which you take when you are grappling a creature

You pick up the target you are grappling and drop it on the ground in front of you. The target takes 6d6 bludgeoning damage, falls prone in its space, and the grapple ends. Plus, the force of the attack sends a shockwave in all directions. Each creature other than you within 10 feet of the target must make a Constitution saving throw. On a failed saving throw, the target takes 6d6 thunder damage and fall prone in its space. On a successful saving throw, the target takes half as much damage and doesn't fall prone.

Powerslam
2nd-level throw
Power Point Cost: 3
Performance Time: 1 action which you take when you are grappling a creature

You pick up the target you are grappling and drop it on the ground in front of you. The target takes 5d6 bludgeoning damage, falls prone in its space, and the grapple ends.

The damage caused by this move increases by 1d6 when you reach 9th level (6d6), 13th level (7d6), and 17th level (8d6).

Punt

4th-level strike

Power Point Cost: 5

Performance Time: 1 action

Make a melee wrestling attack against a creature within 5 feet of you that is one size category smaller than you or smaller. On a successful hit, the target takes 4d6 bludgeoning damage and is flung up to 30 feet away from you in adirection of your choice (including up) and knocked prone. If the punted creature strikes an object, such as a wall or floor, the target takes 1d6 bludgeoning damage for every 10 feet it was punted. If the target lands on another creature, thatcreature must succeed on a Dexterity saving throw against your move save DC or take the same damage and be knocked prone.

Ragdoll

5th-level strike

Power Point Cost: 6 plus 1 for each subsequent round you continue the effect

Performance Time: 1 bonus action which you take while you are grappling a creature whose size category is no larger than your own

You lift the creature up by its legs and use it as an improvised weapon until the end of your next turn. A Large or Medium creature has a reach of 10 feet and the two-handed weapon property. A Small or smaller creature has a reach of 5 feet and can be wielded with one hand. You can use your action to make a melee wrestling attack with the creature. On a hit, both the creature you hit and the creature you are using as aweapon take 6d6 bludgeoning damage if the creature is Medium or Larger, or 3d6 bludgeoning damage if the creature is Small or smaller.

One each subsequent turn as long as the creature remainsgrappled by you, you can use your bonus action to spend

1 power point to continue to use the creature as an improvised weapon.

Side Headlock

1st-level hold

Power Point Cost: 1

Performance Time: 1 bonus action, which you take immediately after you hit a creature with an unarmed strike or improvised weapon

You make a grapple attempt against the target. On a success, the target has disadvantage on ability checks made to escape your grapple as long as it remains grappled.

Side Kick

1st-level strike

Power Point Cost: 1

Performance Time: 1 action

You make a single unarmed strike against one creature. The reach for this attack is 5 feet plus your unarmed strike'snormal reach. On a hit, the target takes the damage normal for your unarmed strike. If you score a critical hit using this move, the target takes extra damage as normal, plus it falls prone in its space and is stunned until the start of your next turn.

Sleeper Hold

1st-level hold

Power Point Cost: 1 power point plus 1 additional power point each round **Performance Time:** 1 bonus action, which you take immediately after you hit a creature with an unarmed strike or improvised weapon

You make a grapple attempt against the target. If the grappleis successful, at the start of the target's next turn, it must make a Constitution saving throw or fall unconscious.

On subsequent turns, you can use your bonus action to spend 1 power point to maintain this effect, forcing thecreature to make another Consti-

tution saving throw at the start of its next turn.

Spin Kick

3rd-level hold

Power Point Cost: 4

Performance Time: 1 action

You make a melee wrestling attack against one target within 5 feet of you. If the attack hits, you deal 4d12 bludgeoning damage.

The damage this attack deals increases by 1d12 at 13th level (5d12) and 17th level (6d12).

Stomp

2nd-level strike

Power Point Cost: 2

Performance Time: 1 action You make a single unarmed strike against one prone creature within reach. If the attack hits, you deal the damage normalfor your unarmed strike plus an additional 2d10 bludgeoning damage.

The damage dealt by this attack increases by 1d10 when you reach 9th level (3d10), 13th level (4d10), and 17th level(5d10).

Suplex

3rd-level strike

Power Point Cost: 4

Performance Time: 1 action which you take when you are grappling a creature

Make a wrestling ability check contested by the creature's Strength check. If you win the contest, you and the creature fall prone in your respective spaces and the creature takesbludgeoning damage equal to 6d6 plus your Strength modifier and the grapple ends. If you lose the contest, nothing happens and your power points are wasted.

The bludgeoning damage this move deals increases by 3d6at 13th level (9d6) and 17th level (12d6).

Stooges

4th-level strike

Power Point Cost: 5

Performance Time: 1 action

You force two creatures within 5 feet of you to make a Strength or Dexterity saving throw (target's choice). If both creatures fail their saving throws, you slam both creature's heads together; each creature takes 6d6 bludgeoning damageand is stunned until the end of your next turn. If one or more creatures fail its saving throw, the move has no effect and your power points are wasted.

Sweep
1st-level throw
Power Point Cost: 1
Performance Time: 1 action or bonus action which you can take while you are grappling a target
The target must succeed on a Strength or Dexterity savingthrow (target's choice) or fall prone in its space.

Superman
4th-level special move
Power Point Cost: 5
Performance Time: 1 bonus action
You gain a fly speed of 60 feet until the end of your current turn. While flying, if you move 10 feet in a straight line towards a target and then make a successful unarmed strikeagainst the target, the target takes the damage normal for your unarmed strike plus an additional 3d10 force damage.
At level 17, the force damage this move deals increases by 1d10 (4d10).

Tangle
5th-level hold
Power Point Cost: 7
Performance Time: 1 action
You attempt to entangle multiple foes at once. Each creature within 5 feet of you must make a Strength or Dexterity saving throw (target's choice). On a failed saving throw, the creature takes 4d10 bludgeoning damage and is incapacitated. While the creature is incapacitated, its move speed is 0, and it canrepeat its saving throw at the end of each of its turns ending the incapacitated effect on itself with a success. On

a successful saving throw, the creature takes half as much damage and isn't incapacitated.

Teleport Kick
3rd-level strike
Power Point Cost: 4
Performance Time: 1 action
You magically teleport up to 30 feet to an occupied space you can see. After you teleport, you can make a single unarmed strike attack as part of the same action.
The distance you can teleport increases by 15 feet at 13th level (45 feet) and 17th level (60 feet).

Thunder Stomp
5th-level strike
Power Point Cost: 7
Performance Time: 1 action
You leap into the air and stomp the ground with both feet.Each creature within 30 feet of you must make a Constitution saving throw. A creature takes 8d6 thunder damage on a failed saving throw and is pushed 10 feet away from you. On a successful save, the creature takes half as much dam-ageand isn't pushed.
In addition, unsecured objects that are completely within the area of effect are automatically pushed 10 feet away from you by the move's effect, and the move emits a thunderousboom audible out to 300 feet.

Whip
2nd-level throw
Power Point Cost: 3
Performance Time: 1 action or bonus action which you can take while you are grappling a target
The target must succeed on a Strength saving throw. On a failure, the target is flung up to 20 feet away from you in adirection of your choice and the grapple ends.

If a thrown target strikes an object, such as a wall or floor, the target takes 1d6 bludgeoning damage for every 10 feet it was thrown. If the target is thrown at another creature, thatcreature must succeed on a Dexterity saving throw or take the same damage and be knocked prone.
On a successful saving throw, the target is not flung and the grapple ends.

Whirlwind Attack
3rd-level strike
Power Point Cost: 4
Performance Time: 1 action
You can make one unarmed strike against each target within reach.

Wrist Lock
2nd-level hold
Power Point Cost: 3 plus 1 for each subsequent round you maintain the effect
Performance Time: 1 bonus action, which you take immediately after you hit a creature with an unarmed strike or improvised weapon
You make a grapple attempt against the target. On a success, you pin the creature's arm behind its back and force it to make a Constitution saving throw. On a failed saving throw, the target takes 2d6 bludgeoning damage and it can't makeattacks using its arms until the end of your next turn. A creature is immune to this effect if it is immune to bludgeoning damage, it doesn't have or need an arm, has legendary actions, or the GM decides that the creature is too big for its arm to be pinned with this move. Such a creature takes an extra 1d6 bludgeoning damage from the effect instead. On a successful saving throw, the target takes half as much bludgeoning damage and can still make attacks usingits arms.
On subsequent turns, you can spend 1 power point to maintain this effect, requiring the creature to make an additional Constitution saving throw. Ω

Monastic Tradition

At 3rd level, a monk gains the Monastic Tradition feature. The following Way of the Mind option is available to a monk, in addition to those normally offered.

Way of the Mind (Psi-Knights)

Practitioners of the Way of the Mind spend years exercising their control over ki. As such, they become powerful psions. Capable of defeating foes with both their fists and telekinetic powers, these remarkably humble psi-knights act as the defacto guardians of the multiverse.

Bonus Proficiencies. Starting when you choose this tradition at 3rd level, you gain proficiency with energy swords (see the sidebar), which counts as a monk weapon for you. In addition, whenever you make an ability check that uses tinker's tools related to repairing or crafting an energy sword, you are considered proficient in tinker's tools and add double your proficiency bonus to the check, instead of your normal proficiency bonus.

Energy Sword Training. At 3rd level, your training as a psi-knight grants you special abilities that you can use while wielding an energy sword.

Energy Deflection. If you are wielding an energy sword and you are targeted by a *magic missile* spell, a ranged weapon attack that deals force or radiant damage, or a spell that requires a ranged attack roll, you can use your reaction to deflect the attack. When you do so, the damage you take from the attack is reduced by 1d10 + your Dexterity modifier+ your monk level.

If you reduce the damage to 0, you can spend 1 ki point to repel the effect. The effect is reflected back at the attacker as though it originated from you, turning the attacker into the target.

Empowered Sword. You can use a bonus action on your turn to increase the power of your energy sword. When you do so, any target you hit with a melee weapon attack using your energy sword takes an extra 1d4 radiant damage. You retain this benefit until the end of your current turn.

Mind Over Matter. At 3rd level, you can cast the *mage hand* spell, requiring only somatic components. When you use this feature to cast thes pell, the hand is invisible.

Mind Tricks. At 6th level, your mental powers grant you greater control over weak-willed creatures. As an action, you can spend 3 ki points to cast *suggestion*, requiring only verbal components.

Ki Connection. At 11th level, you can focus your mind on your ki's connection to the greater multiverse. As a bonus action, you can spend 3 ki points to cause all of your attack rolls to be made with advantage. And for the duration, your attack rolls score a critical hit on a roll of 19-20. This effect lasts for 1 minute or until you use this feature again. This feature has no effect on a magic weapon that has a bonus to attack and damage rolls.

Ki Telekinesis. When you reach 17th level, your control over the ki surrounding all things improves. You can spend 6 ki points to cast *telekinesis*, needing no components.Ω

Energy Sword

An energy sword is a martial melee weapon. It costs 250 gp and weighs 3 lbs. The weapon deals 1d8 radiant damage on a hit. It has the versatile (1d10) property.

Martial Archetype

At 3rd level, a fighter gains the Martial Archetype feature. The following Ki Tyrant option is available to a fighter, in addition to those normally offered.

Ki Tyrant

There are rare fighters throughout the multiverse who hone their inner ki, the energy that pervades all things and channel it to make their attacks deadlier. Unlike monks, specifically psi-knights, who struggle to maintain balance and discipline, ki tyrants bind their ki with anger, aggression, and fear. As such, most ki tyrants lean towards the evil and chaotic alignments, however, there are those who manage to maintain neutrality.

Bonus Proficiencies. Also at 3rd level, you gain proficiency with energy swords (see the sidebar). In addition, whenever you make an ability check that uses tinker's tools related to repairing or crafting an energy sword, you are considered proficient

in tinker's tools and add double your proficiency bonus to the check, instead of your normal proficiency bonus.

Ki. Starting at 3rd level when you choose this archetype, you can harness the mystic energy of ki. This grants you access to a number of kit points. Your fighter level determines the number of points you have, as shown in the Ki Points column of the Ki Tyrant table.

Similar to monks, you can spend these points to fuel various ki features. You start knowing three such features: Aggressive Strike, Ki Choke, and Ki Defense. You learn more ki features as you gain levels in this class.

When you spend a ki point, it is unavailable until you finish a short or long rest, at the end of which you draw all of your expended ki back into yourself. You must spend at least 30 minutes of the rest dwelling on those who've wronged you to regain your ki points.

Some of your ki features require your target to make a saving throw to resist the

feature's effects. The saving throw DC is calculated as follows:

Ki save DC = 8 + your proficiency bonus + your Wisdom modifier

Aggressive Strike. You use your ki to empower one of your attacks. Once per turn, when you hit a creature with one of your attacks, you can spend 1 ki point to deal one extra die of damage of the weapon's damage type.

You can spend additional ki points to deal an extra die ofdamage of the weapon's type. Each point you spend, to a maximum of 3, increases the number of the weapon's damage dice you roll by one.

Ki Choke. As an action, you can spend 1 ki point to targeta creature within 30 feet of you. The target must make a Constitution saving throw. On a failed saving throw, the creature takes 2d6 bludgeoning damage and begins to suffocate until the end of your next turn, almost as if you were choking it with your own hand. On the creature's turn, it can use its action to repeat its saving throw, ending the effect on itself with a success. On subsequent turns, you can use your action or bonus action to spend 1 additional ki point in order to maintain the choke, dealing an additional 2d6 bludgeoning damage. The effect lasts as long as you concentrate on it (as if concentrating on a spell), for up to one minute or if you don't use your action or bonus action to maintain the choke on your turn.

You can increase the choke's damage and recurring damage by spending ki points. Each point you spend, to a maximum of 3, increases the damage by 2d6.

After you reach 18th level, the target is also restrained while you maintain the choke.

Ki Defense. You can use your reaction to deflect ranged weapon and spell attacks when you are hit by one. When youdo so, the damage you take from the attack is reduced by 1d12 + your Wisdom modifier.

You can increase the damage that you reduce with this effect by spending kit points. Each point you spend, to amaximum of 3, reduces the damage by an additional 1d12.

Mind Over Matter

At 3rd level, you learn the *mage hand* cantrip, requiring only somatic components. When you use this feature to cast the cantrip, the hand is invisible.

Forceful Charge

At 7th level, your anger and hatred thrust you into combat, allowing you to strike hard and fast against your foes. As a bonus action, you can spend 1 ki point to take the Dashaction on your turn. While using this feature, if you move 10 feet straight towards a creature, you can also make a single weapon attack as part of the same bonus action; you make this attack with advantage.

If you hit the target, it must make a Wisdom saving throw. On a failed saving throw, nothing happens. On a successful one, the creature has advantage on its next attack roll against you until the end of its next turn.

Relentless Fury

Starting at 10th level, when you roll initiative and have no ki points remaining, you regain 1 ki point.

After you reach 18th level, the ki you regain with this feature increases to 2 ki points.

Tyrant's Presence

At 15th level, you can spend 3 ki points to unravel your enemyies' confidence. When you do so, each creature within 30 feet of you that is hostile towards you must make a Wisdom saving throw. On a failed saving throw, the creaturebecomes frightened of you. The creature remains frightened of you until it moves 100 feet or more away from you or it uses its action to repeat the saving throw, ending the effect on itself with a success. A creature that succeeds on its savingthrow or the effect ends for it is immune to this feature's frightening effect for 24 hours.

Improved Mind Over Matter

At 18th level, you can spend 3 ki points to cast telekinesis. Ω

THE KI TYRANT

Level	Ki Points	Features
3rd	1	Bonus Proficiencies, Ki, Mind Over Matter
4th	1	-
5th	1	-
6th	2	-
7th	2	Forceful Charge
8th	2	-
9th	3	-
10th	3	Relentless Fury
11th	3	-
12th	4	-
13th	4	-
14th	4	-
15th	5	Tyrant's Presence
16th	5	-
17th	5	-
18th	6	Improved Mind Over Matter, Improved Ki Features
19th	6	-
20th	6	-

APPENDIX B
EQUIPMENT & MAGIC ITEMS

By Dave Hamrick
Primary Art by JD Russell and The Griffon's Saddlebag

Neuroprojector
Wondrous item, rare

This cylindrical metal device has 3 charges, and it regains 1d3 expended charges daily at dawn. You can use your action to attach this item to the head of one willing creature, or a creature that is grappled by you, incapacitated, or restrained. At the expense of 1 charge, for 1 minute, you can access and view the thoughts and memories of the target creature. The creature's thoughts and memories are projected as a slightly transparent illusion (as the spell major image) in a 5 foot space within 10 feet of the creature. Viewing the creatures thoughts with the neuroprojector works similar to the detect thoughts spell—you initially learn the surface thoughts of the creature, what's most on its mind, and if you probe deeper, the target must make a DC 15 Wisdom saving throw. On a failure, you gain insight into its reasoning, emotional state, and something that looms large in its mind. If it succeeds, the effect ends. The creature can use its action on its turn to make a DC 15 Intelligence check, ending the effect on itself with a success. A creature that succeeds on its saving throw or the effect ends for it is immune to the neuroprojector's effects for 24 hours.

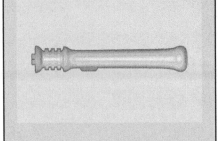

Fire Fire!
Weapon(crossbow, light), rare (requires attunement)

This hollow metal crossbow was created by a team of kobolds and contains an enchanted ember at its core. While holding this magic crossbow, the ember burns brightly inside, causing flames to lick out from various gaps left along the weapon's frame. The crossbow has 3 charges and continues to burn while it has at least 1 remaining charge. While it burns, the crossbow emits bright light in a 20 foot radius and dim light for an additional 20 feet, and any nonmagical bolt fired from the crossbow catches fire and deals an extra 1d6 fire damage to any target it hits.

You can expend 1 charge from the crossbow as an action to cause the flame to spew forth and send out a devastating wave of fire. Each creature in a 30-foot cone must make a DC 15 Dexterity saving throw. A creature takes 4d6 fire damage on a failed save, or half as much damage on a successful one. The fire ignites any flammable objects in the area that aren't being worn or carried.

The crossbow regains 1d3 expended charges each day at dawn. If you expend the last charge, roll a d20. On a 1, the magic ember inside the crossbow dies, and the weapon becomes a nonmagical crossbow.

Red Claw's Regalia
Wondrous item, legendary (requires attunement)

This tough dragon scale robe is miraculously insulated and comfortable.

While wearing the robe, you gain the following benefits:

- You can withstand temperatures as low as -50 degrees Fahrenheit without any additional protection.
- Your Constitution score increases by 2, to a maximum of 22.
- You have advantage on Constitution saving throws.
- You have resistance to fire damage.
- You can walk on lava as if it were solid ground, without taking fire damage from it. Ending your turn on lava causes you to sink into it and take fire damage as normal.

The hem of this robe glimmers with slowly shifting embers. While wearing this robe, your steps leave behind small motes of magical fire and scorched earth. The flames and marks left behind are harmless and disappear 1 second after they appear.

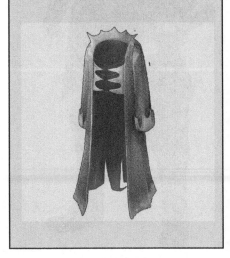

Talyard The Great's Wand of Power

Wand, uncommon

This normal-looking spruce stick is actually the wand of a famous drunkard. A drunken creature that sees the stick perceives it as a magnificent, colorful wand that radiates with an awesome power.

This wand has 3 charges and regains 1d3 expended charges each day at dusk. While you're drunk and are holding the wand, you can use your action to cast one of the following spells from the wand, even if you are incapable of casting spells: "heroism" (1 charge), "lesser restoration" (2 charges), or "thaumaturgy" (no charges). If you don't have a spellcasting ability modifier, Charisma is your spellcasting ability when casting these spells (minimum 1).

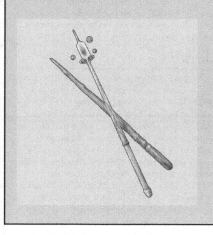

Energy Sword

An energy sword is a martial melee weapon. It costs 250 gp and weighs 3 lbs. The weapon deals 1d8 radiant damage on a hit. It has the versatile (1d10) property.

Rad pistol

Martial Ranged Weapon: Range 50/150 ft. *Hit*: 2d6 radiant damage. Instead of dealing damage, you can force the target to make a DC 11 Constitution saving throw or become stunned until the end of its next turn.

APPENDIX C
MONSTERS & NPCS

By Team Superhydra and Dave Hamrick
Art by Wilson and Grond, Bodie Hartley, and JD Russell

Kobold's Cauldron Monsters

If you run a distillery and you have any concern for safety, you know that one thing you definitely would not mix with high-proof alcohol is an open flame.

However, if you're a kobold distiller, you don't care too much for safety. Which is why at the Kobolds' Cauldron brewery and still, situated conveniently on the side of a stately volcano, you'll not only find plenty of loose alcohol, you'll also find plenty of open flames!

Kobold Brewers

The kobolds that run the Kobolds' Cauldron seemingly have absolutely zero awareness of the hazardous conditions under which they work day in and day out. Stills filled with explosive, high-proof liquor rest on the building's dry, splintered wood floors. These ramshackle vessels then steam and rattle next to uncovered torches and open chasms of flowing magma.

The kobolds themselves are similarly cavalier with their combat tactics, rolling casks filled with unstable moonshine at attackers, and hurling flaming cocktails of booze with reckless abandon.

BOOZE SERVER KOBOLDS
Small humanoid (kobold), lawful evil

Armor Class 13
Hit Points 5 (2d6 - 2)
Speed 30 ft.

STR 7 (-2)	INT 7 (-2)
DEX 16 (+3)	WIS 6 (-2)
CON 9 (-1)	CHA 10 (+0)

Saving Throws Dex +5
Skills Acrobatics +5
Senses darkvision 60 ft., pass. Percept. 8
Languages Common, Draconic
Challenge 1 (200 XP)

Pack Tactics. The kobold has advantage on an attack roll against a creature if at least one of the kobold's allies is within 5 feet of the creature and the ally isn't incapacitated.

Sunlight Sensitivity. While in sunlight, the kobold has disadvantage on attack rolls, as well as on Wisdom (Perception) checks that rely on sight.

Flammable Spirits. The kobold carries many bottles filled with highly-flammable alcohol. As a bonus action on each of its turns, the kobold can stuff a rag into the opening of an alcohol bottle it is carrying and ignite it using a nearby open flame, causing its next Hurl Bottle attack to use its ignited effects.

ACTIONS

Broken Bottle. *Melee Weapon Attack:* +5 to hit, reach 5 ft., one target. *Hit:* 5 (1d4 + 3) slashing damage.

Hurl Bottle. *Ranged Weapon Attack:* +5 to hit, range 20/60 ft., one target. *Hit:* 5 (1d4 + 3) bludgeoning damage.

If the bottle was not ignited, the target is soaked in flammable alcohol. The next time a soaked target takes any fire damage, that fire damage is increased by 3 (1d6) as the alcohol burns away. If not ignited, the alcohol evaporates harmlessly after 1 minute.

If the bottle was ignited, hit or miss, it shatters in a fiery explosion. The target and each creature within 5 feet of it must make a DC 13 Dexterity saving throw. A creature takes 5 (2d4) fire damage and is ignited on a failed save, or takes half as much fire damage and is not ignited on a successful one. An ignited target takes 2 (1d4) fire damage at the start of each of its turns, and can end this damage by using its action to make a DC 10 Dexterity check to extinguish the flames. A flammable object in the area ignites if it isn't being worn or carried.

CASK HAULER KOBOLDS
Small humanoid (kobold), lawful evil

Armor Class 12
Hit Points 7 (2d6)
Speed 25 ft.

STR 9 (-1)	INT 7 (-2)
DEX 15 (+2)	WIS 6 (-2)
CON 10 (+0)	CHA 10 (+0)

Saving Throws Str +1
Skills Athletics +3
Senses darkvision 60 ft., pass. Percept. 8
Languages Common, Draconic
Challenge 2 (450 XP)

Pack Tactics. The kobold has advantage on an attack roll against a creature if at least one of the kobold's allies is within 5 feet of the creature and the ally isn't incapacitated.

Sunlight Sensitivity. While in sunlight, the kobold has disadvantage on attack rolls, and on Wisdom (Perception) checks that rely on sight.

Volatile Cask. The kobold carries a cask of flammable alcohol on its back. While it does so, the kobold can't use its hands to make attacks or use actions, and fire damage the kobold takes is also taken by the cask.

When the cask takes fire damage, roll a d10. If the result is less than the fire damage dealt, the cask erupts in a 10-foot radius explosion. Each creature in the area must make a DC 13 Dexterity saving throw, taking 14 (4d6) fire damage on a failed save, or half as much on a successful one. Flammable objects in the area not being worn or carried ignite.

ACTIONS

Dagger. *Melee or Ranged Weapon Attack:* +4 to hit, reach 5 ft. or range 20/60 ft., one target. *Hit:* 4 (1d4 + 2) piercing damage.

Roll Cask (1/Day). The Kobold rolls its carried cask in a straight line 15 feet in a direction of its choice. The cask then continues to roll 15 feet at the start of each of the kobold's turns, accelerating, decelerating, or changing direction with the terrain at the GM's discretion.

The cask is an object with an AC of 10 and 10 hit points (immunity to poison and psychic damage, vulnerability to fire damage), and which retains the applicable portion of the Volatile Cask trait above. If the cask collides with a creature or a solid surface, both it and what it collides with take 5 (1d10) bludgeoning damage for every 10 feet it moved this turn.

If the cask is destroyed by fire damage, the Volatile Cask trait is triggered automatically. If it is destroyed by damage of a different type, it creates a 5-foot radius pool of flammable alcohol on the ground where it was destroyed. Any fire damage dealt in the pool's area ignites it, forcing each creature in the area to succeed on a DC 13 Dexterity saving throw or take 7 (2d6) fire damage as the alcohol burns up.

Variant: Simple Versions

If you find the above versions of the kobold brewers too mechanically complex for smooth use in your game, you can opt to use these simpler versions instead.

BOOZE SERVER KOBOLDS
Small humanoid (kobold), lawful evil

Armor Class 13
Hit Points 5 (2d6 - 2)
Speed 30 ft.

STR	INT		
7 (-2)	7 (-2)		
DEX 16 (+3)	WIS 6 (-2)		
CON 9 (-1)	CHA 10 (+0)		

Saving Throws Dex +5
Skills Acrobatics +5
Senses darkvision 60 ft., pass. Percept. 8
Languages Common, Draconic
Challenge 1 (200 XP)

Pack Tactics. The kobold has advantage on an attack roll against a creature if at least one of the kobold's allies is within 5 feet of the creature and the ally isn't incapacitated.

Sunlight Sensitivity. While in sunlight, the kobold has disadvantage on attack rolls, as well as on Wisdom (Perception) checks that rely on sight.

ACTIONS

Broken Bottle. *Melee Weapon Attack*: +5 to hit, reach 5 ft., one target. *Hit*: 5 (1d4 + 3) slashing damage.

Burning Spirit (Recharge 4–6). *Ranged Weapon Attack:* +5 to hit, range 20/60 ft., one target. *Hit*: 5 (1d4 + 3) bludgeoning damage. Hit or miss, the bottle then shatters in a fiery explosion. The target and each creature within 5 feet of it must make a DC 13 Dexterity saving throw. A creature takes 5 (2d4) fire damage and is ignited on a failed save, or takes half as much fire damage and is not ignited on a successful one. An ignited target takes 2 (1d4) fire damage at the start of each of its turns, and can end this damage by using its action to make a DC 10 Dexterity check to extinguish the flames. A flammable object in the area ignites if it isn't being worn or carried.

Kobold Winged Management

Supervising the Cauldron's sizable brewing workforce are a handful of winged kobold sorcerers. These middle-manager kobolds use their flight to keep watch over the laborers, and use their magic to repel attackers—as well as to keep lazy or insubordinate kobolds in line.

CASK HAULER KOBOLDS
Small humanoid (kobold), lawful evil

Armor Class 12
Hit Points 7 (2d6)
Speed 25 ft.

STR	INT		
9 (-1)	7 (-2)		
DEX 15 (+2)	WIS 6 (-2)		
CON 10 (+0)	CHA 10 (+0)		

Saving Throws Str +1
Skills Athletics +3
Senses darkvision 60 ft., pass. Percept. 8
Languages Common, Draconic
Challenge 2 (450 XP)

Pack Tactics. The kobold has advantage on an attack roll against a creature if at least one of the kobold's allies is within 5 feet of the creature and the ally isn't incapacitated.

Sunlight Sensitivity. While in sunlight, the kobold has disadvantage on attack rolls, and on Wisdom (Perception) checks that rely on sight.

Volatile Cask. If the kobold takes fire damage, roll a d10. If the result on the d10 is less than the fire damage dealt, the kobold's cask erupts in a 10-foot radius explosion. Each creature in the area must make a DC 13 Dexterity saving throw, taking 14 (4d6) fire damage on a failed save, or half as much on a successful one. A flammable object in the area ignites if it isn't being worn or carried.

ACTIONS

Claws. *Melee or Ranged Weapon Attack*: +4 to hit, reach 5 ft., one target. *Hit*: 3 (1 + 2) slashing damage.

Ignite Cask. The kobold ignites the cask it carries on its back, triggering its Volatile Cask trait as if it had taken 10 or more fire damage.

KOBOLD WING SORCERER
Small humanoid (kobold), lawful evil

Armor Class 15 (studded leather)
Hit Points 36 (8d6 + 8)
Speed 30 ft., fly 30 ft.

STR	INT		
7 (-2)	10 (+0)		
DEX 16 (+3)	WIS 9 (-1)		
CON 12 (+1)	CHA 16 (+3)		

Saving Throws Dex +6, Int +3, Cha +6
Skills Acrobatics +5, Arcana +2
Senses darkvision 60 ft., passive Perception 8
Languages Common, Draconic
Challenge 5 (1,800 XP)

Pack Tactics. The kobold has advantage on an attack roll against a creature if at least one of the kobold's allies is within 5 feet of the creature and the ally isn't incapacitated.

Sunlight Sensitivity. While in sunlight, the kobold has disadvantage on attack rolls, as well as on Wisdom (Perception) checks that rely on sight.

Sorcery Points. The kobold has 5 sorcery points. It can spend 1 or more sorcery points as a bonus action to gain one of the following benefits:

Heightened Spell: When it casts a spell that forces a creature to make a saving throw to resist the spell's effects, the kobold can spend 3 sorcery points to give one target of the spell disadvantage on its first saving throw against the spell.

Subtle Spell: When the kobold casts a spell, it can spend 1 sorcery point to cast the spell without any somatic or verbal components.

Spellcasting. The kobold is a 5th-level spellcaster. Its spellcasting ability is Charisma (spell save DC 14, +6 to hit with spell attacks). It has the following sorcerer spells prepared:

Cantrips (at-will): *acid splash, fire bolt, mage hand, minor illusion, prestidigitation*
1st level (4 slots): *burning hands, expeditious retreat*
2nd level (3 slots): *misty step, scorching ray*
3rd level (2 slots): *counterspell, fireball*

ACTIONS

Dagger. *Melee or Ranged Weapon Attack*: +5 to hit, reach 5 ft. or range 20/60 ft., one target. *Hit*: 5 (1d4 + 3) pierce dmg.

Dropped Rock. *Ranged Weapon Attack*: +5 to hit, one target directly beneath the kobold. *Hit*: 6 (1d6 + 3) bludgeoning damage.

Dire Weasel

As deadly as they are adorable, dire weasels are used by the kobolds at the distillery as mounts and beasts of burden. In the wild, dire weasels primarily hunt small game such as jackrabbits and wild dogs, but have also been known to kill and eat individuals of the smaller humanoid races.

DIRE WEASEL
Medium beast, unaligned

Armor Class 15 (natural armor)
Hit Points 32 (5d8 + 10)
Speed 20 ft.

STR 15 (+2)	INT 4 (-3)
DEX 18 (+4)	WIS 12 (+1)
CON 14 (+2)	CHA 5 (-3)

Skills Perception +3, Stealth +6
Senses darkvision 60 ft., passive Perception 8
Languages none
Challenge 1 (200 XP)

Keen Hearing and Smell. The weasel has advantage on Wisdom (Perception) checks that rely on hearing or smell.

ACTIONS

Bite. *Melee Weapon Attack:* +6 to hit, reach 5 ft., one target. *Hit:* 7 (1d6 + 4) piercing damage. If the target is a creature, it is grappled (escape DC 12).
Violent Shake. *Melee Weapon Attack:* +6 to hit, reach 5 ft., one Small or Tiny creature grappled by the weasel. *Hit:* 14 (3d6 + 4) piercing damage.

Molten Ooze

Volcanoes are not-too-seldom used as dumping grounds for all sorts of undesirable objects or materials. Their unfathomable temperatures and churning magma make them ideal for the disposal of just about anything that one doesn't want to see again.

Sometimes creatures can even be created in this extreme crucible of immeasurable heat and elemental energy. These creatures are born from the elemental heat and amorphous nature of magma, and they take the form of a writhing blob of any number of (now unidentifiable) substances melted in the volcano's caldera. A blob that wanders with intention - an intention to melt and absorb more material into its mass.

MOLTEN OOZE
Large ooze, unaligned

Armor Class 8
Hit Points 115 (11d10 + 55)
Speed 20 ft.

STR 16 (+3)	INT 1 (-5)
DEX 7 (-2)	WIS 7 (-2)
CON 20 (+5)	CHA 2 (-4)

Damage Resistance bludgeoning, piercing, and slashing from nonmagical attacks
Damage Immunities fire
Condition Immunity blinded, charmed, deafened, exhausted, frightened, prone
Senses blindsight 60 ft. (blind beyond this radius), passive Perception 8
Languages none
Challenge 6 (2,300 XP)

Amorphous. The ooze can move throught a space as narrow as 1 inch without squeezing.
Heated Body. A creature that touches the ooze or hits it with a melee attack while within 5 feet of it takes 5 (1d10) fire damage.
Molten Form. Nonmagical metal objects lost in the oozes body melt after 1 round. If the ooze takes 10 or more cold damage in one turn, its speed is reduced to 5 feet and it loses its Amorphous trait and nonmagical damage resistances until the end of its next turn.
Spider Climb. The ooze can climb difficult surfaces, including upside down on ceilings, without needing to make an ability check.

ACTIONS

Slam. Melee Weapon Attack: +6 to hit, reach 5 ft., one target. *Hit:* 8 (1d10 + 3) bludgeoning damage plus 7 (2d6) fire damage.
Constrict. Melee Weapon Attack: +6 to hit, reach 5 ft., one Large or smaller target. *Hit:* 7 (1d8 + 3) bludgeoning damage plus 10 (3d6) fire damage, and if the target is a creature, it is grappled (escape DC 14). Until the grapple ends, the target is restrained, the ooze can't constrict another target, and at the start of each of the ooze's turns, the target takes 21 (6d6) fire damage.

Doctor Kalaxan

Doctor Kalaxan is the mysterious quest giver in the adventure *The Mystery of Hoegar's Hollow*. While he often appears as a wizard that goes by the moniker Kalaxan the Magnificent, Kalaxan is actually a human-like construct known as an android. He was the lead science officer aboard the *Paramount* when the ship crashed.

Construct Nature. Kalaxan does not require air, food, drink, or sleep.

DOCTOR KALAXAN
Medium construct (android), neutral

Armor Class 15 (natural armor)
Hit Points 36 (6d8 + 12)
Speed 30 ft.

STR 15 (+2)	INT 18 (+4)
DEX 15 (+2)	WIS 12 (+1)
CON 15 (+2)	CHA 10 (+0)

Skills History +6, Insight +3, Investigation +6, Medicine +3, Nature +6, Perception +6
Damage Resistances radiant
Damage Immunities poison, psychic
Condition Immunities exhaustion, paralyzed, poisoned
Senses darkvision 60 ft., pass. Percep. 16
Languages Common
Challenge 2 (450 XP)

Innate Spellcasting (Protocols). Kalaxan's innate spellcasting ability is Intelligence (spell save DC 14). He can innately cast the following spells, requiring no components:
- At will: *comprehend languages, disguise self, silent image, shocking grasp, true strike*
- 3/day each: *invisibility (self only), shield, Tenser's floating disk*
- 1/day: *dimensional door*

ACTIONS

Multiattack. Kalaxan makes two slam attacks.
Slam. *Melee Weapon Attack:* +4 to hit, reach 5 ft., one target. *Hit:* 5 (1d6 + 2) bludgeoning damage.
Radpistol. *Ranged Weapon Attack:* +4 to hit, range 50/150, one target. *Hit:* 12 (3d6 + 2) radiant damage. Instead of dealing damage, Kalaxan can attempt to stun the target. The target must make a DC 10 Constitution saving throw or become stunned for 1 minute. At the end of each of the target's turns, the target can repeat its saving throw, ending the effect on itself with a success.

Patreon Alien Requests

Every month, I turn to my Patrons over on *www.patreon.com/dmdave* for cool ideas. Last month it was monsters and they certainly delivered. Now, it's aliens. Here are some of the cool aliens that they came up with to help populate the science fiction campaign setting of Blueshift.

Each alien may be found in Bodieh's interstellar tavern illustration on p. 82.

1 – Tava

Requested by Nathaniel W.

Tava, also known as doom obelisks, are a race of tyrannical, living obelisks beset with a single glowing eye. All tava look the same; they stand close to 26-feet tall. Their outer shell appears to be a cross between black stone and flesh.

When a Tava teleports onto a planet, it immediately begins to use its psionic abilities to dominate and enslave all living organisms it comes across. It first takes control of the planet's military and government, using it as its own eradication force. Once the population has dwindled down to only its strongest survivors, the Tava then uses its knowledge of genetic engineering to perfect the remaining slaves. From there, the Tava moves on to its next target.

Tava have no known homeworld. The doom obelisks can exist in any environment, including the vacuum of space.

Regional Effects. A planet containing a tava is warped by the obelisk's alien mind. When a creature falls asleep on the same planet as a tava, it must make a DC 18 Wisdom saving throw. If the creature fails its saving throw, it is charmed by the tava. While the target is charmed by the tava and 50 feet or further away from the tava, the target must do everything it can to move within 50 of the tava. The creature takes 5 (5d10) psychic damage each time it acts in a manner directly counter to moving towards the tava.

Whenever the target takes damage from a source other than the tava, the target can repeat the saving throw, ending the effect on itself with a success. A target that successfully saves is immune to this tava's regional effects for the next 24 hours and has advantage on its next Wisdom saving throw made against any of the tava's attacks, including its aura of enslavement.

TAVA
Huge aberration, lawful evil

Armor Class 23 (natural armor)
Hit Points 207 (18d12 + 90)
Speed 0 ft.

STR	DEX	CON	INT	WIS	CHA
28 (+9)	1 (-5)	21 (+5)	23 (+6)	20 (+5)	18 (+4)

Saving Throws Con +11, Int +12, Wis +11
Skills Arcana +12, History +12, Insight +11, Perception +11
Damage Resistances acid, cold, fire, radiant, lightning
Damage Immunities poison; bludgeoning, piercing, and slashing from nonmagical damage
Condition Immunities charmed, poisoned
Senses darkvision 120 ft., passive Perception 21
Language understands all but can't speak, telepathy 120 ft.
Challenge 17 (18,000 XP)

Innate Spellcasting (Psionics). The tava's innate spellcasting ability is Intelligence (spell save DC 20). It can innately cast the following spells requiring no components:
- At will: *blur, detect magic, detect thoughts, magic missile (the tava creates 5 missiles), shield, telekinesis*
- 3/day each: *cloudkill, hold monster, phantasmal killer, wall of force*
- 1/day each: *control weather, darkness, forcecage, plane shift (self only)*

Magic Resistance. The tava has advantage on saving throws against spells and magical effects.

Aura of Enslavement. The tava emits an aura of psychic energy in a 50-foot radius sphere centered on itself. Each creature that enters the aura for the first time or starts its turn in the aura must make a DC 20 Wisdom saving throw or become magically charmed by the tava for 1 day, or until the tava dies, or is on a different plane of existence than the tava. The charmed target obeys the tava's commands and can't take reactions, and the tava and the target can communicate telepathically with each other as long as they are on the same plane of existence. Whenever the charmed target takes damage, it can repeat the saving throw, ending the effect on itself with a success. A creature that succeeds on its saving throw or the effect ends for it is immune to this tava's aura for 24 hours.

ACTIONS

Multiattack. The tava can use its disintegration ray. It then makes three telekinetic grasp attacks.

Telekinetic Grasp. *Melee Spell Attack:* +12 to hit, reach 100 ft., one target. *Hit:* 14 (4d6) force damage and the target is grappled (escape DC 16). While the target is grappled it is restrained. Once the tava is grappling three creatures or objects, it can't use its telekinetic grasp on another target.

Disintegration Ray (Recharge 5-6). The tava shoots a ray of force energy in a 100-foot line that is 5-feet wide from its eye. Each creature in the area must succeed on a DC 20 Dexterity saving throw or take 45 (10d8) force damage. If this damage reduces the creature to 0 hit points, its body becomes a pile of fine gray dust. Large or smaller nonmagical objects or creations of magical force in the area are disintegrated without a saving throw. If the target is a Huge or larger object or creation of magical force, this ray disintegrates a 10-foot cube of it.

LEGENDARY ACTIONS

The tava can take 3 legendary actions, choosing from the options below. Only one legendary action option can be used at a time and only at the end of another creature's turn. The tava regains spent legendary actions a the start of its turn.

At-Will Spell. The tava casts one of its at-will innate spells.

Teleport. The tava magically teleports, along with any equipment it is wearing or carrying, up to 300 feet to an unoccupied space it can see.

2 – Peedlebee

Peedlebees are friendly creatures that live on the hyperevo planet Primordia. They are short, covered in fur, and have long, fluffy tails, similar to a Terran squirrel or chinchilla.

Overall, peedlebees are nomadic creatures. They survive by living in the trees of Primordia, out of reach of the dangerous predators that roam the floors of the planet's swamps and jungles. Occasionally, peedlebees coexist with grunk-grunks who protect and assist the peedlebees.

Many peedlebees are natural sorcerers (called Moopees in the peedlebee tongue), who draw their power from the radio waves that constantly assault Primordia. Moopees enjoy traveling with other interstellar beings, seeing it as their duty to use their arcane powers for good.

PEEDLEBEE	
Small humanoid (peedlebee), neutral good	

Armor Class 15 (tek-armor)
Hit Points 14 (4d6)
Speed 35 ft., climb 35 ft.

STR		INT	
STR	8 (-1)	INT	11 (+0)
DEX	14 (+2)	WIS	12 (+1)
CON	10 (+0)	CHA	13 (+1)

Skills Perception +3
Senses darkvision 60 ft., passive Perception 13
Languages Common, Peedlebee
Challenge 1/2 (100 XP)

Keen Hearing. The peedlebee has advantage on Wisdom (Perception) checks that rely on hearing.

Safety in Numbers. While the peedlebee is within 5 feet of an ally, the peedlebee has advantage on saving throws against being charmed or frightened.

ACTIONS

Dagger. *Melee or Ranged Weapon Attack:* +4 to hit, reach 5 ft. or range 20/60 ft., one target. *Hit:* 4 (1d4 + 2) piercing damage.

Radpistol. *Ranged Weapon Attack:* +4 to hit, range 50/150, one target. *Hit:* 12 (3d6 + 2) radiant damage. Instead of dealing damage, the peedlebee can attempt to stun the target. The target must make a DC 10 Constitution saving throw or become stunned for 1 minute. At the end of each of the target's turns, the target can repeat its saving throw, ending the effect on itself with a success.

3 – Space Raptors

Requested by Curse of Sebs

Space raptors (true name unknown) are an ancient-race of hyper-intelligent bipedal lizards. Known for their divination abilities, they are often sought as spiritual guides. It's rare that one ever encounters two or more space raptors in the same place; some believe there might only be one true space raptor, and it pretends to be the entire race.

Space raptors enjoy clever jokes and riddles and will trade valuable knowledge for a joke they've never heard or a riddle they can't easily solve. They also enjoy chocolate. Space raptors will decimate entire colonies for its chocolate supply.

4 – Mantoid

Mantoids are a race of tall, praying-mantis-like aliens that hail from a distant jungle world. While civilized, many of their insect instincts are still intact, including their desire to eat the heads of their enemies (and lovers).

A male mantoid measures nearly 10-feet in length from its head to its tail. The females are larger, measuring nearly 15-feet. However, those are rarely seen. Despite being from a forested planet, the male mantoid's hardshell is brightly colored. Some believe this is to attract females, who tend to have dull shell colors.

5 – Bronbbrog

On the outside, the bronbbrog appears to be nothing more than an ordinary small, domesticated animal, meows, woofs and all. Of course, it's anything but. Within the animal's mouth is a portal to a pocket dimension/gullet of a forgotten horror known as the bronbbrog, a lesser servitor of the elder gods. Bronbbrogs are only ever seen from the inside out. Everything within their gullet exists in its own dimension which the flesh of the bronbbrog surrounds. Once inside a bronbbrog, cutting through it disrupts the fabric of

SPACE RAPTOR	
Medium monstrosity, neutral	

Armor Class 18 (natural armor)
Hit Points 39 (6d8 + 12)
Speed 40 ft.

STR		INT	
STR	15 (+2)	INT	14 (+2)
DEX	15 (+2)	WIS	20 (+5)
CON	14 (+2)	CHA	13 (+1)

Saving Throws Int +5, Wis +8, Cha +4
Skills Arcana +5, History +9, Perception +8
Senses truesight 30 ft., passive Perception 18
Languages understands all but only speaks Common
Challenge 5 (1,800 XP)

Innate Spellcasting (Psionics). The space raptor's innate spellcasting ability is Wisdom (spell save DC 16). It can innately cast the following spells, requiring no components:

- At will: *detect magic, detect thoughts, sending, true strike*
- 3/day each: *clairvoyance, locate object, scrying*
- 1/day each: *foresight*

Pounce. If the space raptor moves at least 20 feet straight toward a creature and then hits it with a claw attack on the same turn, that target must succeed on a DC 13 Strength saving throw or be knocked prone. If the target is prone, the space raptor can make one bite attack against it as a bonus action.

Unarmored Defense. While the space raptor is wearing no armor (not counting its natural armor) and wielding no shield, its AC includes its Wisdom modifier.

X-Ray Vision. The space raptor can see into and through solid matter up to 30 feet. Solid objects within range appear transparent and don't prevent light from passing through them. The raptor's vision can penetrate 1 foot of stone, 1 inch of common metal, or up to 3 feet of wood or dirt. Thicker substances block its vision, as does a thin sheet of lead.

ACTIONS

Multiattack. The space raptor makes three attacks: one with its bite and two with its claws.

Bite. *Melee Weapon Attack:* +4 to hit, reach 5 ft., one target. *Hit:* 6 (1d8 + 2) piercing damage.

Claw. *Melee Weapon Attack:* +4 to hit, reach 5 ft., one target. *Hit:* 6 (1d8 + 2) slashing damage.

Laser Rifle. *Ranged Weapon Attack:* +4 to hit, range 100/300 ft. *Hit:* 15 (3d8 + 2) radiant damage.

the bronbbrog dimension, causing it to implode.

The bronbbrog subsists on creatures that fall into its interior pocket dimension using an extradimensional siphon trait. This attack essentially dissolves the creature into a state of nonexistence. Even memories of the creature fade to nothing.

Mad cultists created the original bronbbrog "host", hoping it would help them connect with the elder gods. Big mistake.

MANTOID
Large humanoid (mantoid), chaotic neutral

Armor Class 14 (natural armor)
Hit Points 78 (12d10 + 12)
Speed 40 ft.

STR		INT	
15 (+2)		10 (+0)	
DEX 14 (+2)		**WIS** 10 (+0)	
CON 12 (+1)		**CHA** 9 (-1)	

Senses blindsight 30 ft., pass. Percep. 10
Languages Mantoid
Challenge 3 (700 XP)

Pounce. If the mantoid moves at least 20 feet straight toward a creature and then hits it with a claw attack on the same turn, that target must succeed on a DC 12 Strength saving throw or be knocked prone. If the target is prone, the mantoid can make one bite attack against it as a bonus action.

Standing Leap. The mantoid's long-jump is up to 30 feet and its high jump is up to 15 feet, with or without a running start.

ACTIONS

Multiattack. The mantoid makes two claw attacks.

Bite. Melee Weapon Attack: +4 to hit, reach 5 ft., one Medium or smaller creature. *Hit:* 8 (1d12 +2) slashing damage. If this attack reduces a creature's hit points to 0, the mantoid eats the creature's head. The creature dies if it can't survive without the lost head. A creature is immune to this effect if it is immune to slashing damage, doesn't have or need a head, has legendary actions, or the GM decides that the creature is too big for its head to be bitten off.

Claws. Melee Weapon Attack: +4 to hit, reach 10 ft., one target. *Hit:* 12 (3d6 + 2) slashing damage.

BRONBBROG
Gargantuan aberration, chaotic evil

Armor Class 16 (natural armor)
Hit Points 101 (7d20 + 28)
Speed 0 ft.

STR	DEX	CON	INT	WIS	CHA
18 (+4)	16 (+3)	19 (+4)	4 (-3)	15 (+2)	20 (+5)

Skills Perception +5
Damage Resistances cold, fire, lightning
Damage Immunities bludgeoning, piercing, and slashing from nonmagical weapons
Condition Immunities blinded, charmed, deafened, frightened, grappled, paralyzed, petrified, prone, restrained
Senses blindsight 60 ft. (blind beyond this radius), passive Percep.15
Languages –
Challenge 8 (3,900 XP)

Grasping Tendrils. The bronbbrog can have up to four tendrils at a time. Each tendril can be attacked (AC 16; 10 hit points; immunity to poison and psychic damage). Destroying a tendril deals no damage to the bronbbrog, which can extrude a replacement tendril on its next turn. A tendril can also be broken if a creature takes an action and succeeds on a DC 15 Strength check against it.

Host Dependent. If the bronbbrog lacks a host, it has total cover against attacks and other effects outside of it, and it can only make attacks against targets that are inside of it. Without a host, a creature cannot escape the inside of the bronbbrog except through magical means.

ACTIONS

Multiattack. The bronbbrog makes two attacks with its tendrils and uses Reel.

Tendril. Melee Weapon Attack: +7 to hit, reach 40 ft., one creature outside of the bronbbrog's host. *Hit:* The target is grappled (escape DC 15). Until the grapple ends, the target is restrained.

Reel. The bronbbrog pulls each creature grappled by it up to 40 feet straight toward its host.

Swallow. Melee Weapon Attack: +7 to hit, reach 5 ft., one creature the bronbbrog is grappling. *Hit:* The target is swallowed, and the grapple ends. When swallowed, the creature falls into a 20-foot radius, 40-foot high cylindrical pocket dimension composed of coarse, rubbery flesh. While swallowed, the target has total cover against attacks and other effects outside of the bronbbrog. At the start of each of its turns, the target must make a DC 16 Charisma saving throw or its Charisma score is reduced by 1d4. The target dissipates into nothing if this reduces its Charisma score to 0. In 1d4 days, all creatures that knew the creature lose any memories they had of the creature. Otherwise, this reduction lasts until a *greater restoration* or similar magic is cast upon the target.

A creature inside the bronbbrog can attempt to escape by climbing to the top of the bronbbrog's insides (towards its "mouth exit"). Once near the interior of the bronbbrog's host's mouth, the creature can use its action to make a Strength check contested by the bronbbrog's Constitution check. If creature wins the contest, the creature escapes the bronbbrog's pocket dimension through the mouth of its host and lands prone in a space within 5 feet of the bronbbrog.

If the bronbbrog's hit points are reduced to 0 from a creature inside it, the bronbbrog's dimensional walls collapse and it implodes. All creatures and objects within the bronbbrog are instantly destroyed, as is the bronbbrog's host which also violently implodes.

Attach to Host. The bronbbrog chooses a Small or smaller beast on a plane of existence bordering its own. The target must succeed on a DC 16 Charisma saving throw or become a host for the bronbbrog. The target is in control of its own body, but the bronbbrog is aware of everything the target experiences and can make attacks with its tendril and swallow attacks using the host's mouth as the point of origin. The bronbbrog otherwise uses the host's statistics. The host does not need to eat, drink, or breathe air while the bronbbrog is attached.

The bronbbrog remains within the host until the target's body drops to 0 hit points, the bronbbrog detaches itself as a bonus action, or the bronbbrog is turned or forced out by an effect like *dispel evil and good* spell. When the bronbbrog detaches, its connection to the host's plane is removed (see Host Dependancy above). The target is immune to this bronbbrog's Attach to Host feature for 24 hours after succeeding on the saving throw or after it detaches itself.

6 – Scuuk

Requested by T.R.D.

Scuuk are a race of armadillo-like scavengers. This curious race originates from a rocky desert planet that shares the same name. A peaceful creature, the Scuuk is more likely to curl into a ball and flee than enter a fight. If cornered, they defend themselves with their sharp claws.

In deserts and rocky badlands, Scuuks gather in clusters known as burrows. Burrows are made of simple tunnels dug by the Scuuk. Scuuk have very little interested in material possessions but might decorate their burrows with interesting objects, especially shiny, reflective metal, rubber, and anything that makes a noise.

Scuuks are primarily insectivores. If finding food proves difficult, it can live off chewing rocks and sand as well, although most scuuks find the habit rather disgusting.

SCUUK
Medium humanoid (scuuk), neutral good

Armor Class 13 (natural armor), 18 while curled
Hit Points 11 (2d8 + 2)
Speed 20 ft. (40 ft. when rolling, 80 ft. rolling downhill), burrow 10 ft.

STR		INT	
STR	13 (+1)	INT	10 (+0)
DEX	10 (+0)	WIS	11 (+0)
CON	14 (+2)	CHA	10 (+0)

Senses passive Perception 10
Languages Common, Scuuk
Challenge 1/4 (50 XP)

Curl. As a bonus action, the scuuk curls into a ball. While curled, the Scuuk can only take the Dash action on each of its turns and it can roll during its move. While rolling, its movement speed is 40 ft. on flat terrain and 80 ft. while rolling downhill (included in its speed). In addition, its AC equals 18 and it has advantage on Dexterity saving throws. The scuuk can use another bonus action to uncurl itself, ending these benefits.

ACTIONS

Claws. *Melee Weapon Attack:* +3 to hit, reach 5 ft., one target. *Hit:* 3 (1d4 + 1) slashing damage.

7 – Crenqrud

Requested by Steve W.

Believed to be from the same homeworld as Jovians, Crenqrud are methane-breathing, glowing, floating jellyfish. These strange creatures are widely considered to be some of the most intelligent creatures in this universe. However, for whatever reason, they don't understand music. (Even Grirrix have music–horrible music, but music nonetheless.)

CRENQRUD
Medium aberration, lawful good

Armor Class 11
Hit Points 18 (4d8)
Speed 0 ft., fly 20 ft. (hover)

STR		INT	
STR	7 (-2)	INT	24 (+7)
DEX	13 (+1)	WIS	10 (+0)
CON	10 (+0)	CHA	11 (+0)

Skills Arcana +9, History +9, Investigation +9, Religion +9
Damage Resistances radiant
Damage Immunities poison
Condition Immunities charmed, frightened, poisoned, prone
Senses blindsight 60 ft. (blind beyond this radius), passive Percep. 10
Languages understands Common and Jovian but can't speak, telepathy 60 ft.
Challenge 1/2 (100 XP)

Aura of Radiation. The crenqrud emits extreme radiation. Any creature that ends its turn within the radius of bright light created by the crenqrud's illumination feature must make a DC 10 Constitution saving throw. On a failed saving throw, a creature takes 7 (2d6) radiant damage and is poisoned. On a successful saving throw, a creature takes half as much radiant damage and isn't poisoned. Constructs and undead are immune to this trait.
Illumination. The crenqrud sheds bright light in a 10-foot radius and dim light for an additional 10 feet.

ACTIONS

Tendrils. *Melee Weapon Attack:* +3 to hit, reach 10 ft., one creature. *Hit:* 4 (1d4 + 2) radiant damage and the target must make a DC 10 Constitution saving throw or become poisoned.
Extend Illumination (Recharge 6). Until the start of the crenqrud's next turn, it can extend the radius of the bright light it emits up to 30-feet and dim light for an additional number of feet equal to the chosen radius.

8 – Space Luchador

See Appendix A for the full character class rules.

9 – Boletan

Boletans hail from the swamps of the hyperevo world of Primordia. They look like tall, brightly colored mushrooms in the rough shape of a humanoid. Each mushroom is connected to the soil of the Primordia; as long as they can feel the soil beneath their root-feet, they can communicate with each other.

The boletans possess a highly reg-

BOLETAN
Large plant, lawful evil

Armor Class 13 (natural armor)
Hit Points 45 (6d10 + 12)
Speed 30 ft.

STR		INT	
STR	13 (+1)	INT	10 (+0)
DEX	9 (-1)	WIS	14 (+2)
CON	14 (+2)	CHA	7 (-2)

Damage Vulnerabilities slashing
Senses darkvision 120 ft., passive Perception 12
Languages Boletan
Challenge 2 (450 XP)

Hive Mind. As long as any part of the boletan touches soft soil, the boletan can telepathically communicate with any boletan within 300 feet of it that is also touching the same soil.
Spores. When the boletan takes damage from a melee weapon attack, it explodes with spores. Each creature within 10 feet of the boletan must succeed on a DC 12 Constitution saving throw or contract the boletan spores disease. The diseased target can't regain hit points, and its hit point maximum decreases by 10 (3d6) for every 24 hours that elapse. If the curse reduces the target's hit point maximum to 0, the target dies, and its body turns to a puddle of rotting flesh overgrown with mushrooms. The disease lasts until removed by the *lesser restoration* spell or other magic.

ACTIONS

Slam. *Melee Weapon Attack:* +3 to hit, reach 10 ft., one target. *Hit:* 4 (1d6 + 1) bludgeoning damage plus 10 (3d6) necrotic damage. If the target is a creature, it must succeed on a DC 12 Constitution saving throw on contract the boletan spores disease as described above.

imented society led by a god-like being known as the Star-Fungus. The Star-Fungus expects unquestioned obedience from its mushroom-subordinates. In the minds of the tyrannical boletans, the Star-Fungus is the one true God; all others gods are false idols and the followers should be destroyed and turned into soil-food.

10 – Jackramit

The jackramit (or ramhare) is the result of a science experiment gone wrong. Combining the DNA of two Terran species, the rabbit and the ram, this large, bizarre, wall-eyed creature has the long ears of the former and the horns of the latter.

Jackramits fiercely defend their territory and their young. Reaching speeds in excess of 35 mph, a strike from a Jackramit can easily break bones of creatures larger than they. They make a sound akin to a cow's moo.

JACKRAMIT
Medium humanoid, unaligned

Armor Class 13 (natural armor)
Hit Points 26 (4d8 + 8)
Speed 50 ft.

STR		INT	
STR	15 (+2)	INT	8 (-1)
DEX	14 (+2)	WIS	11 (+0)
CON	14 (+2)	CHA	5 (-3)

Skills Perception +2
Senses passive Perception 12
Languages Common, Jackramit
Challenge 1/2 (200 XP)

Aggressive. As a bonus action, the jackramit can move up to its speed toward a hostile creature that it can see.
Charge. If the jackramit moves at least 30 feet straight toward a target and then hits it with a ram attack on the same turn, the target takes an extra 10 (3d6) bludgeoning damage. If the target is a creature, it must succeed on a DC 14 Strength saving throw or be knocked prone.
Standing Leap. The jackramit's long jump is up to 30 feet and its high jump is up to 15 feet, with or without a running start.

ACTIONS

Ram. Melee Weapon Attack: +4 to hit, reach 5 ft., one target. *Hit:* 5 (1d6 + 2) bludgeoning damage.

11 – Grirrix
From It Hunts
Requested by Darrion N.

A warrior race, the Grirrix are massive pale-skinned creatures with maws full of dagger-sized teeth. They stand nearly 10-feet tall and weigh close to 500 pounds. Six eyes set into their skulls allow them to see in multiple spectrums.

Long ago, the sun of their homeworld

GRIRRIX HUNTER
Large monstrosity, neutral evil

Armor Class 17 (Grirrix hunting armor), or 15 (natural armor)
Hit Points 200 (16d10 + 112)
Speed 50 ft.

STR	DEX	CON	INT	WIS	CHA
22 (+6)	13 (+1)	24 (+7)	13 (+1)	16 (+3)	9 (-1)

Saving Throws Dex +8, Con +10, Wis +5
Skills Athletics +11, Perception +13, Stealth +11
Damage Resistances cold
Senses truesight 60 ft., passive Perception 23
Languages Grirrix
Challenge 15 (13,000 XP)

Aggressive. As a bonus action, the grirrix can move up to its speed toward a hostile creature that it can see.
Cloaking Device. The grirrix's form is permanently blurred thanks to a device embedded in its armor. Creatures have disadvantage on attack rolls against the grirrix. An attacker is immune to this effect if it doesn't rely on sight, as with blindsight, or can see through illusions, as with truesight. It can disable this trait at any time. If the grirrix takes lightning damage, this trait ceases to function until the armor is repaired.
Targeting System. The grirrix adds double its proficiency bonus to attacks made with its plasmacaster (included in the attack). If the grirrix is blinded or cannot see its target, this feature ceases to function.
Trackless. The grirrix's steps make no sound, regardless of the surface it moves across, and is leaves no tracks behind. It also has advantage on Dexterity (Stealth) checks that rely on moving silently.

ACTIONS

Multiattack. The grirrix makes two attacks with its spear and one attack with its bite.
Bite. Melee Weapon Attack: +11 to hit, reach 5 ft., one target. *Hit:* 14 (2d8 + 5) piercing damage.
Spear. Melee Weapon Attack: +11 to hit, reach 5 ft. or ranged 30/90 ft, one target. *Hit:* 13 (2d6 + 6) piercing damage, or 15 (2d8 + 6) piercing damage when wielded with two hands as a melee weapon.
Plasmacaster. Ranged Weapon Attack: +11 to hit, range 100/300 ft., one target. *Hit:* 28 (6d8) force damage.
Electro-Magnetic Pulse (1/Day). The grirrix's armor discharges a wave of electrical energy. Each creature within 10 feet of the grirrix must make a DC 15 Constitution saving throw. Constructs that are not resistant or immune to lightning damage make this saving throw with disadvantage. On a failed saving throw, a target takes 3d6 lightning damage and is paralyzed for 1 minute. A paralyzed creature can repeat its saving throw at the end of each of its turns, ending the effect on itself with a success. On a successful saving throw, a target takes half as much damage and isn't paralyzed.

REACTIONS

Parry. The grirrix adds 4 to its AC against one melee attack that would hit it. To do so, the grirrix must see the attack and be wielding a melee weapon.

LEGENDARY ACTIONS

The grirrix can take 3 legendary actions, choosing from the options below. Only one legendary action option can be used at a time and only at the end of another creature's turn. The grirrix regains spent legendary actions at the start of its turn.
Attack. The grirrix makes one attack with its spear.
Move. The grirrix moves up to half its movement speed.
Stealth (Costs 2 Actions). The grirrix takes the Hide action.

died, forcing the creatures to live in the cold and complete darkness of their barren planet. Now, the Grirrix move across the galaxy raiding weaker ships for food and slaves (which usually ends up being one and the same).

Grirrix Hunters. Hunters are rare grirrix warriors who possess exceptional intelligence and speed. These dangerous creatures are outfitted with special equipment that enhances their senses and defensive capabilities. A lone grirrix hunter can wipe out an entire squad of enemy soldiers in less than a minute.

GRIRRIX WARRIOR
Large monstrosity, chaotic evil

Armor Class 15 (natural armor)
Hit Points 103 (9d10 + 54)
Speed 40 ft.

STR		INT	
STR	20 (+5)	INT	10 (+0)
DEX	10 (+0)	WIS	12 (+1)
CON	22 (+6)	CHA	7 (-2)

Saving Throws Con +9, Wis +4
Skills Athletics +9, Perception +7
Damage Resistances cold
Senses truesight 60 ft., pass. Percep. 17
Languages Grirrix
Challenge 6 (2,300 XP)

Aggressive. As a bonus action, the grirrix can move up to its speed toward a hostile creature that it can see.

ACTIONS

Multiattack. The grirrix makes one attack with its greataxe and one attack with its bite.
Bite. Melee Weapon Attack: +8 to hit, reach 5 ft., one target. *Hit:* 14 (2d8 + 5) piercing damage.
Greataxe. Melee Weapon Attack: +8 to hit, reach 5 ft., one target. *Hit:* 18 (2d12 + 5) slashing damage.

12 – Doctor Kalaxan
From The Mystery of Hoegar's Hollow

Here may be seen a rare instance of Doctor Kalaxan relaxing after a hard day's work. His stats may be found earlier in Appendix C.

13 – Jovian
Requested by Benjamin A.

Making their homes in the clouds of gas giants, the insectoid species known as the Jovians are natural scientists, frequently traveling across the galaxy to study other species. Jovians produce a hard, silicon-based substance which they use to build their floating satellite homes in the high winds of their worlds. They have a peculiar fascination with planets that have a solid surface since it feels like a massive home/web to them.

Jovians have two sets of bifurcated eyes over a set of jagged, dark red or purple mandibles. Their bodies are covered in a soft chitinous shell beset with what looks like numerous spongey gills. These "gills" serve three functions: flight, respiration, and digestion. They have six legs. The front two legs end in three digits, allowing for manual dexterity. Membranous fibers stretch between each of their legs, aiding them in flight.

A jovian thrives off the particulates it captures in its gills, and does not require normal subsistence. The mouth-like orifice behind its mandibles exists only for communication and is not connected to the rest of the jovian's digestive tract. This, combined with the fact that its brain doubles as the pump for its circulatory system, means beheading a jovian does not kill it.

JOVIAN
Small aberration, lawful neutral

Armor Class 13
Hit Points 7 (2d6)
Speed 10 ft., fly 60 ft.

STR		INT	
STR	8 (-1)	INT	18 (+4)
DEX	16 (+3)	WIS	12 (+1)
CON	10 (+0)	CHA	9 (-1)

Damage Resistances radiant
Damage Immunities poison
Condition Immunities poisoned
Senses blindsight 10 ft., pass. Percep.11
Languages Common, Jovian
Challenge 1/4 (50 XP)

Flyby. The jovian doesn't provoke opportunity attacks when it flies out of an enemy's reach.
Innate Spellcasting (Psionics). The jovian's innate spellcasting ability is Intelligence (spell save DC 14). It can innately cast the following spells, requiring no components:
• At will: *detect thoughts, mage hand* (the hand is invisible)
• 1/day: *hold person, telepathy*
Wind Sailers. Jovians have advantage on ability checks and saving throws against being pushed or knocked prone.

ACTIONS

Mandibles. Melee Weapon Attack: +1 to hit, reach 5 ft., one target. *Hit:* 1 (1d4 − 1) slashing damage.
Jovian Zap Gun. Ranged Weapon Attack: +5 to hit, range 30/90 ft., one target. *Hit:* 5 (2d4) lightning damage.
Web (Recharge 6). Ranged Weapon Attack: +5 to hit, range 15/45 ft., one creature. *Hit:* The target is restrained by webbing. As an action, the restrained target can make a DC 10 Strength check, bursting the webbing on a success. The webbing can also be attacked and destroyed (AC 10; hp 5; vulnerability to acid damage; immunity to bludgeoning, poison, and psychic damage). Ω

APPENDIX D
PLAYER HANDOUTS

By Dave Hamrick

The Hunt: Sark Peninsula

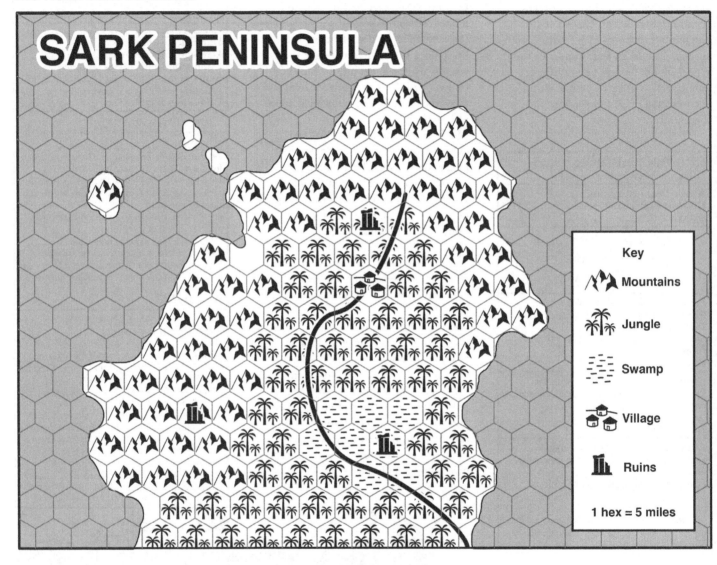

Tomb of the Kirin-Born Prince: Nebtka's Story

Nebtka's Story

Nebtka, the Kirin-Born Prince, began his life in shadow
Where moon devils tried to deceive the young prince.
Eventually, Nebtka discovered the light and found his way.
Nebtka sent the light to the north, illuminating the world.
But the devils continued to follow him.
They whispered in his ear, trying to drive him mad
But Nebtka plugged his ears to their cruel words.
In time, Nebtka grew strong;
Nebtka labored and new paths opened to him
Then Nebtka had a vision
All of his past and all of his future was revealed to him;
Nebtka knew his destiny was in the east.
Nebtka joined four brothers, elemental priests:
Loa-te, the Priest of Fire, who heated the very air around him,
Amun-afa, the Priest of Water, whose touch could extinguish even the mightiest flame,
No-za-ora, the Priest of Earth, who could part the seas with a word, and
Gan-dan, the Priest of Air, who could wither the mountains to sand with a whisper
The priests were powerful;
"We dare not use our powers all at once," they warned Nebtka
Lest we destroy the world. "Only one of us may use our powers at any given time."
So the five set out, seeking Empeku, God of Death.
Powerful winds pushed the party back until Loa-te's heat removed the wind.
Then Loa-te led Nebtka to the feet of Empeku, God of Death;
Standing at the edge of shadow, Empeku demanded sacrifice.
Thus, Gan-dan offered himself as a sacrifice to Empeku
Gan-dan spoke, "My powers cannot help the Prince on his quest."
His brothers protested, but he promised he would join them again
At the end of their journey. Gan-dan died.
In exchange, Empeku awarded Nebtka the Scepter of Time Immortal
With it, Empeku promised, Nebtka could change the direction of the sun.
Loa-te, saddened by the death of his brother Gan-dan, went mad.
The fire priest buried himself in a tomb full of scarabs with golden shells
Flames surrounded the tomb and
Only Amun-afa could cross the flame to see his brother.
In time, Amun-afa grew saddened, and he, too, rested in a tomb to the south.
The sea swallowed Amun-afa's tomb, preventing Nebtka from reaching his destiny
No-za-ra, the surviving brother, whispered to the sea, parting it
Nebtka stepped beyond the sea into the vale of night
There, the dead haunted Nebtka, draining his life
Finally, No-za-ra laid on the ground and slept.
No-za-ra dreamt of his brothers; and, in time, their ghosts joined him.
First, came Gan-dan's ghost riding the wind, just as he'd promised.
Then, came Loa-te, arriving in a burst of flame.
Last, came Amun-afa, appearing with the rain.
One last time, the four were together.
Alone, Nebtka stepped into the unknown.

OPEN GAMING LICENSE & SUBMISSION GUIDELINES

Send all submissions with a signed and filled-out Standard Disclosure Form to:
submissions@broadswordmagazine.com

BroadSword Monthly
Submission Guidelines:

https://bit.ly/2kIv9wn

Made in the USA
Columbia, SC
24 January 2020